Death at the Dutch House

Also by Barbara Whitehead

Crime fiction (The York Cycle of Mysteries)
Playing God (Quartet, 1988)
The girl with red suspenders (Constable, 1990)
The dean it was that died (Constable, 1991)
Sweet death, come softly (Constable, 1992)
The killings at Barley Hall (Constable, 1995)
Secrets of the dead (Constable, 1996)

Historical fiction
The caretaker wife (Heinemann, 1977)
Quicksilver lady (Heinemann, 1979)
House of green dragons (Methuen, 1982)
Ramillies (Methuen, 1983)

Timeswitch fiction
Shadows end (Kimber, 1983)

Non-fiction
Dig up your family tree (Sphere, 1986)
Charlotte Brontë and her 'Dearest Nell'
(Smith Settle, 1993)

DEATH AT THE DUTCH HOUSE

Barbara Whitehead

Constable · London

First published in Great Britain 1997
by Constable and Company Limited
3 The Lanchesters, 162 Fulham Palace Road
London W6 9ER
Copyright © 1997 by Barbara Whitehead
The right of Barbara Whitehead to be identified as the author of this work
has been asserted by her in accordance with the
Copyright, Designs and Patents Act 1988
ISBN 0 09 477190 1
Set in 10pt Palatino by CentraCet, Cambridge
Printed and bound in Great Britain
by Hartnolls Ltd, Bodmin, Cornwall

A CIP catalogue record for this book
is available from The British Library

For John, Alan and Roger

Author's Note: The Dutch House on Ogleford, a small, forlorn
building, was the inspiration for the house in this book. I moved
it, enlarged it and added various features. It represents the fast-
vanishing architecture of Dutch influence in this area.

1

Julia Bransby was the kind of person who stops at green traffic lights and vaguely waits for them to turn red. Which is why she had never passed her driving test. Her moped, which she rode on L plates with great caution, was away having its MOT. So at the end of her few days in Manchester, at a reunion of old school friends, she was walking home from York station.

It was a lovely evening. Intermittent late frosts and cold days had delayed the northern spring, but more recent warmer, sunny weather had brought everything into bloom together so that fading Kanzan cherries coincided with horse chestnuts, and late daffodils with early May blossom on the hawthorns.

As she crossed the River Ouse Julia admired the west end of York Minster on the skyline. The stone tracery of the west window formed the shape of an elaborate heart, and she wanted to use it in one of her embroidery designs – perhaps as the pattern on a quilted cushion. She kept glancing at the cathedral until she turned left to descend to the river, that led her home to her suburb of Clifton by the riverside path. As she walked, the smart black suitcase she carried grew heavier and heavier and she shifted it from hand to hand.

Fifteen minutes' walk ahead was the complex of old buildings collectively known as the Dutch House, now partly turned into flats, in one of which she lived with her son Adam. The complex held a small community. Julia and Adam were part of this mixture of old and young, male and female, married and unmarried. On the whole they got on well together.

As Julia walked by the river she passed through sheets of scent from snowy hawthorn blossom and lilacs white or purple and from drifts of other scented flowers, all fooled by the weather into blooming late or early so that this year everything, whether dying down or unfurling, was out at once, compressing much of the long spring display into three short weeks. Soon she was walking parallel to Ouse Avenue, which ran a few hundred yards from the river bank. There her friends Linda and Robert

Southwell (pronounced Suthell) lived. As it happened they were talking about her.

'Have you seen your friend Julia Bransby lately?' asked Detective Chief Inspector Robert Southwell. He was sitting lazily on a plastic chair in his garden, while his wife Linda sat on the swing seat with a canopy, which they had bought the week before. Linda had made a jug of lemonade which now stood on the table between them. She was looking at the garden with the expression which Bob knew meant plans, and plans meant work, usually for him.

'I haven't seen Julie for a while. Any special reason for asking?'

'Not really. When I passed the Dutch House on my way back from seeing the children off on their trip this morning I saw that there was a notice by the gate and I wondered what Julia thought about it.'

'What kind of notice?'

'The kind of notice that says "HOUSE OPEN TODAY, 10 a.m. to 5 p.m. ADMISSION £2".'

'She'll be furious,' Linda said with conviction. 'She asked them not to. They haven't the faintest idea of how to set about it and won't take any notice of what she tells them.'

'Who's "they" in this case?'

'Oh, you know, Miss Ducket-Penrose and that old bat Mrs Honor.'

'I know that the goings on among that particular community are the cause of endless gossip around here.'

'It is like a soap opera, or one of those family saga novels, except that they aren't a family. None of the tenants in the flats are related to any of the others and several of them are loners.'

'Lone lorn women?'

'I wouldn't describe any of them like that,' Linda said carefully. She wasn't married to a policeman for nothing. To avoid his sometimes sharp questioning she'd grown into the habit of considering her words when retailing any sort of story or gossip. 'Lone women – and men – they might be but lorn, no way.'

'Independent old bats?'

'Very independent old bats.'

'Can old bats be men as well as women?'

'In the Dutch House they can.'

Linda swung lazily to and fro in her new swing seat sheltered from the surpringly hot setting sun. Curled up against her thigh a Siamese kitten, very small and sweet, seemed to like the swinging as much as she did. Linda was wearing a light, floaty summer dress instead of her usual jeans. She looked across at her husband affectionately. For once he looked relaxed. He was a tall, thin man with an intelligent face which was wide at the temples, narrower in the lower part. His grey eyes were hidden by the reflections on his glasses, reflections of green lawn and pale flowers and sunlight.

'Why haven't you seen Julia lately?' asked Bob.

Just in time Linda stopped herself from answering abruptly. This golden afternoon was almost over already, shadows were lengthening. She didn't want to spoil it.

'She was going to go away for a few days and it was the first time she'd left Adam to look after himself, so she was cooking and filling the freezer and flying all over the place getting her professional jobs done. I haven't seen her for three weeks.'

Julia felt too hot and unbuttoned the jacket of her fine wool suit. She wished she'd taken a taxi, or that Adam had come down to meet her and carry the case. Pushing the button at the road crossing she waited for the traffic to pause for a moment to allow her to pass over. The Dutch House was hidden from her and would be until she was actually on top of it, for it was set back from the road behind high hedges and the recessed drive entrance could not be seen either.

Julia was returning home knowing that she had changed in her few short days away, but never thinking that home would have changed, that irrevocable movements in time had taken place. She reached the end of the hedge and came in sight of the gate. In one glance she took in two things, a pair of young lovers who stood there, and at the same time the notice poised above them, black letters carefully handpainted on white, saying 'HOUSE OPEN TODAY, 10 a.m. to 5 p.m. ADMISSION £2'.

The young man and the girl reminded Julia of a Victorian painting she had once seen, called *The Idyll*. They were lip to lip, and one of the girl's hands hung down gracefully against the tiny flowerheads on her long lawn dress. Petals from the tree above fell round them like confetti.

7

Julia stood still for what seemed like endless minutes but was a second only. That crystallized moment reminded her of the sweetness of love, and the unfathomable behaviour of human beings. The two parts of what she saw, taken together, made sense – unbelievable, shocking sense. In her absence they had done it, they had opened the house to the public and if she knew anything about it her son Adam had lettered that board, and these two young people – it being a little past six o'clock with the first tints of dusk creeping gently over the early summer land – had recently come out from a tour of the Dutch House.

There was no way she could open the gate without disturbing them.

She put her hand on the gate and said gently, 'Excuse me.'

They started slightly at her voice and moved a foot or so. She could now open and squeeze through the wrought-iron gate. She smiled and asked, 'Have you been round?'

'Yes,' answered the young man, 'but it's closed now.'

'I realize that,' Julia answered. 'Do tell me what you thought of it.'

The girl's dreamy eyes, as they focused briefly on Julia, told her plainly that had the Dutch House been a hovel it would have been all the same to her, sheer heaven, because she was with the young man.

'It's very quaint,' she said in a warm, soft voice.

'Nice that it hasn't been modernized,' added the young man. 'You get a real feeling of age.'

'Oh, you do.' Julia was looking up the short drive to the main part of the Dutch House. 'You certainly do.'

The garden at the front of the house was much wider than it was deep. Bisected by the gravel of the drive were two flat lawns of grass, adorned only by symmetrical pairs of yew trees trimmed to the shape of pyramids.

'Home,' thought Julia, and the indecision, the feeling of being at a crossroads, which had plagued her while she was away, was so overwhelming that she did not know exactly what her reaction to the new home development was.

She walked up to the front door of the Dutch House, climbed the few steps and opened the white-painted panelled door by its large faceted brass handle. The handle shone like gold. She

8

walked through the hallway floored with white and black marble tiles set diamondwise and out through the glass-paned door at the back.

Ahead of her now was a wide garden walk straight as a ruler, between large square beds cornered by trimmed yews and divided as neatly as a chessboard by smooth paths. Over the garden wall on the left she could see the billowing blossom of the avenue of great old white cherry trees in the garden of the Homestead, a nearby property. Julia blamed the fact that the Homestead garden was open to the public for putting the whole idea into Cherry Ducket-Penrose's head. No way was the Dutch House ready to be opened to the public, and you had to do the thing properly if you were going to do it at all and make the place earn its keep.

Two people and a cat were approaching the house on the central garden walk, a tall serious gangling boy of seventeen, a short round woman of about sixty, and a very beautiful Siamese tom-cat who was trying to rub up against their ankles as they walked. It must be feeding time, thought Julia. Oberon is only as friendly as that when he's really hungry.

The boy and the woman were deep in conversation. Every now and then Cherry Ducket-Penrose glanced up at Adam from under the brim of her large garden hat. It was a while before they noticed Julia, looking accusingly at them as they walked towards her. When they did see her they both jumped and looked guilty, which she found extremely satisfactory. It produced a mellowing in the tone she had intended to use.

'I can't turn my back, can I?' she asked quite mildly.

Cherry Ducket-Penrose, the owner of the Dutch House, had already decided on her strategy for this moment. She was going to fight any criticism, fond though she was of Julia.

'You know, Julia dear, it *is* my house, and I can open it if I like,' she said, 'and dear Mrs Honor has been so kind and helpful. She sat at the door and took the money while I conducted people round the ground floor and Adam showed them the kitchens. They went round the garden by themselves because Mr Spicer wanted to be paid overtime to be there.'

'Let's make a cup of tea,' put in Adam. 'Lovely to see you, Mum.' He kissed his mother's cheek as a propitiatory gesture.

9

'It's been great fun opening the house this weekend, it's given me something to do. I'm dying to tell you all about it. How was your holiday?'

'I'm dying to tell you about that, too,' Julia replied. What was done was done. She'd have to see that next time it was done properly, that was all she could attempt. But if Cherry was on her high horse, and Mrs Honor backing her up, there wasn't going to be much she could do about it – was there?

'I'd like to go home,' she said suddenly. 'Will you join us in a cup of tea there, Cherry? I'm a bit tired after the journey.'

'I'll see you tomorrow,' said Cherry Ducket-Penrose. 'Oberon wants his meal. Have you seen Titania?'

Perhaps it would be best to postpone socializing. Julia could feel untimely words rising to her lips. They were all in the hall of the Dutch House now, and Julia picked up her suitcase. It had left a cleaner oblong in the layer of dirt that spread over the marble tiles and she knew that meant dusting it carefully before she took it into her bedroom at home. Looking down she could see bristle marks on the floor as though someone had made efforts with a dustpan and brush, and the marks of the visitors' feet. Glancing at the stone staircase leading down to the base-ment kitchens she noticed that the cobwebs were still floating like ancient tattered banners two feet long from the enormous stag's antlers which hung high on the wall, and she shuddered. You don't *open* a house in this condition and expect it to become a tourist attraction. You just *don't*.

Adam took the suitcase without being asked and they walked to their flat without speaking except to their neighbour Dr Bright, who passed them with a cheery greeting, Mr Spicer who was standing looking at the herbs in the flower beds, and Ms Haygreen who leaned out of her window and waved to them.

The modern – relatively speaking, it was actually Victorian – wing of the old house had been converted beautifully by John Trim, the architect, into eight flats. The area in front of the wing had a large paved parking space, and square beds which were outlined with box and planted with herbs and other things of the unsophisticated kind: marigolds and columbines, Esther Read daisies and nasturtiums and helenium. The second entrance from the road led to both this wing and the stable block along-side. This was now mainly garages with another two flats over.

10

Miss Cherry-blossom Adelaide Honoria Ducket-Penrose still owned the freeholds, but the housing society owned the flats, although Cherry insisted on calling the members of the society her tenants.

Julia Bransby and her son Adam lived in a central ground-floor flat in the wing. Julia, now in her late thirties, had been a widow since Adam was five; her husband, a lecturer at the university, had died and she had chosen the newly converted flat as a suitable home for the rest of Adam's childhood and youth.

She had been able to work up a good connection in her own line, which was textiles. Essentially she was a designer of modern embroideries, but she had acquired a good working knowledge of conservation. She could advise, and give valuations of inherited pieces. She was sought by old families in country houses stuffed with fabrics, by churches about their vestments, by small museums who could not afford full-time specialists, by art galleries mounting textile exhibitions, by trade unions with moth-eaten banners, and by charities given old pieces of costume or patchwork quilts which might be something special. She wrote articles when she found something which needed writing about, or when commissioned.

It had been a useful type of work to have found, or created, for herself, because she had been able to refuse jobs during Adam's holidays unless she could take him with her, and had always been at home when he returned from school. If she had writing to do it could be done in the evenings when he was in bed. He had attended St Olave's, a nearby prep school, and was now in the sixth form at St Peter's, and would be sitting A levels that summer. Then, she supposed, he would be going off to university the year after, and then there would be girlfriends, and his own career, and she would find herself alone . . .

She had been facing that prospect, among other things, during her few days away. After all, they had to be apart some time. It had been the first time, but would not be the last – no, only the first of many, leading eventually to the time when he would be married with children of his own and living in another town or even a different country, busy with a career, remembering sometimes that he had a mother and giving her a telephone call. It would be, 'You all right, Mum?' 'Yes, fine, Adam . . .'

As they opened their door the net curtains of their neighbours twitched, showing that Mrs Honor knew they were back.

'I'll make the tea,' Adam said now. 'You sit down, Mother. I know you're cross, but what could I do about it?'

'Nothing. I'm not blaming you.'

'If I hadn't painted the notice they would have paid someone to do it and Cherry can't afford anything at all.'

'I'll take my suitcase in,' said Julia, who had been dusting it. She looked around her bedroom with a sense of peace and joy. It was so calm, a lovely room. And clean. Returning to the living room she sat down and listened to Adam making the pot of tea in the kitchen and gazed out of her patio window through the now perceptible dusk, across the roughish grass of what had been an orchard to the garden wall which stretched across, dividing them from the Homestead. Near the wall grew a tall old group of silver birches which were always moving in the wind. Julia felt that she could sit and watch them for ever.

Adam brought a tray through bearing some of their pretty Susie Cooper tea set, a deep blue with white spots, and set it down on the low coffee table.

'I need this,' Julia remarked as she poured tea for both of them and picked up a piece of her own home-made fruit cake. 'Have you taken anything out of the deep-freeze for the evening meal, Adam?'

'All taken care of. I'll cook it if you like.'

'Since it only needs to go in the microwave that won't be difficult,' she teased him.

'I've become quite good at microwaving since you've been away.'

'And painting notice boards.'

'That was fun, and it couldn't be helped, I told you.'

'I wouldn't mind if only she would take heed of my advice,' Julia said, but found that the anger had gone out of her voice. 'You don't open a house which is never cleaned from one year end to the other and looks like a jumble sale.'

'Cherry polished the brass,' Adam defended.

'She always polishes the brass. I think it is the only thing she ever learned how to do.'

'She says she can't afford help in the house, that's why she's opening it, to make some money. Anyway, Mother, it was only an experiment; she wanted to try it for Bank Holiday weekend to see how it went, and then open it properly in the summer.'

'You mean it will be closed for the next few weeks? Good.' Julia drank her tea and nibbled her cake. 'How did it go, anyway?' she asked, unable to restrain her curiosity.

'Very well, considering it was all done in a rush without much advertising.'

'Is she giving you anything for your trouble?'

'I don't want anything.'

'Or old Mother Honor?'

'She doesn't want anything either. Quite a few people came. One man came every day. He told Cherry that if she wanted to sell any of her antiques he would advise her on values, that's his job.'

Julia was alarmed at once. 'That kind of approach is exactly what I warned her against . . .'

'He's respectable. He gave me his card.' Adam found it on the top of a bookcase and handed it to his mother.

'Taffinder Walker. Specialist Antique Valuer. Paintings, silver, ivories and general.'

The address was a small nearby market town and Julia realized that she knew the shop. She had often walked down that road through the town centre and passed a place full of middling quality old furniture. Presumably when he found anything of really superior class Walker sold it on to one of the dealers in London.

'You liked him then?' she asked doubtfully, still alarmed. 'You say he came every day?'

'The house has been open three days and he came each day and talked to Cherry for ages. He had a big estate-type car and a chauffeur.'

'Did he now. Did she say he was specially interested in anything?'

'No. He wasn't offering to buy. He seemed genuinely friendly and anxious to advise her if she wanted it. He listened to her talking mostly. Oberon liked him.'

This was the kind of approach Julia had been dreading. The Dutch House only had good security in the Victorian wing, where the occupants had installed their own locks, bolts, or electrical systems. The older part, Cherry's part, could be broken into, she was sure, by a five-year-old child with its father's credit card or its mother's hair grip. Even if Cherry remembered to lock the door. And now that Cherry had opened the house to the public, if any of the chaotic grubby contents were valuable, they could be seen by anyone who paid two pounds to enter. Julia wished her own expertise was wider. She felt that she knew nothing more than the average person about antiques apart from textiles and Cherry had never been willing to let her go through the building examining those properly.

'So you see everything's perfectly all right,' Adam concluded and Julia wondered about her son. She knew that he was brilliantly intelligent in an unusual way, perverse, kind, obstinate, independent; but was he a good judge of people?

'Now what's your story?' asked Adam.

'It's lovely to be home.' She stretched her arms and yawned. 'Well, it has been tiring and rather strange really. You haven't met most of the crowd and I don't suppose you'd want to. We were at school together, in the same form for about five years. Some of us stayed on longer than others. There were seven of us who were The Gang. It's all a long time ago – twenty years, actually, since we were all in the same form. You know why we met now – because Joan is emigrating to Canada to live near her son and it seemed to be a moment of change. Although those moments have come before, I suppose we are all now at a time when our lives are changing direction.'

'How many of you did you say there were at Manchester?' asked Adam.

'Four of us.' Julia looked sad. She certainly seemed tired, more so than would be accounted for by the train journey, or the shock on arrival. Rousing herself a little, she said, 'I discovered that one of my best friends at school has died of a brain tumour. I never met her husband and, do you know, she had three sons. Although I hadn't seen her for so long I feel I miss her being in the world. We were inseparable for several years, yet after my marriage we lost contact, and I don't remember ever mentioning her to you. Odd, isn't it?'

Adam agreed that it was odd.

'And then another friend has committed suicide. One can't imagine that of one's friends and specially not of her, she had so much going for her. I think in a way I loved her more than I've ever loved anyone, yet we weren't nearly as close as say Joan and I. But there are some people you can't help loving. If they exist, you love them.'

'So there were five of you there,' said Adam.

'No. Four of us. Brenda went to South Africa many years ago, you know that, she and I keep in touch by letter. There was Joan who's going to Canada and Madeleine, the most beautiful girl I ever knew, who lives in Cornwall now, she came up specially. And Pat who is a dear, and lives in Sheffield. And me. So there we were. I don't believe we stopped talking from the moment we met until the moment we parted. We certainly didn't waste much time sleeping, that must be why I'm so shattered now.'

'I'll do everything tonight,' Adam said generously, feeling for once in charge of his efficient mother. 'We'll eat in half an hour and you had better have an early night if you are going to work tomorrow.'

'Do I ever work when you're on holiday? But you are right, Adam. You are a dear, too. Let's open a bottle of wine. Not that I'll need anything to help me sleep. By about nine o'clock I'll be dead to the world. Have we any of that rather nice German wine we liked from Sainsbury's?'

'Yes. There's a bottle in the fridge. Something else that's ready, Mother, your moped. I fetched it back from the garage for you. It's passed its M.O.T.'

'You didn't ride it back?'

'It's all right with L plates and I'm seventeen. Not that I'd be seen dead riding it usually, but it was a favour to you.'

'Thank you, darling,' said Julia meekly.

She let his superior jokey tone pass without comment. There was no doubt about it, Adam was a dear. Not that she understood him, or always approved of him – helping Cherry against his mother's wishes didn't please her at all.

There was another thing she hadn't told Adam, though. For the last few months, she and Tom Churchyard, the telephone engineer, had gradually been seeing more of one another.

'There's some post for you.' Adam jerked his head in the direction of the bookcase, as he went out to the kitchen.

Picking up the little pile, Julia recognized the handwriting on one of the envelopes, and knew at once that the letter was from

Tom. They had known one another for a while in a vague kind of way, but since the last performance of the Mystery Plays – the Plays when there had been a murder – they met increasingly as friends.

Tom had played the part of God and she had advised on the costumes. There had been the odd coffee together, and sometimes a lunch, which had become a very pleasant habit for her, and for Tom too she supposed. She had jumped at Joan's invitation to this reunion not only because she wanted to see the old gang again, but also because things had progressed further with Tom and they were on the brink of becoming more than friends, and she wanted to be right away from York for a while in order to think about it, to gain a new perspective, to decide in short, whether to or not . . .

She still had not reached any conclusion. Slipping into her bedroom she put Tom's letter under her pillow to read later in privacy, then returned to sit and gaze out of the patio window.

'Meal's ready, Mother,' said Adam, putting his head round the door. He had laid the table properly in the dining area at the end of the kitchen. The wine was open and the steaming dishes were standing on thick heat-proof mats.

'This is lovely, darling.'

For a moment, sitting down at table, Julia felt like a visitor in her own home.

'Look, Mother,' said Adam when he had eaten most of his plateful, 'there's something I want to say.'

'Go on then,' said Julia.

'It's time you started treating me like a grown-up. I'm seventeen, not thirteen. All my friends do lots of stuff you don't let me do.'

She looked at him in surprise.

'Give me an example, dear.'

'They look after themselves a lot more. Their mums let them use the washer, iron, all that, look after their own clothes. You still buy things for me. I can go and choose my own.'

'I thought you always had chosen your own? You've had a clothes allowance for years.' One thing she hadn't expected was a palace revolution. 'And what's so great about doing your own laundry?'

'It's a matter of self-sufficiency. I'm going to Uni next year and don't know how to look after myself. I'll feel a right pillock. And I want to learn to drive.'

'Book yourself lessons tomorrow. Though it might be more sensible to wait until after the exams. Start doing your own washing and ironing. Again, I suggest you wait until after the exams. It's only a few days really.'

'You don't mind?'

Did she mind? Julia rather thought she did. Seeing Adam well turned out was one of the pleasures and prides in her life. Knowing his smart appearance was thanks to her was part of it. He was right, though. Modern days, modern manners. Washing and ironing was no longer a skilled job. He didn't want her along on clothes-buying expeditions. Fair enough.

'I don't mind,' she said.

'And this cooking caper. You sweated blood leaving food ready in the deep-freeze. I want to learn to cook. You might teach me, I wouldn't be daft enough to refuse. Why should you go to all that trouble? Why can't we both come and go as we please?'

'Where were you thinking of going?' she asked conversationally.

'Out,' he said.

'That vast mysterious region known as Out? But at the risk of babying you, it is always wise to let your base camp know something of where you are and what you're doing.'

'I made a pudding,' he said, getting up and clearing their plates.

2

The following morning Cherry-blossom Adelaide Honoria Ducket-Penrose was sitting in Julia's living room sipping coffee and watching her do the ironing.

'I've never done that,' she remarked.

'You've done ironing, Cherry, I'm sure you have.'

'I've never ironed sheets. We always sent them to the laundry.'

Cherry had the habit of saying 'we always'. She meant, 'When

Mummy was alive,' for Cherry and her mother had lived for many years in a loving household of two, plus supporting staff.

'You still send them to the laundry, I suppose.'

'Yes.'

'And towels and things?'

'I wash my stockings and undies every night,' said Cherry, who was personally very clean, whatever her house might be like. 'We always did that ourselves, even when we had staff. It is called daily dipping,' she informed Julia.

Without answering Julia refolded the white cotton sheet and pressed a further quarter of the surface. She enjoyed having Cherry there watching her; she was fond of the older woman, and looked at her now with affection. Cherry still wore her large-brimmed garden hat and her perpetual cigarette stuck to her bottom lip ready for a quick draw in between mouthfuls of coffee. The whole of her projecting bosom was strewn with cigarette ash, as usual. She was decorated by large brooches and rings and sat with dainty ankles crossed in front of her. Odd, thought Julia, how fat women often have dainty ankles and beautifully shaped small hands and feet. Cherry had very beautiful grey eyes, too, in a rather pale puddingy face.

'Did I ever tell you how I came to be called Cherry-blossom?' she asked.

She had told the story many times, but Julia said, 'No, how was it?'

'Mother had me at home and the fan-trained tree up to the window was in full flower, you know the tree on the house wall at the back. So she called me after it.'

'Very pretty,' said Julia.

'That was before the war, which unsettled everything, particularly Daddy. He ran away with that dreadful woman. Do you know, when I was staying with them, I saw her in a black lacy nightdress?'

'That must have been a shock,' said Julia, who had bought a black lacy nightdress herself three days before, thinking she would Be Prepared. Her heart had thumped as she made the purchase.

'I could never forgive her for that.' Cherry took a drag on her cigarette. 'Mummy wouldn't have been seen dead in such a garment.'

18

Julia thought the obvious comment but said nothing, while folding the sheet firmly into a rectangle and giving it a final rub over the top. Three of Adam's shirts were on wire hangers waiting to be hung in the airing cupboard. Her own undies and blouses from holiday were finished, and so were the few odd-ments of household linen. She thought she would relax over the remainder of her coffee, and it was time to have it out with Cherry about opening the house.

'It isn't so much that I mind you doing it,' she started without preamble, 'it's the way of doing it that was all wrong.'

'You mean without you helping,' said Cherry sweetly, mean-ing 'interfering'.

'You should have had a cleaning woman in.'

'I can't afford one.'

'And a professionally painted notice and at least a leaflet, if not a guide book, and postcards on sale, and proper advice on the history of things on display, and their age.'

'And pot pourri and tea towels and that artificial scent all over the place? You don't get much smell from flower petals on their own, you know. It must be chemical perfume when it is so penetrating,' said Cherry darkly.

'I'm not going to be side-tracked, Cherry.'

'It is a home and that's what I showed people. They'd rather see a home than a museum, and there are lots of antiques and things in it if they want to look at those.'

Julia drained her coffee cup and rose in answer to a knock on the glass of the patio door. Mrs Honor from the adjoining flat loomed outside, tall and elegant. As usual she had about her an air of superiority which Julia found annoying.

'Do join us,' Julia invited. 'I'll fetch more coffee.'

'Such a success, dear Cherry,' beamed Mrs Honor. 'Such fun helping you run it. I haven't enjoyed anything so much since Blue Moon won at Crufts.'

'Where is Blue Moon?' asked Cherry.

In answer, it seemed, the small face of a white Pekinese appeared on the other side of the glass.

'May he come in, Julia?' Cherry called.

'Of course.' Julia reappeared with more coffee and a cup for Mrs Honor.

Adam came from his room, looking half-dazed with study,

19

and poured himself a mugful of coffee. He threw himself into a low chair and his angular young masculinity struck a harsher note in the group of women. His legs were now too long for his socks and trousers so that a band of white flesh showed, and his arms also were too big for his shirt and jersey so that bony wrists stuck out for a good three inches. His hands seemed to be longer every time Julia looked at them. His throat had shot up – 'like a giraffe's', his mother thought, most unfairly, and even the bones of his skull had grown, she was sure, and his hair, instead of lying neatly on his head, erected itself in spikes and lumps.

Although he smiled at everyone he said not a word. Blue Moon came and rested his feathery forepaws on Adam's lap and the two indulged in a little non-verbal conversation.

It was half an hour before Adam returned to his swotting, Mrs Honor and Blue Moon to their flat and Julia could take issue again with Cherry.

'Come over,' invited Cherry, 'and I'll show you exactly how it all went, where I took them and what I showed them.'

'Well, if it won't take too long. Could we do it before lunch?'

'I thought you wanted to be involved?' Cherry said rather coldly. 'Although you don't need to be. Mrs Honor is most helpful and Adam of course, and Mr Walker, such a nice man, came to see the house and will tell me anything I want to know about the history of things, as you put it.'

Julia was quelled.

The original passage from the servants' wing into the main house had been blocked, so they went out at the front and along the paved parking area. They paused in Cherry's front garden, on the grass between two of the trimmed pyramids, and looked up at the façade of the Dutch House.

They saw a house of two storeys plus attics and basement, of mid seventeenth-century date, built of richly textured brick. The brick was varied and glowing in colour and formed into unusual shapes, curved pediments over lower windows and triangular pediments over upper windows. An inverted pyramid of brick supported the oriel window in the centre. The heavily moulded white-painted front door was set within a doorcase of chamfered brick.

Julia turned her head to the right and once again admired the way the Victorian wing had been melded unobtrusively to its older parent while retaining the simple frontage of a socially inferior building.

'It is a lovely house,' Julia said. 'I've always thought you very lucky to live here, Cherry.'

'It doesn't strike me the same way, of course,' Cherry said. 'To me it is home – the only home I've ever known. It is like an extension of myself, I suppose – can you imagine that?'

Julia nodded. 'But I can't help remarking that the windows should really have been cleaned before you showed it.'

Cherry, having triumphed over Julia by opening the house in her absence, was now conciliatory. 'Mr Spicer was supposed to do it. He is a lazy hound. I'll tell him off today. It is always the outside man's job to clean the windows.'

The two women went inside.

'Mrs Honor sat here,' Cherry pointed to a small wooden table brought up from the kitchen into the hall, 'and took the money. She left Blue Moon at home and Oberon sat on the table, looking terribly aristocratic. Which he is, of course.'

All Siamese cats are aristocrats, but Oberon was a king among Siamese, Julia knew.

Behind the table was a carved William and Mary chair in walnut, one of the dining-room set of twelve. Julia reached out and stroked the back of it, then looked ruefully at her hand.

'It's all right.' Cherry misinterpreted her action. 'That's only the one with a broken stretcher, not one of the perfect ones.'

'I expect Titania hid,' Julia said. 'She's so much shyer than Oberon.'

'Yes. She did not deign to appear. Oberon showed off all the time, he loves the limelight. I was pleased the last of the kittens had gone, or she would have been under everyone's feet.'

'You found a home for Peaseblossom, then?'

'Didn't you know? It was arranged before you went off, such a nice family called Suthell, spelt S-o-u-t-h-w-e-l-l. They collected her on Friday.'

'My friends?' asked Julia. 'Do they live on Ouse Avenue? Bob Southwell and Linda?'

'Yes. I'm glad you know them. I like to be sure to whom my kittens have gone.'

'Peaseblossom will have a good home with the Southwells.'

The main rooms of the house were on this floor, and in Mrs

21

Ducket-Penrose's later years she and Cherry had treated their home like a bungalow and not used the upper rooms. Although there had been many alterations through the centuries one basic plan could still be adhered to; it was possible to walk round inside the house from room to room, beginning in the main hall but not returning to it until the circuit had been completed.

Cherry and Julia accordingly walked left into the long gracious drawing room, with its tattered silk-upholstered furniture, its crumbling cornices once gilded with pure gold, its mist of dust and its clutter. Julia did not know what to say, but out of all her reactions to this particular apartment being open to the public she gasped only, 'That cornice ought to be repaired and re-gilded, Cherry.'

Cherry did not appear to hear.

'What did you say to them in here?' asked Julia.

'I showed them the painting of Mummy.' Cherry waved at a large oil painting by de Laszlo of a slender young girl dressed in the fashion of the late twenties. It was a painting of vague shapes and cloudiness, with the girl seeming to come out of a fog into distinctness only round her head and shoulders, which had a wistful beauty. Her stick-like arms melted into the surrounding soft and apparently random brushstrokes. Her dress looked as if it might be fringed and beaded. It exuded the glamour of its time.

'The dress is somewhere put away,' said Cherry, and here Julia caught her up quickly.

'If it is in good condition it could be worth hundreds of pounds, do you realize that, Cherry? Have you much of her clothing from that period?'

'Oh, I don't know!' said Cherry, with another look round the drawing room. 'I showed them that chair because my grand-mother embroidered it and that case of medals because they were grandfather's. There isn't anything else of interest in here really.'

Julia had only once passed through the drawing room before, when the curtains had been closed and old sheets thrown over the furniture. At least Cherry had had enough sense to remove those and let in some light, though light could damage fibres if not strictly controlled. Looking at the tattered silk of the upholstery and the shredded remnants of curtains Julia decided that light wouldn't matter at this stage.

Next Cherry led the way to the little corner room which had originally been called a 'cabinet'. It was usually referred to nowadays as 'my little den', and was the bit of the house Julia knew best. Normally she walked across the hall, entered the short back hall which led to the garden door, then turned left through the dining room into this tiny apartment, where Cherry spent much of her time.

There was a corner fireplace with, over it, one of those high wooden structures popular in the time of William and Mary for the display of china – very appropriate in the Dutch House. The original Chinese Famille Verte porcelain pieces were still there, for the Dutch House had never changed hands. The property had passed through the female line on occasions, but it had been handed down generation to generation, and because it was small as important houses go it had been retained and loved when grander properties had been demolished or sold off. Through time some of the Famille Verte china had been broken or chipped, some was fastened together with centuries-old rivets, some glued with modern adhesives, and the whole of it was interspersed with old letters, postcards, and invitations which Cherry had pushed up there.

The table had not been cleared since Cherry had breakfasted in front of the tiny fire grate, with its summer fan of folded paper filling in the space where for eight months of the year there was a cheerful little fire. On the hearth were a brightly polished copper kettle and sparkling brass fire irons.

Julia looked at the table with interest and picked up the sugar basin. She felt very drawn to the object for some reason. Artefacts are evocative to those who are sensitive to such things, and as it nestled in her hand the sugar bowl spoke to her of a long-ago time and the craftsman who had made it, and all the human life it had shared. She liked the tiny irregularities, the raven's mask on the curve of the side, the minute traces that told her it had been made by hand. 'This looks old, Cherry, do you know anything about it?' she asked idly.

'That's worthless,' said Cherry with contempt. 'Can't you tell it is only moulded glass? Here, I'll show you proper glass.'

Going to a corner cupboard she took out some tall delicate old wine glasses with elaborate stems. 'Feel underneath. Can you feel a sort of scar – probably polished smooth? That is where they break the glass from the pontil rod when they have finished making it. Hand-blown glass might be valuable, particularly if it's cut. Moulded never is.'

'I still like your sugar basin – it appeals to me, somehow – though these are very lovely, of course.'

Cherry took another glass bowl out of the cupboard. 'Feel the crisp edges of this cutting,' she said, taking Julia's hand and rubbing her finger ends over the pattern. 'Now feel the sugar basin. Can you tell how smooth it is in comparison? Never be taken in by moulded glass.'

'I won't be,' promised Julia humbly, wondering if the antiques expert, Taffinder Walker, had seen those beautiful tall wine glasses with the pontil mark underneath. She wished she had spent more time on antiques other than textiles. No one likes to feel stupid and that was what Julia felt at that moment. But something obstinate in her still liked the sugar basin better than the other glass.

'What did you point out to your tourists in here?' she asked.

'My guests, dear. I like to think of them as my guests.'

'What did you point out to your guests?'

'Those embroideries,' replied Cherry with immense pride, indicating two framed panels, one on either side of the door. 'Mummy embroidered those.'

Julia said nothing. The panels had been embroidered in the nineteen thirties from bought transferred kits and stitched in stranded cotton. Not that there was anything wrong with that. She had done her first embroideries that way herself. But these panels of crinoline ladies in cottage gardens, both surrounded by hollyhocks, were by any standards worthless. They were not even well stitched. She always averted her eyes from them when she was visiting Cherry in this room.

'Are those the only things you pointed out in here?'

'No. I showed them the miniatures by the fireplace, that one is of Mummy and that one is of Daddy.'

'Who are the others? They look interesting,' asked Julia, mentally dating the tiny portraits by their costume.

24

'I suppose they are some sort of relatives,' said Cherry thoughtfully.

After this they went into the dining room, which Julia knew well. The long walnut table with its twelve chairs – eleven at that moment – had its top wiped free of dust but the film was settling on it again already.

'In here I showed them the picture over the fireplace and told them it is supposed to be of Utrecht,' said Cherry, anticipating Julia's question. The painting was darkened by centuries of smoke, but a line of houses and the masts of ships could be made out vaguely. There was no comment to make. Julia was familiar with the festooned curtains of pure silk hanging in ribbons – such a very perishable fibre, but so lovely who could resist it, and they would cost a fortune to replace – and the worn old Spanish leather on the walls, which had once been gilded but was now stained by what looked suspiciously like damp.

They then walked past the door into the garden at the back of the house, and penetrated into rooms on the right of the hallway, which Julia had never seen before. The 'cabinet' room at this end was simply furnished as a small bedroom and appeared to be in use. The wallpaper was a charming one which reminded Julia of fabric patterns.

'Is this a handpainted Chinese wallpaper?' she asked.

'Oh, yes,' Cherry replied over her shoulder as she hurried through the room without commenting on it.

The next door led very surprisingly into a bathroom. It took Julia a minute to realize that it had been created by cutting off the end of the adjoining bedroom. There was an enormous pottery vase in the corner filled with plumes of pampas grass, many years old for they were grey and thick with spiders' webs. Even so they cast an aura of glamour, and the walls and floor tiled with genuine peach-coloured marble, the sunken bath with its low sides painted with simulated black marble, the loo covered discreetly by a specially made white wicker chair, gave Julia a distinct impression of the film sets of the thirties. But it was an eerie glamour, for she felt the pampas plumes might crumble away, the painted ceiling drop on her head. Over the bath someone had fixed a length of string from two clumsy cup hooks and on it Cherry's daily dipping was hanging presumably to dry.

Julia was overcome by the bathroom. She was even more overcome by the bedroom into which it led.

'Cherry!' she cried in outrage. 'You didn't show your guests round this?'

'Of course I did. It's the State Bedroom. It isn't the one where I was born – that's upstairs – but this is the best. We used to save it for grand visitors but when we moved down here Mummy used it and I took the little corner room. We shared the bathroom. This is fun, isn't it?'

The bed was incredible. It was a four-poster and the canopy over it must have touched the ceiling. Obviously made by a master cabinet-maker, probably French, the hangings were of grey velvet and slate-blue brocade. But! But the condition it was in!

'I hope you made the bed before you showed anyone round.' Julia was straightening the crumpled bedding.

'Yes,' said Cherry shortly.

'Cherry, this I really do know something about. You have the most marvellous bed here – I was in charge of renovating one very similar recently. All those velvet borders round the canopy – those that are hanging away in great loops – do be careful you don't ever catch them or they will fall down entirely – they are exquisite work. What a pity the curtains are mostly off their rings – they must be getting spoiled dragging down like that and trailing on the floor in heaps. And the cover – it is not the one made for the bed of course, that would be velvet – but it is a beautiful example of appliqué from about 1800 – do you realize this cover alone is worth about nine hundred pounds in auction?'

'Don't be ridiculous,' Cherry said firmly. 'It's only an old thing Mummy used because the velvet one had come in two. And how do you think I could possibly afford to have the hangings mended? No, they'll do my time and that's that.'

Julia thought that the whole bed looked as though there had been an attempt at deliberate destruction, the hangings ripped – the whole of the piece of furniture held together only by threads of fabric and scraps of glue – leaning at a crazy angle – it was in a terrible state. It looked as though a gang of vandalistic teenagers had been asked to do their worst. But Julia could see that Cherry was quite unaware of the look of the thing.

She had become convinced that her friend never saw anything

above eye level, or Cherry would have noticed the flaunting cobwebs; and never below the top surfaces of the furniture, for where there had been polishing done it was only the tops that had been touched and everything below was crying out for beeswax and turpentine applied with a good soft rag.

Apart from that enormous and startling piece of vandalism that went by the name of the bed, there were pretty chests of drawers in the room and delicate watercolours on the walls, looking as though they were gradually fading away into the wallpaper, which itself was at least a hundred years old and had once been boldly patterned with birds and foliage. Against the walls were piled many cardboard boxes and mysterious bundles. Julia realized that Cherry moved round her house in little tracks, like those of an animal in undergrowth, and that everything not used by her every day was mounded up and forgotten.

The bedroom windows looked out at the front of the house and wandering over, Julia could see that a station wagon had just arrived and parked on the grass, exactly at the spot where she and Cherry stood when they gazed at the façade of the house. A tall handsome man was climbing out of it, and another man, wearing a peaked cap, sat in the driving seat.

'Oh, it's Mr Walker,' cried Cherry, who had come to stand beside her. 'Now you'll meet him, Julia, and you will see that "the history of things" is in good hands. He's very knowledgeable.'

She bustled through the door which led from the State Bedroom back into the hall and opened the front door to the antique dealer. Following behind, Julia thought she would be able to sum him up and decide whether he was befriending Cherry in good faith or for what he could get out of it.

'Julia, I'd like to introduce Mr Walker. Mr Walker, my tenant Mrs Bransby. She is a textile consultant.'

'Really?' Walker took Julia's hand in a brief clasp. His hand felt pleasant, dry and warm. 'Delighted to meet you.' Turning to Cherry, he held out a picture which had been under his left arm. 'A charming scene, Miss Ducket-Penrose, but unfortunately the expert to whom I showed it feels that its commercial value is negligible. As its sentimental value is so great to you, it doesn't seem worth while selling it.'

Cherry looked disappointed as she took the picture.

'Mummy painted it,' she explained to Julia. 'Do I owe you anything, Mr Walker? Did you have to pay your expert friend?'

'Oh no, that's quite all right. We do one another little favours from time to time. I did tell you that pictures aren't my particular area.'

The smile was charming, Julia admitted, even while she was thinking, 'Little favours, I bet you do.'

'I'm sorry it isn't valuable, but I wouldn't have sold it anyway. A cup of tea?' suggested Cherry. 'I'm afraid I can't offer you lunch.'

'Thank you, but I only dropped by in passing to return your lovely picture. So nice to have met you, Mrs Bransby.' Taffinder Walker bent down to caress Oberon, who was rubbing against his legs and yowling for attention in the weird voice of the Siamese.

Cherry sighed wistfully as she closed the door behind the antique dealer. 'I hope you didn't frighten him away, Julia, with those stern looks of yours. I don't have so many attentive good-looking young men in my life.'

'He is certainly very good-looking,' agreed Julia gently. She didn't have very many attentive good-looking men in her life either. Except for Tom Churchyard . . .

'I suppose you're going to go now as well,' Cherry added sadly.

'Adam will be ready for his lunch and I want to entice him out for a walk this afternoon. It is a shame to waste this lovely weather and he neglects his exercise when he's working for exams. I've seen it before. Have lunch with us, Cherry?'

Julia felt almost motherly towards the older woman, who had this morning admitted her further into her friendship than ever before – but no further than dozens, possibly hundreds, of tourists over the previous three days. She wondered why the antique dealer had bothered to take away Cherry's mother's amateurish water-colour – he must have known it was worthless even if his speciality wasn't pictures. Even she knew that it was a daub and not worth the paper it was painted on. 'I wish I had more free time to offer to help you, Cherry. I could put some of your textiles in order at least.'

'Why should you? You have Adam to look after and a busy career. Mrs Honor has nothing to do except look after herself and Blue Moon. I won't have lunch today, dear. Another time, perhaps. I've had coffee with you already this morning.'

Cherry's delightful smile warmed her words, but Julia left the house wondering where she stood with her friend. Where, after all, did she stand with anyone? Adam would soon be able to manage without her and bringing up a child single-handed had meant severe limitations on social life. She discovered when her husband died that most of their mutual friends had been his rather than hers, and when she was alone with Adam and preoccupied with making a career, they had gradually dropped away. She had made a scattering of new ones. The other occupants of the flats had been good and friendly neighbours through the years. People she met professionally were often congenial and became friends. Near at hand was Linda South- well, who was perhaps the person she felt closest to on a 'drop in for coffee and never mind the family disorder' basis.

One thing was sure. She didn't want to talk to Linda about all this. Tom Churchyard lived next door to the Southwells, and her feelings about Tom were far too unsure and private at present to be aired. A father confessor might be handy, she thought, then shook her shoulders and held her head up proudly. What nonsense she was thinking! Shouldn't today be one of happiness? Hadn't she had a letter from Tom, suggesting they spent an afternoon together, away from York, away from their own settings, to get to know one another a little better . . .

So! She now knew that she had decided to let her relationship with Tom go further, and to keep quiet about it. The gossip amongst the other inhabitants of the Dutch House would be unbearable if they knew, and as for Adam, she wasn't sure how he would react. Better to be sure herself first. Mrs Honor now, that supercilious old skeleton, patronizing . . . Julia had to pull herself up sharply. She didn't want to descend to the level of some people, just because she herself could never get on with Mrs Honor, though Adam managed perfectly well.

All the same, the very thought of being talked over by the other inhabitants of the Dutch House made her skin crawl. She loved them – well, most of them. Cherry, unconditionally. Mrs Honor, not at all. Mrs Robinson, mostly. Miss Haygreen and Miss Hodson, indulgently. Dr Bright, Mr Spicer, Mr Markhall, the Brothers Lloyd, in a neighbourly way, though Mrs Bright, who descended on York from time to time from her usual residence in the south of France, she felt she hardly knew. The new resident, Susannah Wilmet, seemed fine so far. It was nice to have a young woman about the place. Julia looked forward to knowing her better.

Adam agreed to come for a walk on condition they took Blue Moon. As they went out at the front they met Dr Bright coming in, and he lived up to his name with his expansive gestures and radiant smile.

'You aren't taking that perambulating powderpuff out with you, are you?' Dr Bright exclaimed on seeing Blue Moon, who didn't like him either, and put on a show of growling and general antagonism.

'We are, actually,' said Adam rather stiffly.

'You might at least borrow a proper dog. A German Shepherd dog, Adam, or a labrador. Labs always want exercise, they eat too much.'

'Blue Moon's the only dog at the Dutch House,' said Julia. 'And he knows you think he's a powderpuff. He's trying his best to behave like a Rottweiler.'

'Oh well, each to his own,' said the doctor with another smile as he went upstairs to his flat over the Bransbys'.

They walked along the river bank. The day was calm, the willows almost without movement, the meadows and St Peter's playing fields flat and green. The scene was like a Dutch painting. Blue Moon decided he wanted to fight a German Shepherd dog, who looked surprised at his presumption.

As they walked Julia asked her son if he minded being on his own for a while the next day. 'I want to make a trip into the West Riding,' she said, not wishing to volunteer more in the way of explanation.

'I'll be all right,' he said casually.

Julia felt it sounded as if she went off and left him constantly.

'Don't get into mischief,' she couldn't help saying.

'Mother! Stop it! What have we agreed? I'm seventeen, not seven, right? Anyway, Cherry isn't opening the house again until July.' He grinned at her teasingly.

'So she told me. I must say it was a relief. How anyone could think of opening a house in that state I don't know.'

'It's different,' said Adam.

'True.'

'She says it is a home, not a museum.'

'I have heard her say that.'

Adam enjoyed most things in life in his own way. Now that he had asserted his independence he particularly enjoyed teasing his mother. 'That telephone engineer rang up while you were in Manchester,' he said.

'Telephone engineer?'

'Tom Churchyard, he said his name was. The one who wrote to you. I gave you the letter when you got home.'

'How did you know that letter was from Tom?'

'Well, I said you were away until the following Monday, and he said, "I'll write to her then," and the letter came the next day by hand. There isn't a delivery on Sunday. Didn't you notice there wasn't a stamp? The writing looked like a man's to me, and doesn't he live next door to your friend Linda? That's so close that he might have dropped it in on his way home, or something.'

'As it happens the letter was from Tom, thank you for your interest, Adam.'

'That's all right, any time.'

'How are your General Studies going on?' she said repressively. Really, having a private life was almost impossible with a teenage son about.

'Fine. There isn't much preparation you can do for General Studies except read the newspapers and watch current affairs programmes on television.'

'You seem to have quite a few lessons programmed in it.'

'We're supposed to understand the society we live in.'

'Hopeless, I would have thought.'

For a while they were silent, then Julia said, 'Apart from Cherry's doings, there must be some happenings amongst the neighbours you haven't told me about.'

'They are like the Tribes of Israel, always falling out.'

'I don't know that the tribes did fall out, did they?' Julia felt on very unsure ground for the second time that day.

'Mr Spicer and Mrs Honor have been at it again, hammer and tongs.'

31

'They always are. Do you remember last year when the apples were ripe and she would go on taking them when she thought no one was looking, and Mr Spicer kept catching her at it?'

'It was the shrubs this time, over by the wall. Some of them have been flowering and she cut some for flower decorations and as usual he told her they were for everyone's enjoyment and the garden round the flats was not run for her amusement only. Then it was the herbs in the box beds at the front, she was stuffing a duck and wanted some sage leaves.'

'The sage is doing beautifully, she could have had as much as she liked, I would have thought.'

'Not in the gospel according to Spicer.'

'Well, that deals with our next-door neighbours. Sometimes I wish I wasn't the punchbag in between them. What about upstairs?'

'Mrs Robinson on the end fell down and broke her ankle . . .'

'Oh, Adam, how awful. I must buy her some flowers tomorrow. I noticed she wasn't waving out of the window when I came home. It isn't like her to miss anything that's going on. She will feel lonely.'

'It's all right, Mother, she's gone to her daughter's to recuperate. The daughter didn't seem very keen. Doctor Bright above has been trying to help old Oddsocks on the end . . .'

'Darling, he does have a name. You really shouldn't call him Oddsocks.'

'Anyway he's been trying faith healing for his rheumatism and Doctor Bright's been telling him cod liver oil would be just as good.'

'Internal or external?' asked Julia. 'Help me with this dratted dog, Adam, he's spoiling for a fight.'

'Doctor Bright's wife was here for a couple of days. I heard her voice. They were talking away on Saturday night.' Sounds from the flat above theirs were very muted, but Mrs Bright had a voice of distinctive timbre and no one could mistake it, even coming dimly through brick and plaster. 'Cherry came in on Friday night and watched television with me, and Mrs Honor came in with Blue Moon on Saturday night.'

'She's got her own television.'

'There was nothing on, so we played Scrabble and talked.'

It was a superb afternoon, and there was still plenty to hear, about the inhabitants of the two flats over the garages, who were going to be at daggers drawn any minute. The partition wall was not quite as sound-proof as John Trim had intended it to be.

The mother and son walked slowly along the river bank, out of the city and over the Ings, the meadows which were flooded in winter. A faint, good, sweet scent seemed to rise from the earth itself. The sun gave new life to everything, the beginning of summer; the river sparkled, the grass shone as if newly groomed, the trees seemed to rejoice. They passed fishermen sitting motionless under umbrellas, lovers walking hand in hand, and family parties surrounded by boisterous children and barking dogs. A few dogs seemed to be busily taking themselves for walks. Blue Moon rolled over onto his back, wriggled in ecstasy, and decided that he loved everyone.

Back at the Dutch House trouble was brewing. The newest tenant, Miss Susannah Wilmet, music teacher, being on holiday, was taking the opportunity to spend eight hours practising the piano. She intended one day to be a concert pianist. She was five feet nothing, slim but with large breasts, a stormy mass of dark brown hair and eyes to match in storminess and colour. Her most promising attribute as a concert pianist was her temperament.

Next door to her in the other flat over the stable block lived the Brothers Lloyd, Gawain and Lancelot. They had been very taken by the idea of living next to such a charming and talented girl, and having the opportunity of listening to her playing the piano – the sound came very clearly through the party wall. On this particular day it was coming clearly for the full eight hours, and after about five their nerves were starting to fray.

In the evenings during term time they had discovered that Susannah took pupils, and that was bad enough, but at least it was intermittent, with Susannah's voice (sharper than they had ever expected) interrupting the learner's performance at regular intervals. There were not usually more than two pupils during the evening, either, and last thing at night Susannah often gave herself a short recital, which on the whole the brothers enjoyed, though sometimes it stopped them getting to sleep. It was just unfortunate, they told themselves, that as they grew older they needed to go to bed earlier.

They didn't like to complain, having begun by being so

welcoming, but they did wish as the afternoon wore on that Susannah would go over to drink afternoon tea with Mrs Honor, as she sometimes did.

Cherry was sitting in her garden, wearing her garden hat and reading an eighteenth-century book in French. She wasn't sure that she agreed with its sentiments, as it was *Essais de Theodicé sure la Bonté de Dieu, la Liberté de l'Homme, et l'Origine du Mal*, but the tiny little engravings on the title page and at the beginning and end of every chapter were entrancing. She thought she would ask Julia to make them into embroidery designs for her, then she could sit out here on summer days and stitch canvas-work cushions.

A few yards away Mr Spicer was busy clipping the box edging. They were both content.

Mrs Honor was arranging a bowl of flowers on her dining table. She had picked them from the flower beds in front of the flats, and Mr Spicer was going to be furious. In the flat above her Mr Markhall, who was a retired architect, was rearranging his books on their shelves and at the same time pondering a chess puzzle. The flat over Mr Spicer's was empty, because Mrs Robinson was at her daughter's. The attic flats, where Ms Haygreen and Ms Hodson lived, were sunny and peaceful, perhaps because both ladies were out. If they had been at home, Ms Hodson would have been complaining about the smell of stewing weeds with which Ms Haygreen intended to dye fabric, and Ms Haygreen would have been incensed by the smell of turpentine from Ms Hodson's oil painting. At that moment, though, Ms Haygreen was still picking her weeds and Ms Hodson had set up her easel in the garden of the Homestead and was trying to capture the spring blossom.

Two old, short, stocky men in dark-blue suits were knocking on Mrs Honor's door. During the war – so long ago – she and her husband had both been involved with the French Resistance, a fact she mentioned rather often, and from time to time there was a pleasing contact with former colleagues.

By the time Julia and Adam were turning for home, Mr Markhall had given up his chess puzzle as a bad job and finished rearranging his bookcase. As his concentration relaxed, he became conscious of voices drifting up from below, Mrs Honor's cultured tones and Ms Susannah Wilmet's passionate contralto.

Moving onto his balcony, he could hear perfectly because their voices were growing louder as the discussion went on. The two women were sitting out on Mrs Honor's patio and drinking tea, only a few feet below him.

Susannah was explaining that it was the burning desire of her life to become a concert pianist, teaching being only a temporary stopgap, and how could she achieve her goal when the two old men next door to her were constantly interrupting her necessary practice?

Mrs Honor was soothing and encouraging her, repeating her conviction that Susannah had enormous talent and would one day be famous worldwide. She was urging the girl to be firm and egotistical, to regard her ambition as paramount, much more important than the piffling interests of the two Lloyd brothers.

'My dear,' she said, 'one day I will be very proud of having known you. When I hear your name mentioned I will tell my friends that I once had the privilege of being your neighbour. You will have the world at your feet.'

Mr Markhall listened. As he stood there he noticed that Mrs Honor's clematis montana was rapidly mounting his balcony and about to invade his windowframes *again*. He fetched his kitchen scissors and began to snip off the intruding tendrils of clematis, throwing them one by one down onto the tea-table below.

On the whole it was a typical kind of day at the Dutch House.

3

When Taffinder Walker first met Cherry Ducket-Penrose, he also made the acquaintance of Mrs Honor. She was, as Julia had found, much more formal than her friend, but being anxious to have his expertise, she invited him to drink tea with her on several occasions. The pattern was always the same. If Taff Walker's chauffeur and handyman, Duncan Fraser, who often went with Taff like an accompanying child or puppy dog, turned up at Mrs Honor's door, it was shut in his face. Duncan often had to resign himself to sitting in the motor trying to read the books Taff gave him, which were all on antiques. Inside Mrs Honor's flat, Taff would be treated to an account of Mrs Honor's courtship and marriage.

'He and I began as pen-pals,' she would explain. 'A lot of girls in those days wrote to servicemen. They appreciated it, particularly if they had no families. Toto was in Bomber Command, stationed at Heslington, and had a lot to do with the French squadrons flying from Elvington. Strangely enough, three years after our correspondence started, I was posted to France myself, to take part in running one of the Resistance's escape routes for shot-down airmen. I had a French governess, you see, so my accent is perfect. Our correspondence lapsed of course and I quite thought he would be dead when I returned at the end of the war.'

'So he was still alive and waiting for you, as who would not,' responded Taff Walker gallantly.

Mrs Honor was always flattered by his remarks. She was intensely self-absorbed, and too aristocratic to believe that she could possibly be influenced by anyone lower than herself in the social scale. The result was that she could be influenced very easily.

'We met and married – a usual enough story, Mr Walker. We were very happy. He died four years ago and I moved into this flat, bringing the best of my pieces with me. That is why I invite you to visit – I know you appreciate my bits and pieces.'

'They are as charming as their owner.'

Taff was not lying. The flat was charming in the way which most appealed to him. The armchairs were like stately thrones, the desk florid in the Empire style and he put it down as genuine, the ornaments were rare and valuable, the best of their kind. The effect was like the private boudoir of the owner of a castle.

'How your touch would improve the Dutch House!' he ventured to say, hoping that the remark would not get back to Cherry Ducket-Penrose. Somehow Mrs Honor seemed to draw it out of him.

The Pekinese looked up and snuffled doubtfully. Mistress liked this man, but Blue Moon was not so sure. He was not keen on men in general, and this one had a distinct smell of Oberon about his trousers. While mistress was out of the room brewing the tea and the man was lifting up the ornaments and looking underneath, he, Blue Moon, ventured to remonstrate and was given a sharp push for his pains. He yelped and when his mistress hurried back into the room, the man explained that the dog had got under his feet and nearly made him fall over.

'I was admiring your Dresden, Mrs Honor,' he said, 'and did not notice he was so close.'

'It is very gratifying to have an expert admire it,' she said, setting down the tea-tray. It was loaded with the best china cups, saucers and tea-plates, and fancy cakes. 'Don't fuss,' she said sharply to Blue Moon. 'Give Mr Walker a paw. Naughty dog, come out! Don't hide behind the chairs. A paw, I said!'

The paw was offered reluctantly.

'All that wartime life comes back to me at this time of year,' said Mrs Honor, pouring the straw-pale tea. 'There is a reunion at Elvington shortly, and we always took part, Toto and I. When he died I stopped going to the reunion, but some of our French friends from long ago have called to see me each year. So kind of them. We are all getting older, there are fewer and fewer of us. I am really old and frail, Mr Walker.'

'That is not the impression you make at all,' he said, still gallant. 'When I first saw you I thought you were the owner of the Dutch House, you were so very "grande Dame".'

'It is kind of you to say so.' Mrs Honor agreed with him completely. She would have made a much better owner of the Dutch House than Cherry did; plump, untidy, ash-strewn Cherry Ducket-Penrose. She would have liked to own and show off the Dutch House. 'More tea?'

Mrs Honor often changed the subject abruptly. 'Cherry tells me you are related.'

'Not exactly. We may be. Her mother's maiden name was Becuda so she was certainly descended from one of the settler families of the seventeenth century. My mother was a Taffinder, another settler family who like the Becudas came over from the Low Countries after the Thorne Levels were drained by Vermuyden, to farm the newly available land. We might be related.'

'A long time back, obviously,' Mrs Honor said.

'In the second half of the seventeenth century there was a lot of intermarrying amongst the settler community.'

'Hardly relevant nowadays.'

At comments like this Taff was driven to protest. 'It means a great deal to those of us descended from the immigrants. They left their traces, buildings and drainage in the Dutch style. One thinks of many houses and barns stretching from the Isle of Axholme up the Vale to York, where we have the Treasurer's House, the Old Manor House here in Clifton, and of course the Dutch House itself.'

Mrs Honor did not bother to listen to this kind of conversation. She followed her own thoughts. 'Cherry has a great deal of valuable stuff in there,' she said thoughtfully. 'I know you will give her the best advice, Mr Walker. She has no idea of value.' She shot a very perceptive look at the antique dealer.

'I will advise her to the best of my ability.'

'I expect you charge for advice?' Mrs Honor had a few items put away which she would be glad to change into money.

'One must live.'

A ring at the doorbell usually interrupted these tête-à-têtes, and when Mrs Honor returned to the sitting room, she would say, 'It is your chauffeur, to remind you of your next appointment.'

'I can't believe how the time has flown! I must say goodbye, Mrs Honor.'

Her habit was to extend her hand, like minor royalty, and, holding the tips of her fingers, he would touch the wrinkled back of her hand with his lips. Once outside, Taff Walker seemed more jaunty, quite pleased with himself. He exchanged meaningful looks with Duncan Fraser and tipped him a wink.

When the momentous Thursday came, the day which was later to be analysed so closely, Julia caught a mid-morning train to Leeds. As she passed through the ticket barrier at the end of her journey, she could see ahead the bulky figure of Tom Church-yard, waiting for her in the wide foyer. They had gradually grown into friendship since the last performance of the Mystery Plays; were they now to become lovers? Before he caught sight of her she had time to study him, to remind herself of the craggy face, the slightly waving hair, the air of dependability and competence, the grey tweeds he liked to wear which, she was sure, made him look older than he was.

As she walked towards him he caught sight of her and his face lit up with a kind of quiet happiness. She felt as nervous as a young girl on her first date. They both put their hands out awkwardly, clasped briefly, and felt thrilled and shaken by the contact.

Their eyes met and then glanced away again, met and glanced away.

'Would you like a coffee?' asked Tom.

'I'm dying for one.'

'There's the station buffet here, it isn't too bad these days. Or we could go to the Queen's Hotel on the corner, they serve coffee in the lounge bar, I've been checking it out and it looks all right.'

Julia thought about her current relationship with Tom. Was it close enough yet for the comfort and intimacy of the Queen's Hotel? She plumped for the more ambiguous surroundings of the British Rail cafeteria and they stood in line to harvest their two cups of coffee.

'Today's my treat,' said Tom.

She decided to accept that, although she had made a point, when they met previously, of paying her own way. Sitting opposite one another at the tiny table she was conscious of Tom's gaze on her bare arms and wished that she was still wearing the jacket of her suit. He seemed fascinated by her hands and forearms; she wondered if they really were attractive, or did he only want to avoid eye contact?

'Where are we going then?' she asked.

'More than one place if you like and there's time,' he said. 'I thought first a bit of sightseeing – Oakwell Hall not many miles from here has recently been done up and it has reopened to the public. Have you ever been there?'

'No, that sounds like fun. I don't think I've even heard of it.'

'It was made famous by Charlotte Brontë when she used it as the setting for her novel *Shirley*, but they have concentrated on an earlier period in the refurbishing – there was an excellent inventory surviving from one of the Batt family who lived there in Jacobean times. Then I know a pub at Heckmondwyke that does good bar lunches. After that we can see how much time there is and decide.'

'Great.' Julia found that she liked having her day planned for her, with due consideration of her wishes. She knew that had she rejected out of hand the idea of going round a historic house Tom would have given in at once and suggested something else.

They finished their coffee and left the station.

'I've got a car here,' said Tom, leading the way to the car-park.

'Not yours,' she stated when he went to a small saloon and unlocked the door. Tom had a vintage Rolls, which was why he usually travelled round York by bicycle. The Rolls was a little too precious to treat as a general runabout, and cycling was quicker in the narrow medieval city streets snarled up with late-twentieth-century traffic.

'We will go out in the Rolls one day.' Tom smiled, opening the near-side door for her. 'But I must admit I try to keep my mileage down in it. If we were going on an expedition near York it would be different. This is a hire car.'

Julia's heart was thumping again. That casual suggestion, as though expeditions together were to become a way of life, that quick sidelong look – she stared through the window at the Leeds traffic. It was much better not to talk until they were out of this lot. She folded her hands neatly on her lap.

She is neat altogether, thought Tom. Always neatly dressed, usually in grey which suits her. Her hair nearly black and cut a twenties-type shingle, high at the nape of the neck and hanging in curves onto each cheek. Her figure slim and – yes, neat. Of average height, with grey eyes, which have sparkling whites and long black lashes, she has an air of confidence and capability which I like. . . . Now, her nearness was affecting him a good deal. He had to concentrate hard on the traffic and let the knowledge of their whole afternoon together stay in the back of his mind.

Oakwell Hall was a charming stone-built house with a great deal of woodwork inside. There were no vestiges of twentieth-century features. They felt that they had stepped back in time to a yeoman's house of the seventeenth century. There was a dairy, and the kitchens, and the great hall with its wide many-mullioned window looking out over the countryside. A twisting wooden staircase was partitioned off from the great hall by a gate, to prevent the household dogs of that other century going upstairs. There was the best parlour, where the intricately patterned plaster ceiling had once fallen down on top of a schoolmistress, during the time when the hall was a private girls' school and she slept in that room in a four-poster bed. Tom told Julia how the ceiling had been reconstructed from an old drawing and they both bent their necks backward to admire its craftsmanship, the coats of arms and other designs.

What Julia liked best about the house was the way it had been treated; it did not seem old because of dirt and decay, but because the meticulous refurnishing had given the illusion of a household living and busy in the fashion of that time. Julia admired the modern fabrics, hand-embroidered in India, which reproduced so exactly the feel of Jacobean crewel work as it had been when first made. Some of the furniture was old, some new in the manner of the old, which gave the correct impression. The pottery had been carefully made in the old way and to the old patterns.

'I wish I'd studied general antiques more,' she said to Tom. 'One becomes very narrow minded as a specialist and I seem to have developed tunnel vision. I know in my bones that they have done this exactly right but I could not have decided myself on what they ought to do, except for the fabrics.'

'Aren't you one of the voluntary tourist guides in the Minster?' asked Tom. 'You must be knowledgeable.'

'Yes, I do guide, but apart from the fabrics and those marvellous carpets, I repeat what I've been told and wish I knew whys and wherefores. I have absorbed a bit about Gothic architecture,' she finished hesitantly.

'When I've heard you lecture you have always been most authoritative.'

'Yes, but I only lecture about things I know backwards.'

The two were very conscious each of the other. It was impossible while going round the house to do what Tom wanted to do and Julia thought she would like him to do, which was to hold her hand; but he was attentive in little ways, holding doors, or guiding her with a light momentary touch on her shoulder, and several times his hand slid down her arm after such a contact and there was a slight pressure on her fingers. The staff of the building made them acutely self-conscious. There seemed to be a man in uniform in every place where they thought they might be sufficiently alone for Tom to take her hand and squeeze it, and the men looked at them knowingly, as though they guessed

41

that going round Oakwell Hall was a pretext for being together, a prelude to something, an opening movement in what might or might not become a symphony. The staff had no doubt seen the same opening movement played before their eyes many times.

'I'm rather pleased to be out of there,' Julia said at last as they left the building and headed back to the car.

'I know what you mean.' Tom looked at her. Then, 'Are you ready for lunch?'

'Starving. I'm glad I saw the house, though. It makes it even plainer what is wrong with the Dutch House.'

'Oakwell isn't a home.' Tom hesitated. He hadn't been into the Dutch House. 'You expect a real home to be more cluttered if it holds the possessions of many generations of a family.'

'There is such a thing as being too cluttered. There is also such a thing as being swept and dusted.'

'Oh,' said Tom.

It was not many miles to Heckmondwyke and the building, now a pub, which the great Dr Priestley had lived in as a boy when he was boarding in the household of his schoolmaster, the Revd Kirby. Much of the interior was now open to the rafters, giving a light open feeling which must have been absent earlier when many of the rooms were low and dark.

Julia swung up on a great crescent of happiness. It was lovely to be taken out by Tom to places where she hadn't been before and fussed over and – yes, why deny it? – courted. Once more their hands touched briefly in passing and she wondered if he felt the hunger she felt for further contact. She looked down at her ham salad to hide her thoughts, sure that they would show only too plainly in her eyes. Julia's husband had died twelve years before and it was no use pretending that she had met no other men who had showed an interest in her, because she had. Usually she turned the budding interest aside pleasantly but firmly. Now a tingling sensation told her that this was something serious which might alter her life. If he did hold her would she like it? There was no way of knowing short of trying it and if she did not enjoy his closeness it was going to be very difficult to reject him without hurting him severely.

'What would you prefer to do this afternoon?' asked Tom. 'What time do you need to be home? Don't you like that salad, shall I fetch you something else, you don't need to eat it?'

'The salad is fine, I need to be home for about four o'clock, I don't mind what we do but one open house was enough. The countryside round here is lovely, could we see a bit of it?'

'There are some pleasant woods not far away. We could go for a walk,' suggested Tom. 'They are actually the grounds of a small museum but we don't need to go into the building. It's turned out so warm and sunny.'

'Right.' Julia ate up her salad and accepted a sweet and a coffee.

The sunshine illuminated the woods, shining through the new young leaves to make them glow like stained glass but more heart-touching, more ephemeral, more fragile. Shafts of sun struck the ground where there were open spaces. Sheer joy in living seemed to irradiate the downward slope towards the river, and as the two walked, the tall bulky man and the slender woman, the other people here and there in the wood seemed insignificant, as though they were on another planet.

Silence fell between them.

At last Tom stopped on the sloping path, turned towards Julia, and without preliminary his arms went round her and for a second they looked into one another's faces before their lips met. It seemed to them that the world changed in that moment.

Having once come into close contact Tom and Julia could not break away. After a while, when two dark-clad elderly ladies approached them on a parallel path, their arms dropped and they walked on a little, linked only by their hands, but as soon as they were reasonably screened by the young beech leaves they turned to each other once again. Time stopped obligingly. The sun was going to shine for ever. It seemed a minute instead of an hour when Julia pulled away and looked at her watch.

She spoke in a voice that was a caress in itself. 'Do you know what time it is? I have to prepare an evening meal.'

'I'll take you straight back to the station.'

Hand in hand like children they walked quickly to the car, drove into Leeds, and Tom bought a platform ticket so that he could put Julia onto the next train.

'It might seem a little ridiculous', he said hesitantly, looking down and barely touching her hand, 'to try to keep this secret at the moment but do you think we can?'

'It will be much better for the present.'

43

'Yes. Someone might see us here on the platform and jump to conclusions – the right ones of course – but—'

'But we've only just found out ourselves.'

'Exactly.'

'And we don't want to be the subject of talk yet . . .'

'No.'

'You'd better go, then,' said Julia, but Tom hung on until the train arrived and she saw him last through the carriage window as it moved off towards York. She leaned back on her seat and thought how sensible they both were, and then she moved into the kind of magic daydream which comes only too rarely in a lifetime, and looking out of the window, over the fleeting countryside, she saw that the sky was covered with clouds which looked exactly like the breadrolls in the sky of a painting by Magritte, which surprised her because never before had she seen clouds in that formation spaced evenly over the blue of the heaven, and she longed to tell everybody about it but the only person she really wanted to tell was Tom.

4

While Julia and Tom had been discovering their love in the wood, other things had been happening in the Dutch House flats on that Thursday afternoon.

Ms Haygreen and Ms Hodson were in the middle of a dispute about smell. This always happened after they had both engaged in a bout of their own activities. Ms Haygreen said that she was allergic to the smell of turpentine and oil paint and Ms Hodson said, 'Tough! What about that stink of stewing weeds I've been having to put up with?'

'You could have closed your door,' said Ms Haygreen. 'At least my Work produces something both beautiful and useful, as William Morris would have agreed.'

'He would have thought my paintings were beautiful,' countered Ms Hodson. 'And as for *use*, they give people pleasure, and what could be more *useful* than that.'

'Scrawls,' said Ms Haygreen, flipping her fingers at a mural which decorated the landing they shared at the top of the house. 'Mere scrawls. What skill does that piece show?'

'If that's a scrawl, your effort is only fit to be a duster,' said Ms Hodson heatedly, gesturing wildly at a batik hanging which hung opposite the mural.

At which Ms Haygreen remarked that Ms Hodson had no taste, no taste at all, and Ms Hodson retreated into her flat and banged the door, after which Ms Haygreen, left in possession of the landing but feeling that she had a very hollow victory, went into her own flat and banged her door too.

In the flat below Ms Haygreen's and above the Bransbys', Dr Bright heard the bangs with relief. Now there would be a bit of peace and quiet until the two ladies had their next row, which might not be for some time. He knew that in the morning they would both have forgotten about today's little episode. Forgotten or forgiven, he was never sure which, but the result was the same in either case. He looked at his watch and found it was half-past three. Time he had his afternoon tea. He made himself a pot of Lapsang. All was delightfully tranquil.

Although he could hear the sound of distant music, it blended with the gentle swish of the wind in the trees and the calling of a cuckoo. His wife had gone away again – this time to her sister's in Brighton. He had been pleased to see her, of course, but not as pleased as he had been when she went away again. Later, during the evening, he intended to go to a lecture on medieval cesspits, and he was looking forward to that very much. If his wife had still been in York he would not have felt that he could desert her, and the lecture was not on her type of subject. The Medical Society had lectures on some very interesting topics. He would meet a number of his friends, and probably adjourn to someone's house afterwards to carry on a discussion and enjoy a glass together. A bachelor existence was a very pleasant one.

Mr Spicer was having an afternoon nap in his flat. He knew that Cherry Ducket-Penrose was asleep in her chair in the garden, and thought that sauce for the goose should be sauce for the gander. Mrs Robinson's flat above his was empty. He closed his curtains against the sun and convinced himself that no one would know he was taking an hour off duty.

The most unhappy people in the Dutch House flats were the Brothers Lloyd, who had been driven out of their dwelling by the unrelenting pounding of the piano next door. They had complained on the previous day about the noise, and Susannah's reaction had been to take it out on the poor piano (and of course, themselves). She was in a passionate sulk. The brothers decided the only thing to do was to go for a walk, and later Gawain had to make the weekly visit to the supermarket. They put on their identical hats and their identical pale blue jumpers under light summer-weight jackets (worn for the first time that year) and went out, discovering that the sound of the piano was surprisingly pleasant at a distance. They returned to their flat separately, only to be overwhelmed once more by the volume of sound, and driven to make a further protest.

Susannah Wilmet rushed out in a highly emotional state to Mrs Honor's flat after this second complaint in one day from the Brothers Lloyd, and was welcomed in and cosseted by Mrs Honor. She was not there many minutes; the itinerant hairdresser was due, late though it was. He did Mrs Honor's hair every week at the same time. Susannah had to leave, with a last compliment from the older woman ringing pleasantly in her ears. As she lingered in the hallway, tying a flapping shoelace, Adam passed and spoke to her, and was snapped at.

Julia's return was soon after that. She rejoined the flow of events in the Dutch House still in a daze from her afternoon with Tom. She went into her flat quietly, wishing that she could be alone.

Her son Adam was typing on her portable typewriter on top of the dining table. Looking casually over as she stood with a tablecloth in her hand she saw that he was using a very small piece of paper, in fact it was – yes, it was – a large sticky label.

'What are you typing, dear? Have you nearly finished because I want to spread the cloth?'

'Just a second, Mum,' said Adam. The sound coming up to her was filtered through the falling curtain of his hair.

Julia went away and found something else to do for a few minutes. She was hardly conscious of her son. Her mind was full of the moment when Tom had taken her into his arms . . .

'Adam,' she said again.

With a deep breath he announced that he had done now, and standing up he moved the typewriter to its accustomed place on the lower shelf of the dinner trolley.

'It's this book, you see,' he said, holding up a library book. 'It's such rubbish something really has to be done about it.'

'Why is it rubbish?' She remembered Tom's hand brushing hers.

'It is supposed to be a history book but it is full of inaccuracies. When I reached this one it really got on my wick. Listen to this: "The Crystal Place was destroyed during a bombing raid during the blitz in the 1939–45 war."'

'That's wrong,' said Julia at once. 'It was burned down in the thirties well before the war started. Everyone knows that. I can't remember the exact year.'

'That sort of thing is infuriating. Read this.' Adam stuck his label down onto a suitable partly blank page at the beginning.

Julia took the book and read, 'There are a number of historical errors in this book, of which a typical example will be found on page 193 line 4. The publishers are offering an annual prize to the person finding the most. Please send your list to us before December 31st in the year you read the text.'

'Do you think you ought to have done this?' she asked dubiously. It was hard to concentrate on Adam, but she thought he was making more fuss than was warranted.

'Serve them right. I've made several labels and I'm going to visit as many libraries as I can looking for copies.'

'Well, whatever turns you on,' said Julia, who was sure he would soon tire of this occupation. She shook out the cloth and smoothed away its creases. That moment, she thought, when Tom had ... and then she'd said ... with a wrench she came back to the present. 'Thanks for switching the oven on, dear. Everything is ready.' She carefully refrained from asking if he'd washed his hands. She must remember not to treat him like a child. How would he and Tom get on? Thank goodness she didn't have to face that problem yet.

'How was your day?' Adam enquired amiably as they began their meal.

'Good.' Very good indeed, she thought, and tried to control her face so as not to look too enthusiastic. 'Oakwell Hall has been done up beautifully in the style of a yeoman's house of the seventeenth century.'

'So it is about the same age as the Dutch House?'

'I suppose so, but the style is quite different. It is typically English. The Dutch House is typically Dutch.'

'Cherry has been telling me. She has traced her foreign ancestors back to 1640, did you know that, Mum? And they were probably here twelve years earlier than that, only the record doesn't survive. The first ancestor she found spoke Dutch and she thinks he was a Walloon, nowadays that's part of Belgium.'

Her son's voice was a kind of buzzing in the background of Julia's mind. She was going over, second by thrilling second, her walk through the woods at Carlinghow with Tom. She had to make herself concentrate for the moment on Adam.

He was saying, 'There was a big Dutch – or Walloon – influence all the way up from Hatfield and Thorne to here. There was a brick manufactury near Drax and some of the settlers lived there. Peter Smaque, isn't that a fun name? Can't you see him in his wooden clogs waiting for a cargo to come up river? He lived at Drax. And his grandson, Abraham de la Prime, he writes about relatives near York.'

Dutch architecture, thought Julia. That's what he's on about. I should be able to make an embroidery out of those lovely curly Dutch gables, with those diagonally placed bricks, 'tumbled gables', I think they're called. Aloud she said, 'The Old Manor House across the green shows Dutch influence, doesn't it?'

'There's scores of them, buildings all the way up the Vale of York. There was a row of lovely Dutch-type brick gables on a building on Skeldergate but the city council had it pulled down. Almshouses, I think. They don't seem to realize that they are destroying the whole ambience which is what was valuable.'

'All right, get off your soap box. Is all this from Cherry?' For the first time since she got back home his mother had actually been listening to him.

'I've been reading it up. Do you know, Mum, I think I'd like to be an architect.'

'I thought you were going to be a philosopher.'

'I don't know if philosophers can do anything to stop the ancient housing stock being destroyed. Once destroyed that's it, gone for ever.'

'Pass me your plate if you've finished.'

'I haven't quite,' said Adam hastily.

Julia dreamily got up and fetched a dish of baked apples from the oven and cream from the fridge as Adam scooped up the last of his first course. She automatically put on the coffee pot.

'Are you swotting again after this?' I hope you are, she thought. I want to think about me and Tom. Blow Dutch architecture.

'I'm taking the dog for a walk and then there's something I ought to watch on the telly – for my General Studies.'

'I believe you, thousands wouldn't,' Julia remarked. She looked forward to the television being on. Then she would be able to sit and gaze in the right direction and think undisturbed about her afternoon, and look forward to the next time she met him . . .

In fact after a short time the noise of some sort of fracas in the hallway between Mrs Honor's flat and her own disturbed Julia's train of thought. Voices were being raised in anger. At first Julia was not going to move from her chair, but after a little while she got up and went to the front door of her own flat. Adam, absorbed in the television, didn't seem to notice the disturbance.

Julia listened. There was silence. Those who had been falling out must have either made it up or gone away. For the first time she wished that there was a pane of glass in her front door, so that she could have seen what was going on. She opened the door a crack. Now, in the darkening entrance, she could see the figure of a man. A thin man, stooping over as though he had been pressing his ear to the door opposite. His knuckles were raised, he knocked. Julia could see that he was Mr Markhall from upstairs, the flat over Mrs Honor's. Probably he had come down to complain about the noise – he must have heard it more clearly than she had herself. Julia closed her door softly and went back to the television. Adam had not moved. She sat down again and meant to go on with her happy, dreamy thoughts about her day and Tom Churchyard, but the disturbance had made it impossible. She could not help thinking about her neighbours.

Julia had not made up her mind, even after four years, whether she liked or disliked Mrs Honor. Perhaps it was both. They were in constant contact. Apart from their doors facing one another across the hallway, which also housed the staircase to the four flats above, the ground-floor flats themselves were mirror images of each other. The two tiny private patches of garden outside their patio doors were only a few feet apart.

A short projecting wall divided Julia's garden from her neighbour on the left, Mr Spicer. (He used a separate entrance, which

49

included the short flight of stairs to Mrs Robinson's above him). On the right, a similar short projecting wall separated Mrs Honor's patio from the adjoining block of garages and flats, which had been made from the old stables.

Julia wished for another wall, at least six feet long and high, between her own tiny terrace and patch of rose bushes, and Mrs Honor's patio, rampaging clematis, and other climbers. Unfortunately the garden door from the hallway prevented this. This door was for all the residents, to give them access to the shared grass and trees, and the distant shrub border next to the boundary wall.

The apple tree which had been such a bone of contention between Mr Spicer and Mrs Honor in previous years stood a few yards from Mrs Honor's patio door; the other apple trees which were dotted about were the remains of a previous orchard, surviving at intervals in the grass. Julia was always grateful she did not have an apple tree in her vicinity; the worry of it would have been too much to bear. As it was she was the recipient of bitter complaints from her neighbours to left and right: Mrs Honor who would insist on taking the apples and Mr Spicer whose job it was to harvest them from all the trees and distribute them equally amongst the inhabitants of both flats and main house.

Added to such small crises as this, there was the problem of Mrs Honor often appearing unexpectedly at the patio of Julia's flat and demanding admittance, whereas she – Julia – was expected to telephone to announce that she wished to call on Mrs Honor, and was it convenient? Adam was treated more indulgently by the other inhabitants than was Julia, and she found this infuriating. She was regarded with a critical eye and constant curiosity. Visitors to her flat were scrutinized as they approached and the length of time they stayed was noted. She was tacitly expected to account for her absences. Julia knew, really, that the interest was kindly – or she thought that it was. But there were times when she rebelled against this surveillance, and she was pleased that another young woman had come to the flats, so that the spotlight was moved from herself, at least temporarily.

It was not surprising that she did not want to publicize the

50

budding, changing relationship between herself and Tom Churchyard.

It was not until last thing that night, when Adam was already in bed and she herself undressing, that there was a resurgence of joy.

The phone rang. She snatched it up, not wanting the noise to disturb Adam.

'When are we meeting again?' Tom said urgently.

She hesitated, and finally spoke very low.

'In ten days' time – the weekend after this,' she murmured tentatively. 'I am attending a conference in Nottingham – at the university there. I thought of going down early on the Friday. That may give me some time free during the day, but I expect you will be working.'

'It isn't long since you left Adam last, is it?'

Julia was disconcerted by this reaction, so like her neighbours'. She realized, though, that Tom was only mirroring her own concern for Adam's welfare.

'It isn't long, but he feels I baby him, he wants the chance to be more independent ... luckily he has been invited out by a school friend. There's a concert they want to go to in Edinburgh – they travel to the ends of the earth to hear pop groups – and the friend's father has been rash enough to say that he'll take them up by road, stay with them, and bring them back. It means Adam will be away that whole weekend. He will go there straight from school on the Friday.'

Tom's mind had been working overtime. 'I'll have the day off on that Friday,' he said. 'Let's travel down together on the train. It will be fun. Then I'll see you to the university after we've had lunch in Nottingham.'

Unspoken between them was the idea that at some point in those hours the chance would arise for an embrace, for those long sweet kisses which had seemed more like a drug than a caress still lived in both their minds with every intimate detail still intact.

'They won't open the Dutch House again while you're out of the way?' he whispered teasingly.

She supposed that he found it difficult to understand how much agitation that episode had caused her. She explained, 'The opening is to start properly in July. I'm hoping that I can be of some influence between now and then.'

'So you will be able to forget it for the day?'

'Perhaps I will have other things to think about,' said Julia softly.

'Conferences are absorbing,' he said, still in that light, teasing tone. She had not realized that stately Tom could sound so jokey and affectionate. His usual speaking voice was deep and grave – and earlier that day she had found it could be very loving. Combined with his large stature and dignified manner, this deep voice had made him ideal for the part of God, which he had played with distinction in the Mystery Plays.

'And ten days is a long time,' added Tom.

5

It was the following day, Friday. Adam had spent the morning taking his General Studies examination. He arrived home at noon as Julia was setting the table for lunch by the window which gave onto their patio and the view of the spread of grass and graceful trees. For the first time that year the window was wide open during lunch – nearly as good as eating outside. They always enjoyed this feature of their summer meals.

Julia had spent the morning working, trying to evolve a satisfactory embroidery design out of the Victorian water trough on Clifton Green. An elaborate fantasy of red marble and old dark stone, the pride of the neighbourhood conservationists, the water trough stands like a miniature mausoleum under the shade of the trees fringing the green, an ancient triangle of grass which still provides grazing for horses. Julia was adding to her panel of photographs and sketches of the subject, working examples of experiments with stitches and fabrics. The working panel might become part of an exhibition.

Julia said to Adam as they sat down at the table that she hadn't seen their neighbour Mrs Honor all that morning. This was unusual. Even if they did not speak, Mrs Honor was normally to be seen through the back windows of the flat, taking her Peke for his early constitutional on the grass at the rear of the flats. Her penetrating voice was normally heard praising him for answering the call of nature, followed by a running commentary as she used her pooper-scooper before taking the little dog inside again.

'She hasn't gone away, has she?' Julia asked. 'She was here last evening, but I must admit I haven't taken much notice this morning.'

Adam was much more likely than she was to be up to date on the intentions and movements of their neighbours. He seemed to view the community in which they lived as if they were rare birds and he was recording them for posterity. Perhaps they were, Julia reflected. It was certainly a civilized, cultured little community, rare birds indeed, whatever their internecine feuds. In her present mood of happiness she viewed even Mrs Honor with appreciation.

'She isn't away as far as I know,' Adam replied with his customary scientific caution.

'I haven't seen her out with Blue Moon, and it's past twelve o'clock.'

'She will be perfectly all right, Mother. Probably she was out before you got up.'

'I doubt it.'

'She might have gone to that reunion at Elvington, but I think it is tomorrow.'

They went on with their meal, which as usual was a light one. Today was typical, salad, wholemeal bread and cottage cheese followed by fruit and dates, with home-made lemonade – Linda Southwell's recipe – to drink. For a while Adam said nothing more, but his mind was evidently working, because as they both finished eating he said, 'We'd better check on her doorstep. If she has gone away she will have put out a note to cancel the milk.'

With one accord, as if suddenly fearful, mother and son left the lunch table and went into the shared hall of the flats. Mrs Honor's door did not in fact have a step, but it had a little red wool mat outside, and on the mat was a pint of milk. Sticking out of the letter-box was the end of the morning newspaper, and the corners of one or two letters and circulars.

'Funny,' Adam said. 'You'd better knock, Mother.'

Julia knocked, first gently and then forcefully, but there was no answering footstep from inside, and what was worse, no bark from Blue Moon.

'If she had fallen down and hurt herself,' Julia remarked, 'Blue Moon would be kicking up a racket, I'm sure, desperate for Outs and for food.'

'Shall we look through her patio door?' asked Adam.

'It isn't the thing, you know. She would be horrified if she thought we were peering in at her windows.'

'She will have to be horrified,' Adam replied. 'Better that than not care about her welfare, surely.'

'Nothing will have happened, Adam. One has these frights with old people and they come to nothing, and then one feels a fool, an intrusive fool. She may have decided suddenly last night to go to see an old friend, and then been invited to stay the night. But I will look into the bedroom if I can.' It only took her a few seconds to discover that the net curtains there were impenetrable.

When she returned, shaking her head, Adam was already leading the way through the door which led from the hallway onto the grass at the back of the block. He held the door and his mother followed on his heels.

As they turned to the right, onto Mrs Honor's patio, they realized at once that something was very wrong, and Julia's conscience ceased troubling her. The patio door was partly open and the curtains carelessly half-drawn in a tumbled way.

'I think we'd better call the police,' said Julia, hanging back.

Adam, however, was already pushing the patio door further open, until the space was wide enough to walk through. Julia followed him. Once inside they stood stock still.

Mrs Honor's body lay with her head near their feet. Blood, now dark red, had flowed over her fine quality Persian carpet. On the floor to one side of the room stood a row of her precious ornaments, some cardboard boxes and packing material.

Julia hoped that this was some sort of hallucination. She knelt at Mrs Honor's side and reached out for her wrist to feel for a pulse.

Adam let out a sound without words and strode over the prone body towards the far end of the room.

'Adam!' Julia almost screamed at him. 'What do you think you're doing?'

He bent over something, then turned towards her. 'Blue Moon,' he said. 'Blue Moon. The bastards.' He knelt on the floor and peered at something. Julia could hear a barely perceptible animal sound.

'Adam, we must get out of here. The police must be notified at once.'

Looking down, Julia had known instantly that she could do nothing for Mrs Honor; no one could. 'We shouldn't touch anything. We really shouldn't have come in.'

Getting up and turning with a burden of some kind in his arms, Adam said, 'Mum, we must get to a vet.'

Oh, God, the dog.

Adam came back the way he had gone through the room. As he approached, Julia slid out again through the patio door. He came edging after her, unaware, it seemed, of her own need for speech, for some kind of interchange, intent on the burden in his arms, a burden of white and rust, of white fur draggled with rusted crimson, which hung as if boneless and without life . . .

They went towards their own flat. Their patio door was also open, in addition to the dining-room window, because on such a summer's day as this it was pleasant to feel the sun and air and hear the birdsong.

Julia sprang to the telephone and pressed 999. 'Police,' she said urgently, and as soon as she was put through gave her name and address, before saying that there had apparently been a break-in next door and her neighbour was lying injured and, she believed, dead.

'They're coming,' she said, turning to Adam.

'We won't be here, Mother.'

'What do you mean?'

'We'll be at the vet's.'

Julia could hardly glance at the burden in his arms. 'The vet can do nothing, love.'

'Blue Moon's alive.'

'He can't be – he looks – Mrs Honor's—'

'He's warm.'

'He'll be too badly injured – he'll have to be put down—'

'We've got to get him to a vet.'

'We've no transport, Adam. The moped's no good for this sort of thing.'

'Get a taxi.'

'Look, surgery will be over anyway. I'll see what I can do. I'll ring them. Perhaps someone will come round. Oh, God. How does one find a vet?' The thought flashed through her mind that the dog's own vet would be listed in Mrs Honor's telephone book, but no way was she going back in there again, looking for a phone number. Adam stood with his eyes firmly fixed on her face.

'All right. I'll do what I can, if you think he's still got any life in him, though I doubt it.'

Trembling, she made her fingers find the right section in the Yellow Pages. Vets. The nearest would be the best, she supposed, though Mrs Honor had almost certainly had her own ideas about which of them was the most suitable to treat her darling. When it was only a matter of a lethal injection though, perhaps one veterinary surgeon would be as good as another?

Julia could hear her own voice shaking as she spoke into the phone. Shock. What she and Adam should be doing now was trying to combat the effects of shock, now they had notified the police, or going to see Cherry Ducket-Penrose and breaking the news to her gently, instead of bothering about a dog who must be dying there in Adam's arms if it wasn't dead already. It was useless dragging out a vet; no animal who looked like Blue Moon did could be alive. What was the point, poor little thing, he would be out of his misery soon enough without any strange man pulling him about and interfering.

Yet she could hear herself insisting to the vet's assistant that the creature must have instant attention, that the man must come round immediately, it was an emergency, she would pay what-ever the fee was for such an inconvenient journey considering he was, so the assistant thought, at home having his lunch now.

'Give me his home number,' she heard herself saying in that ominous tone which she used very rarely but which, when used, got results.

The vet said he would come at once.

'He's coming.' She turned to Adam, although he must have heard the conversation. 'I'll go to the front and watch out for him. If he doesn't know the Dutch House he will waste time finding us.'

'The police are here.' Adam's voice was strange, flat and

56

toneless. Even as he spoke a figure appeared at the patio door, an official figure in uniform.

'Come in, officer,' said Julia. 'You must excuse us. You see we have an injured dog here, Mrs Honor's dog, and the vet is on his way. I must go out to the front and meet him. We will have to speak to you afterwards. Please don't bother my son at present. We will both be at your disposal as soon as we possibly can.'

Afterwards she wondered how she could have produced such calm formal speech at that moment, but formality and politeness are strong supports in time of need. Adam had said nothing at all. After one glance at the policeman he seated himself on a low padded chair which was tucked into a corner of the dining area, a chair she liked to use when sewing by hand. He lowered himself gently, taking care not to move the position of the creature – the thing – in his arms. On Adam's light coloured T-shirt she could see a spreading mark of blood.

The vet arrived quickly, at least there was that much to be thankful for. He saw Julia waiting among all the clutter caused by the police cars and an ambulance, which were standing on the paved area, blocking it so that he had to park his car on the other side of the box-bordered beds and walk through them on the brick paving which separated their bright mixture of blowsiness and formality.

'Mrs Bransby? You have the injured dog?'

'I rang.' Julia led the way through the hall and to her front door. 'As you see we have an emergency here. My neighbour actually. It's her dog. I'm afraid she is dead.'

'Not Mrs Honor?'

'Do you know her?'

The vet stood stock still. 'Are you telling me what I think you are? Mrs Honor's dead, and her dog badly injured . . .'

'I'm afraid she was murdered.' Julia could hardly say the word. It felt as though her throat was full of cottonwool.

'Murdered!'

'Well, I think so. Unless it was an accident. But . . . it looked as though she had disturbed a burglar.'

As she took the vet into her dining area Julia saw that Adam's face was white and ravaged by tears. He lifted it and looked at the vet. A uniformed policeman was standing just inside the patio door, looking sympathetic.

57

The vet took in the situation at a glance and dropped to his heels in front of Adam, long gentle fingers moving Adam's grasp. 'Let's have a look at the little fellow,' he said.

Nobody said anything whilst he examined the dog. Julia was astonished to hear a sound from the animal, hardly more than an intake of breath.

'Looks like the Mersey Boot Syndrome,' said the vet. 'Broken jaw, I'm afraid. Broken legs. Probably broken ribs. This dog has been very thoroughly kicked. How was Mrs Honor . . . ?'

'Her head was bashed in,' said Adam.

'Bashed in? Blunt instrument?'

'I imagine so, though we only found her,' put in Julia. 'We don't really know. I wouldn't have said "bashed in", Adam. Blood had flowed from somewhere, and there was a little on the side of her head, but—'

'Whatever they did, at least they didn't do it to Blue Moon. Probably thought he was a goner anyway.'

'You obviously knew Mrs Honor,' said Julia. 'Were you by any chance the dog's regular vet?'

'Yes, though he's been a very healthy little animal. I've only seen him once a year for top-up vaccinations. My practice is nearly all small animal work.'

'What can we do?' asked Adam.

'The kindest thing might be to put him out of his misery.'

'Isn't there any chance of saving him?'

'It's obviously a while since this happened. He's lost blood and chances. It really depends if he has much in the way of internal injuries. Broken bones we might be able to cope with, if that was all. Exactly when did it happen?'

'Some time ago,' said Julia dubiously. 'We hadn't seen them at all today and usually they are out on the grass first thing.'

'So it could have been last night.' After a pause for thought, the vet went on, 'You see, if he was bleeding badly inside, he wouldn't have lasted this long. It looks to me as though he went for his mistress's attacker and was kicked away. The injuries are all at his front end. That's in his favour.'

'Please try,' Adam said through his tears. 'Please try to save him. Please try.'

Julia had to look away. She had not seen Adam cry since he was small. Suddenly he had shed ten years, and she longed to put her arms round him to comfort. But that time had long gone. He was on his own now, for better or worse.

'He's still a young dog . . .'

'Three, I think,' put in Julia, who remembered the puppy Blue Moon arriving, a tiny ball of white fur with a ridiculous plume of a tail and bravery enough for a lion.

'It will be expensive. We'll have to start with an X-ray, then make up our minds from there.'

'The expense doesn't matter,' Adam said, 'but I'm coming with him.'

The vet hesitated. Julia could see that he wanted to say no; it would be far simpler, let alone more hygienic, to deal with the dog by itself than with a distraught Adam as well.

'If he's going to pull through he'll need me.' Adam blinked away his tears and sounded firm.

Something, perhaps the unusual circumstances, must have made the vet change his mind and his usual procedure; Julia could see an alteration in the expression of his face. She knew many dog owners handed over their pets to a vet's care without seeing the creature again as it went through medical treatment, and perhaps died.

'I'll give him an injection now to dull his pain a bit and keep him calm, then you can have him on your knee in the car.'

Robert Southwell was in the police station on Clifford Street when his boss, Detective Superintendent Joe Birch, rang through from headquarters at Fulford.

'Bob,' DS Birch said, and at his boss's tone Bob Southwell snapped onto full alert. Something serious. Fate was not going to grant him the further ten minutes which were all he needed to finish the paperwork he was doing. That thought went through his mind as his overweight boss took a tiny breath before going on. 'Bob, you know there was another burglary this morning?'

Now Bob knew there were burglaries every morning, give or take a few. By burglary in that particular tone, DS Birch must mean one of the special series of burglaries of antiques which had broken out in York recently.

'Yes, I did hear, sir.'

'Know any details?' asked DS Birch in the way that means, 'I'm going to tell you anyway.'

'I've been busy writing an overdue report,' Bob said. 'I'll have it finished in ten minutes. No, I haven't heard anything much up here in my office, I wanted to concentrate.'

'Same pattern as the others, care and neatness, packing materials, choosy about what they take. But they were interrupted by the owner of the flat.'

'Flat, sir?'

'One of the flats at the Dutch House, near you.'

'My wife has a friend who lives there . . .'

'Name?'

'Julia Bransby. Mrs. Widow. One son.'

'Rang to inform us. The burglary was at her neighbour's, called Mrs Honor.'

'I know her slightly.'

'Not any more you don't, Bob. The old lady died.'

'*Died*?'

'Do you know them too well to be involved?'

'No, no.'

'Get over there, then. I've a Finance Committee meeting I can't get out of, for the next hour, perhaps longer. Dave Smart's there already, plus the Scene of Crime officers. Organize Coroner's Officer, Home Office Pathologist, Forensic Scientist, will you? Take charge until I'm free.'

'Yes, sir. Right away.'

'Don't stop to finish that report,' warned DS Birch.

'I wouldn't think of it, sir.'

Bob realized that he had heard the words 'grievous bodily harm' as he had walked through the other offices *en route* for his own after his midday meal. Obviously the GBH had become murder. The first of this series of specialized thefts of choice antiques to involve the householder. It was a bit close to home, burglary and murder at the Dutch House. The conversation he and Linda had had came back to him. They had talked about the community in the Dutch House.

'An old lady called Mrs Honor,' DS Birch repeated, then added as an afterthought, 'And her dog.'

Bob was silent. Then he began to react smoothly, efficiently. Pushing the unfinished report to one side, he pulled a pad of scrap paper under his hand and began to make rapid notes. DS Birch was still talking.

'You remember the break-in a month ago at Acomb, where the house was only empty for a couple of hours, and the other in Heworth where a delivery van was parked in front of the house so that the villains couldn't be seen to force the front door, and no one realized there was anything the matter, just thought the owners had bought a new piece of furniture or something?'

'I remember them perfectly, and the other cases.'

'Every time the evidence pointed to the items taken – always antiques – having been packed carefully and nothing else disturbed. On one occasion when the burglars must have taken fright and left without finishing the job, some packing materials were still there, and a row of clocks on the coffee table waiting to be stowed away in suitcases.'

'This is the fifth or sixth, isn't it, but in the other cases no one was hurt. How did she die?'

'We think she was struck with a blunt instrument, but that's only pro tem. Guesswork at this stage. When the 999 call arrived we hoped the informant (your Linda's friend) was wrong and that the lady was only injured and unconscious, but it was obvious that she was dead, and that's now been certified.'

'Have any of the other residents been informed?'

'Not yet, but Mrs Bransby might have told them, though I think not.'

Bob knew that the whole of the Dutch House complex must be heaving with people by now, wondering what on earth was happening. There would be police cars outside, probably an ambulance, men coming and going. He looked at his watch. Ten to two.

'I'll see things keep moving, sir.'

Bob put down the phone and left his desk, reaching for his light summer coat as he passed its peg. He was at the Dutch House shortly after two. He was curious, interested. This would be the first time he had entered the complex apart from one dinner-party at Julia's flat, over a year ago. The parked police vehicles reminded him where the entrance was. DI Dave Smart, a reliable, stocky, red-faced officer with crisp black hair, was standing there, looking out for him.

'Let's check progress,' said Bob.

Dave explained the situation. The body had not yet been removed.

'How is the neighbour, Julia Bransby? She's a personal friend.'

'Very upset.'

'I seem to remember that she and Mrs Honor didn't get on very well.'

'Good fences make good neighbours, sir, and their rear bits of private garden are open plan. But she is very upset. I couldn't speak to her son, he's gone off to the vet's with Mrs Honor's dog. Mrs Bransby thought it was dying.'

'A quick look here first, then I think I ought to circulate.'

Bob Southwell's quick, light stride took him in a moment through the entrance door to the block and in at Mrs Honor's front door, with a cursory nod to the uniformed officer on guard there. He looked into the sitting room, which was seething with busy policemen. A glance took in all that was happening and another nod acknowledged the greetings of the men. He left the flat again, looking very serious.

'Nothing for me to do there at present,' he said to Dave. 'I'd better go and speak to people, first of all to Miss Ducket-Penrose. She owns the place. Then I'll come back and have a word with Julia – Mrs Bransby.'

'I think you might find Mrs Bransby's there before you.'

Bob was in time to find both women still together. When he knocked on the white-painted front door of the Dutch House, Julia came to answer it, and showed him into the small corner room where Cherry spent most of her days. On the round pedestal table were tea cups and a half-bottle of brandy.

'My recipe for shock,' Julia explained. 'Will you have some?'

'Tea, yes, please, Julia. No brandy, thanks.'

Julia took a third cup and saucer out of a bow-fronted mahogany corner cupboard and examined them for dust, then rubbed them out with a table napkin before pouring Bob a cup of tea. Glancing round the room, he was pleased that she had taken that precaution. Cherry had not seemed to notice. Perhaps she was used to guests dusting out her tea cups before using them.

'I don't think I can tell you anything,' Cherry said. 'I haven't seen Mrs Honor since yesterday morning when she came with Blue Moon and we walked round the garden.'

Nevertheless, Bob managed to obtain quite a lot of information, as well as giving official sympathy and talking about the procedures which would necessarily take place, but he hoped would not inconvenience and distress the other people in the Dutch House too much. The information he gained might be completely irrelevant, but one never knew. He asked how long Mrs Honor had lived in her flat, and brief details as to where she had lived before and what was known about her.

'None of that matters, though, does it?' asked Julia almost in alarm. 'Burglars don't need to know anything except that there are things in the house worth stealing, do they? In any case, I thought they broke in anywhere they saw a chance; although Mrs Honor was very careful. She never left anything unlocked and she put on her burglar alarm whenever she left the house.'

'In this amazingly warm weather even the most careful householders leave windows open,' Bob remarked, 'particularly when they are at home. That has been most helpful, Miss Ducket-Penrose. Can either of you ladies tell me the names and addresses of Mrs Honor's relatives? We need to inform them.'

'I have a note somewhere,' said Cherry, getting up and searching in her desk. 'Yes, here it is. She had no children or nephews and nieces but this is the address of a brother-in-law in Devon.'

'Thank you. I will take Mrs Bransby away with me now, if you are sure you will be all right.'

Cherry was sure that she would.

'I'll pop back later,' Julia said, and gave Cherry a little pat on the shoulder.

Bob and Julia walked back in silence to the Victorian wing and the flats it contained. When they were in the entrance hallway Bob stood still for a few seconds. Through Mrs Honor's kitchen window and open front door he could see his men busy inside. Julia's door immediately opposite was shut and indeed locked, for he could see her scrabbling in her handbag for the key, and at that moment she produced it.

'I would like you to show me exactly what you did earlier today,' Bob said.

'Come in, then.'

Julia led the way into the kitchen and dining area, where she indicated the table and the still-open window.

'We were sitting here . . .' She talked him through the events, moving as she did so to demonstrate what she and Adam had done earlier. They went out of her flat again as she went to Mrs Honor's front door and mimed a knock, went to peer through the bedroom window's muffling of sheer curtain, then walking through the back door past a grandiose plant tub, onto Mrs Honor's concrete flags, and to the patio door. A glimpse inside turned her pale and she said, 'I don't think I can go on with this, she's still there, it's horrible . . .'

'Go back to your flat, Julia. You've explained beautifully. I'll be with you again in a few minutes. Actually we will need someone to give a formal identification, will you be up to doing that?'

Julia put her hand to her throat, but she nodded.

'We *will* move her as soon as we can. I'll see you soon.'

Bob went back to Mrs Honor's flat. It was indeed a sad, shocking, gruesome sight. Looking in his turn through the patio door, he felt a mixture of anger and sorrow. Sorrow because an old lady had been struck down in her own home and now lay there dead, whereas the day before she had been lively, interested in a million things no doubt, breathing, talking . . . Bob stepped inside the room and the men there made room for him.

The Forensic Scientist and Home Office Pathologist arrived and everyone cleared out of the way as the two men took over. They spent a few minutes standing and observing, also walking round the body to view it from different angles, before moving in for closer examination.

One of them said, 'We'll need to get her down to the mortuary but I can tell you now, Bob, this is a blow or blows with a blunt instrument, which has not yet been found. You haven't found it, have you, Dave?'

'Surely haven't,' replied Dave Smart.

'Time?' asked Bob.

'Yesterday. Late evening, I would estimate at present.'

'Are we ready to move her?'

'Just about. Do you want the identification now or later?'

Dave Smart fetched Julia, and in the presence of the detective constable who was to remain with the body to ensure continuity, the victim was turned over so that Julia had a clear view of the face. Choking a little, she performed the official identification, then escaped back to her own flat. The body was prepared for its journey; hands and head plastic bagged, photographs all long since taken, it was gently inserted into a body bag and carried out to the ambulance with the detective constable in attendance. Everyone was relieved by its removal. The crime could now take on something of the aspect of a problem, freer of emotional overtones.

'I know you won't have finished for a while yet,' Bob said, 'but I would like to have Mrs Bransby back in here for a minute now, while the whole event is fresh in her mind.'

Once more Julia had to pluck up all the courage she possessed. She demonstrated exactly where she had stood, petrified, on Mrs Honor's Persian carpet. She showed how Adam had stepped over the body and walked to the corner where the bundle of stained fur which was Blue Moon had been lying.

'My legs are not as long as his, of course,' she said.

'And that is all you did? You did not touch anything else, or walk anywhere else?'

'No.'

'Neither of you came back in, later?'

'I was tempted, when Adam wanted a vet, and I didn't know which one she used. I thought the number would be in her address book, but no way was I coming back in here for it.'

'Adam didn't come back?'

'No.'

'So all you saw was exactly as it was when we arrived?'

'Yes.'

For a few seconds Julia watched a young man who was lifting fibres from the wall.

'I expect you will find our fingerprints all over,' she said, 'especially Adam's. While he's been swotting for A levels he's spent more time than usual at home and is great friends with everyone at the Dutch House. As for me, Mrs Honor often asks me in – asked me in – for something or other.'

'Normally a very beautiful flat?'

'Oh, yes. She had excellent taste and liked the unusual. She was very particular about the look of things, and would spend a long time altering the position of her ornaments, or trying a piece of furniture a few inches to one side or the other, or arranging flowers, or creating a still-life of fruit.'

'You had the impression that her possessions were valuable?'

'Certainly. She loved showing them off and talking about them to anyone who would listen.'

'So knowledge that she had valuable antiques would be widespread?'

'I'm sure it would. Far more so than, let's say, Miss Ducket-Penrose's possessions, which she doesn't advertise – or at least, didn't, until she got this mania for opening the house to the public.' Julia looked across at the cardboard boxes and tissue paper. 'That seems particularly horrible, somehow, to choose someone else's belongings and come prepared to pack them.'

'Yes. Will you be able to tell us what is missing?'

'I can make a fair shot at it. Not that I know much about antiques. But I have a good visual memory, and Mrs Honor tended to use the same words every time, about her things, I can probably remember her phrases.'

Bob Southwell escorted Julia back to her own flat, thanked her, and installed a policeman to write down her statement. 'Don't think that when the immediate shock is over, you'll be back to normal,' he cautioned her. 'That applies to the whole community. You may never be quite over it, any of you. One of our men is going round at this moment informing the other inhabitants and we are contacting Mrs Honor's relatives. I'll be in touch. Tell Adam I want to talk to him.'

'Adam! I wonder what's happening to him! I must ring the vet's at once.'

'Do that,' said Bob as he left her.

The policeman taking the statement was young and seemed shy, but he worked steadily and Julia repeated all the things she had already told Bob Southwell. It seemed to take a long time. At last, he thanked her and went away.

Julia shrank from ringing the vet. She sat for a while with her hands folded on her lap. Her mind was a blank and the events of the afternoon were the last things she wanted to dwell on. The only warm spot in her mind was the glowing undercurrent of her feeling for Tom, which was always with her now, and gave her comfort. She knew that he would be bound to hear, and that he would contact her as soon as he did. Then she remembered her promise to return to Cherry Ducket-Penrose and got up to go to her. Once in the main building, she went straight to the corner cabinet room.

Cherry was sitting exactly where she had been before, and the three cups and saucers were still on the table. She turned her large and puddingy face towards Julia. The tracks of tears from those beautiful grey eyes ran unashamedly down her ageing cheeks.

'The police think it is burglars don't they?' she asked.

'She had some lovely things, but so do you, Cherry dear. You ought to have a burglar alarm.'

'Mrs Honor had a burglar alarm,' countered Cherry.

Julia felt there was no answer to that. Mrs Honor had turned her burglar alarm on religiously every time she left her home.

'Let's go into the garden,' said Cherry. They left the house by the garden door, and walked in silence down the central path, with Oberon and Titania rubbing their legs and circling round their feet.

'The young policeman who came after you left said something about the dog,' Cherry said.

'Blue Moon had been attacked too, he's at the vet's. The vet thought he'd been badly kicked. He said something about the Mersey Boot Syndrome. Adam went as well, to give Blue Moon a bit of reassurance.'

'Hmmm, well,' and Cherry looked widely over her garden to avoid meeting Julia's eyes. 'I'll have to rely on you, then, Julia, to help me prepare for opening to the public in July.'

Julia couldn't speak. Was that to be the whole of Mrs Honor's obituary? Was she so soon to be replaced? She felt angry words forming on her lips. Then Cherry turned to look at her. Her face looked even more ravaged than it had done in the house.

'Julia,' and her voice was breaking, 'I cannot believe it. I just cannot believe it.'

Next they were in each other's arms, both weeping, in the warm sunshine of the garden.

6

When Cherry and Julia were both feeling a little calmer, Cherry insisted on being told all about the dog.

'In my opinion he was absolutely supine and dying,' Julia said frankly. 'I watched them go away with him in the vet's car. Adam never looked back at me, he only had eyes or thought for the dog. I found a bit of old blanket, they'd wrapped it round him, with his head, all swollen and not looking like his head at all, at one end with a dangling broken front leg sticking out. Otherwise Blue Moon looked like a papoose, you know, those Red Indian babies wrapped up, like ours used to be wrapped in swaddling bands in the olden days. The vet drove very carefully, the car glided smoothly away.'

She wondered how long it would be before she saw her son again, and if he had completely forgotten the other far more important casualty – Mrs Honor over whose dead body he had stepped – Mrs Honor, who was, Julia supposed, no longer lying on her Persian carpet but, broken and dead, in a mortuary.

'Will you come to my flat, Cherry,' she asked, 'for a cup of tea? I know we've had one already this afternoon, but I don't think I'll be able to eat, I don't know about you, so we might as well drink, it will keep us going.'

She thought, you are rambling, woman, what's wrong with you – is it shock? After all you don't find your neighbour murdered every day of the week – that's what this is – this is murder. Aloud, she went on, 'Please forgive me. I don't think I'm quite myself. What with Blue Moon and everything.'

'Let me make it,' said Cherry, who liked messing about in Julia's kitchen. When they reached the Bransby flat she went to the kitchen area and, after filling the kettle, plugged it in and switched it on. 'Tea?' she checked.

'Yes, tea. You'll find some bags in the cupboard. Thank you.'

'They were all there, weren't they,' Cherry said. 'All my other tenants, we saw them all as we came in, hanging about or asking the policemen things.'

'You can't blame them,' said Julia, who was beginning to feel the pounding of a migraine headache. She fetched the brandy and when the cups of tea appeared in front of her she added a generous amount of spirit to both.

'My son and Mrs Honor were friends,' she went on, hoping that she wasn't getting drunk and sounding maudlin. The headache was getting stronger. 'Yet all he seemed to be thinking about was the dog. But he is an unusual young man, I can't always follow the way he is thinking. He takes after his father, I suppose. He taught Logic, you know. Such an odd subject.'

'Adam did what he could to help the living. That was logical in the circumstances. Not many people can react like that. Mrs Honor could no longer be helped by anyone.'

Cherry's face was less pale and she seemed much calmer. 'My grandfather the General would have approved of the way Adam reacted. Probably have recommended him for a medal.'

'Of course.' Julia gazed down into what was left of the tea and decided to have another cup. 'It was obvious that nothing could be done for her.'

'Your garden was looking lovely,' Julia murmured to her tea cup after a pause, her thoughts wandering. 'The flaming colours of the late tulips are beautiful. I must draw them before they drop, and make them into a design. They are such very Dutch flowers. But this Dutch blood you keep talking about, Cherry my dear – or Fleming, or Walloon, or French, or whatever it is – over the centuries it must have been so much diluted . . .'

'It is a Cause,' Cherry said, her voice obviously affected by the generous amount of brandy Julia had given her. 'So much of the architecture has been knocked down in the twentieth-century whirlwind of destruction.' She pronounced her words with great care.

The phone rang, and it was Adam.

'He isn't dead yet, Mother,' he said. 'They've X-rayed him quickly without giving him a general anaesthetic.'

Julia could tell that he had put his hand over the receiver. 'Adam, Adam,' she was saying softly. 'There's nothing else you can do now. Why not come home for a bit?'

'I'm not leaving him. The vet says I can stay as long as I like.'

'You *are* getting special treatment.'

69

'Anyway, Mum – I don't want to come back. I don't think I ever want to come back.'

Julia didn't know what to say to that. 'What's happening now to the dog?' She tried hard to concentrate on what he told her.

'The vet's giving him fluids intravenously. If all is well they hope to operate on him tomorrow. They say he needs twenty-four hours to get over the shock and for his circulatory system to return to normal before they do anything else.'

'If Blue Moon's calm and hardly realizes what's happening I'd like you back with me, Adam.'

'Can't we go somewhere else for the night? A hotel? Or can I stay with Pete?'

'I think my place is at home, really. Cherry is here at the moment. We need to support each other. There are all the other neighbours as well. I'm sure when the police have gone, every-one will be round quick as a dose of salts, wanting to know all about it like distressed ghouls. The police are going to leave a guard on Mrs Honor's flat for tonight, they haven't finished their investigations, so the neighbours will come to me – that will be as near as they can get to the scene – and want a first-hand report. They won't come all together, either. It will be penny numbers all evening.'

'I ought to be with you, Mother,' said Adam.

Julia loved her son seeming protective, it was a delightful reversal of roles and he sounded very mature, but she didn't like the fact that he had come into contact with violent crime and its consequences. Goodness knows what effect it might have. She thought that she would be happier coping on her own.

'Ring Peter and ask if you can go there for the night, if you can't face coming back here. Don't worry, Adam, of course I need you but I'll be fine.'

'I'll come back tomorrow, Mumsy,' said Adam, reverting to his childish name for her. 'I'll stay here as long as the vet will let me, then I'll go to Pete's if that's all right with them.'

Cherry had been quietly sitting drinking her brandyfied tea, but now she put down her cup and rose to go.

'The cats will want their meal,' she said. 'I gather from your conversation with Adam that he isn't coming back tonight. It's just as well, but will you be all right?'

'There will be a policeman in the hallway, so I'm told. You haven't any protection, on your own along there.'

'Burglars won't come back to the same spot so quickly.' Cherry sounded as though she was intimately acquainted with the habits of criminals. 'The whole Dutch House should be safe for some time. Goodnight, my dear.'

In an unusual display of emotion, the two women kissed and Julia saw her friend on her way.

DCI Robert Southwell went home briefly to put his wife Linda in the picture. When there was a murder, particularly since DS Birch's health had begun to break down, Bob worked all the hours there were and the least he could do was to pop in at Ouse Avenue, which was so close by, for a few minutes and break the news. With his long strides he got there in no time.

'Something pretty awful has happened,' he said.

Linda, who had her husband and both her two children within sight, realized that her own little world was not involved. 'Tell me,' she said.

'It's at the Dutch House.'

'Is Julie all right?'

'She's fine. It's her neighbour, Mrs Honor – one of the old bats . . .'

'Oh no!' Linda, a warmhearted girl, was dismayed and upset.

'I'm afraid . . .' Then he told her all about it, or as much as she would learn anyway from Julia.

'What can I do?'

'Nothing. You could give Julia a ring and express solidarity. But I shouldn't go round, not this evening anyway. She'll have enough on her plate. I shouldn't keep her long on the phone, either.'

'All right. Are you going out again?'

'You know what a murder case is like. I doubt if I'll get much sleep tonight. The sooner we get on the trail the better, and time's been lost already. Expect me when you see me. Can you tell Tom we'll have to skip our evening out?'

'Oh, horsefeathers, it's your pub night, isn't it?'

'Was,' said Bob as he went out of the door.

71

Linda looked at the clock. Their neighbour, Tom Churchyard, didn't always work office hours either in his job as a British Telecom engineer, but on his pub night with Bob he tried to be home in good time. He'd probably be back already, in the other half of the semi-detached houses. 'I'm just going next door,' she said to Susan and Paul. 'I won't be many minutes. Be good.'

The children considered that remark not worth replying to.

Ever since he and Julia had broken down the barrier between them, Tom Churchyard had been walking round with a blissful expression on his face. He too had felt some doubt about this relationship, before he had taken the plunge, that moment in the wood when his arms went round Julia at last, as if they had a life of their own and could wait no longer.

He too wanted to keep the new state of things under wraps for a while. Years before, he had been jilted sharply, and the impression left was so deep that his relationships with women since that time had only been superficial. He had become self-sufficient. He owned his house which he had bought when prices were only a fraction of the current level.

Oddly, it seemed to other people, he had settled in without discarding the evidence of the former owners. Children's posters and drawings still cluttered some of the walls. He had bought the carpets and curtains with the house, and not redecorated. The traces of the family who used to live there seemed to keep him company. He was a tidy, though not an excessively tidy, man. His appearance was often slapdash because of his choice of rough-textured grey tweeds, handwoven ties, and rumpled hair. He liked handmade things. Part of Julia's attraction for him was her personal tidiness combined with her occupation, her total professional immersion in textiles, the combination of craft and art. Although he was five years younger than Julia, he looked older. In his leisure hours he wore old tweed trousers, soft slippers, a loose sweater, and loved everything historical and traditional, especially his vintage Rolls Royce and classical music. This counterbalanced his job, where he was necessarily in the forefront of technology, even though holes in the road, ducts and cables, did not always strike the onlooker as at the cutting edge.

His desire for secrecy was partly due to shyness. His friends the Southwells next door, Bob, Linda, Susan, Paul, and the new kitten Peaseblossom, only knew him as a confirmed bachelor and he didn't want to be teased about becoming a lover. Overcoming his old wounding experience at last would not be easy. There were a lot of readjustments to make.

Tom heard a light tap on the front door. He knew it was Linda before he went into the hall, because no one else tapped like that.

'Come into my parlour, said the spider to the fly,' he said, throwing open the door and trying to ignore the fact that he was wearing his striped cooking apron. 'Bob going to be late again?'

'I'm afraid he isn't going to be able to make it at all.'

Tom's disappointment showed in his face.

Linda told him what had happened, and he turned rather pale. It was on the tip of his tongue to ask if Julia was all right, but his caution reasserted itself. 'That's bloody awful,' he said. 'A harmless old woman murdered in her own home for a few bits and pieces.'

'The whole of the Dutch House will be panicking, I'm afraid. I'm going to give my friend Julie a ring now and see how she is.'

'That's a good idea. Tell Bob I'm sorry about tonight but I quite understand. I'll see him as soon as he has some free time.'

'Must dash,' said Linda.

Tom felt like dashing at once to the Dutch House and taking Julia in his arms, sheltering her head on his chest and comforting her. Would she like that? He knew she would. But was it the right thing to do in these circumstances? He'd better ring first and find out.

It was some time before her phone was free. 'It's Tom. I've heard,' he said as soon as he did manage to get through.

'Oh, Tom, darling! It's absolute hell!'

'I'll come,' he said.

'Oh yes! Oh no! You'd better not.'

'Surely a friend can call and . . .'

'Yes, of course, but you've no idea what it's like. The neighbours have all heard and they keep coming here to ask questions and be comforted with cups of tea and I'm going to see Cherry gets some food because if I know her she will forget all about it.'

'You need me and the car.'

'No. No, really, darling. Please no. This isn't the time, it will only confuse matters. Here at the Dutch House we have so much to cope with at present – we're all in this together – there are people here with cars if I want one. We're a little community, you know how it is, at the moment we're all clinging together and though I want you here like mad and only wish I could see you for a minute we'd really better not, at least until tomorrow.'

'I don't like to think of you sleeping next to where a murder's taken place. The Dutch House doesn't seem very safe to me.'

'It's as safe as anywhere else, I suppose. Anyway, Adam and I have already slept here since the murder – the police say it was late last night. Not long after I found that note you popped through my door. That is really gruesome. I came out to see if you were still about. I keep thinking about it. I might have seen the murderer, but I didn't see anybody. Poor soul. Lying there all that time without anyone checking. We nearly didn't go round today because we were afraid of intruding.'

'I'm going to ring again, at eleven o'clock,' Tom said firmly. 'And after that I shall walk round and check that everything looks all right.'

'Don't lurk and get arrested, Tom,' she said. 'It is sweet of you. It will be comforting to think that you are there. I shall go to sleep much calmer for that.'

'What about your conference?' asked Tom.

'It's not for ages yet, is it? Nearly a week. I am going, of course. I'm lecturing apart from taking part generally. You will still come to Nottingham with me?'

'Try to stop me.'

'That's all right, then.'

The warm feeling her relationship with Tom gave Julia was much stronger after this and she knew that it would glow brightly when she was at last alone in bed. But at the moment she had too much to do to allow her thoughts to dwell on it. Late though it was, she prepared a meal for two and took it round to Cherry Ducket-Penrose's part of the house. The cats were sleeping off their meal but sure enough Cherry had been going to make do with a slice of toast. They ate together on the little round table and finished with yet another cup of tea.

'I'd open some wine, normally,' Cherry looked at her, 'but at the moment it doesn't seem right and we've had so much brandy. I feel a bit better now, though.'

'Things are always worse if you miss meals.'

'The hot soup was nice, although the weather is so humid.'

'It's surprising. Now, Cherry, if you are sure you don't want me to sleep here or to come to me . . .'

'No, but thank you for suggesting it.'

Julia left reasonably calmly. It was unlikely that anything else would happen. The burglars would hardly return when they must know the place would be stiff with police. At nine o'clock Adam walked in. He appeared unexpectedly in the sitting room, tall and pale, gaunt like a spectre. Julia was alone. She jumped up and went to him, taking his shoulders in her hands.

'Adam, my dear, I didn't expect to see you again tonight.'

'Pete's family were very good and they gave me a meal but I could see they thought the whole thing so awful that having me there was miserable for them. So I came back. There's nothing I can do at the vet's.'

'You'll want to go there first thing in the morning.'

'Yes.'

'Do you have any lessons you can't miss tomorrow?'

'No, it'll be all right. Can you ring school, Mother, and tell them. Thank goodness the next exam's a week off yet. There's no way I can swot at the moment. I can't think about anything except Blue Moon.'

Julia thought that was obvious, but she agreed with him that for once school and exams could go hang for a few days because A levels could be passed any time and at the moment there were more important things.

Next door everything was quiet. Few sounds ever came through the hallway from Mrs Honor's flat, but now the two Bransbys were conscious of the extreme lack of any stirring. They knew that many items had been taken down to the police station, and that there were two policemen on duty, one in the hall at her front door, and one standing on her patio. Everything was secure. It was the silence, deathly silence, which was oppressive.

'It must have been every bit as quiet last night,' remarked

Julia. 'Should we put on the television or radio or a tape of something? All the neighbours have been in already so we probably won't be disturbed now. I'll go to see Cherry again before bedtime.'

Without answering, Adam found a tape of Chopin's piano music and put it on, with the volume low so that the dreadful silent void was filled up without the feeling that they were making merry.

In the incident room which had been set up at the police station Bob Southwell and Dave Smart were looking at one another seriously over a desk covered by files and notes. Dave had a glass of water in front of him but it was not much cooler than the heavy warm air.

'Progress, boss,' said Dave, who had just returned from the post mortem, and had been giving his report of events. Brian had run true to form and given a running commentary, which Dave had been summing up to Bob.

'We aren't doing too badly. But something's nagging at me, Dave. Do you know what?'

'Can't guess, boss.'

'We've had a whole series of these burglaries, right?'

'Right.'

'They've been reported in the local papers – the *Yorkshire Evening Press* has had a field day with them?'

'Surely has.'

'Lots of detail reported, yes?'

'Yes.'

'Non-violent burglaries?'

'Right.'

'I've asked the intelligence officer to get out all the details and do a search for similarities and differences. He's started that already. But I don't think this is one of the series, Dave.'

Bob got up and paced about, wondering if this was the hottest night of the year. It was dark by now – as dark as an English summer night ever is. From the uncurtained window he could look down on the quiet street. The pubs had long since turned out and the drunks had staggered their way home. The few night clubs were probably still in full swing.

He turned back to the desk and sat down again. Dave, sipping his water and wishing for some ice in it, had said nothing.

'Well?' Bob said crisply, wanting some comment.

'If you mean what I think you mean, you are suggesting that this has been got up as a copy-cat crime, using the details published by the press, but that it's been done by different people for a different purpose?'

'Exactly. Without being able to put my finger on it, this doesn't feel the same as those others.'

'When they were interrupted once before, they ran for it,' added Dave.

'They could have run this time. Mrs Honor must have been in bed or preparing to go there, she was in night clothes and dressing gown. Presumably they made enough noise, selecting their booty, to wake her if she was asleep, or alert her if she was still in the bathroom. She walked in on them with her little dog. They could have scarpered through the open patio doors.'

'The other times they've made darn sure that the place was empty.'

'Breaking in at that time of night – not very late, but plenty late enough for a good many people to be going to bed – they were running the kind of risk they haven't run before. They've been bold, rash even, but it has been in daylight when they were sure the householder was from home. No, I don't like it, Dave. It could be deliberate murder. Planned, I mean. Not carried out in the heat of the moment as we were meant to think.'

'So do we change our procedure?'

'Yes, I think so.' Bob fiddled about with the things on the desk. 'First thing in the morning we'd better organize a press conference, the super and I will speak to them.'

'What am I to do?' asked Dave after what seemed like a long interval.

'We've spoken to all the other people in the Dutch House, haven't we?'

'They were all asked whether they had heard anything suspicious during the previous evening. If they had been out we asked what time they had left and returned, and if they saw anything out of the ordinary either time.'

'We'll go back and ask them a bit more. You can organize it tomorrow, Dave, or rather' – glancing at his watch – 'later today.

This time try to get background on Mrs Honor. Does she see many people, have many visitors, who are her friends, who has been to that flat in the last few weeks? What did they know about her antiques or other valuables? What did they know of her personal history?'

'Right, boss.'

'Can you get on to Mrs Bransby first thing and tell her I want to see her and her son Adam this morning? I'd like both the Bransbys to hold themselves available.'

'OK, boss.'

'Now I'm going home to have a few hours' sleep. I want this cracked quickly, Dave. We all need to be on our toes later today. Get yourself home as well. Sandra can stay in charge here.'

Sandra, who liked working nights because her husband could look after the children while she was away, came into the office for instructions.

'Nothing special,' Dave told her. 'Carry on filing and sorting this lot. You're in radio and telephone communication if anything turns up which needs either me or the boss. Don't disturb the DS unless it is absolutely essential, he's been a bit off colour and the doctor told him this afternoon to take things easy. His blood pressure's sky high but he refuses to stay off work, so we are trying to save him as much as we can. I expect Mr Southwell and I will both be back here before you go off shift.'

Then he left her to the hot but peaceful quiet of the incident room during the night hours.

In an adjoining office one of the drug squad, hairy and wearing jeans, was listening for messages from his mates who were still out among the subdued nightlife of the city. Downstairs the uniformed police were sorting traffic problems and monitoring the occasional accident caused by drunken drivers or teenage car-thieves, with more bustle and conversation than there was on the upper floors.

The milkman delivered during the night and usually arrived at the Dutch House at two in the morning. No one had told him about the burglary and he turned up at Mrs Honor's doorstep with her pint of milk to find a large wide-awake uniformed officer standing on the red wool doormat.

'What's going on?' he asked in surprise.

'Don't you know? Do you always deliver your milk at this time?'

'Yes, I do actually. What's it to you?'

The milkman sounded truculent. The policeman took out his notebook. 'Delivered last night, did you?'

'Yes.'

'What time?'

'About the same as this, give or take ten minutes.'

'Name and address, please.'

Shrugging his shoulders the milkman gave the information. 'Now will you tell me what's happening?'

The policeman told him.

'Bloody hell,' said the milkman. He looked pale and shaken. 'She won't want no milk then.'

'Did you hear or see anything unusual when you came last night?'

'Not a thing. It's always quiet at this time, here at the Dutch House. They're not night owls. Not like some flats I could mention, where you might run into a fight or owt, hear music belting out, babies crying, anything.'

'I'll tell you what to do,' said the policeman. 'Make up your bill to include yesterday and put it in the letterbox next time you're here, whoever sorts out the estate will settle it. And that pint you've got there, I'll buy it now for cash.' He fished in his pocket for some coins. 'We're going to make ourselves a cuppa soon and those Scene of Crime officers, greedy buggers, finished all the milk in the flat when they had a drink of tea yesterday.'

'I didn't think they were supposed to do things like that,' said the milkman.

'Only go sour, wouldn't it? And I expect they'd gone over the bottle for fingerprints.'

In the next door flat Adam was wakeful and listening to the indistinct voices as they came through the front door from the hallway. He had opened his bedroom door and window to try to create a through draught of air in the hot and humid night. As he heard the chink of a milk bottle at their own door he realized who had been talking. He turned over, flipped his pillow so that the cool side met his cheek, and tried to settle to sleep again. The shock and emotion which had resulted in tears had gone. He was now in command of himself. Lying with his eyes open in the darkness, covered by a single sheet, he thought about the Dutch House and the rhythms of life there, the interwoven patterns of the thirteen people – now twelve – who lived within the old walls. Although the fabric had been ripped apart it was reweaving itself. The milkman would only be leaving their own bottle in the hallway for a while but, before many months had passed, someone else would live next door and there would again be the two chinks of milk bottles in the small hours, followed by two more from upstairs and two more from the attic floor.

Even as Adam pondered this, he could hear the footsteps of the milkman on the stairs, descending after his deliveries were done. As he passed through the ground-floor hallway he called out a goodnight to the constable, who replied to him as the outer door closed behind the milkman. Quiet descended and Adam slept.

Not everyone was asleep in the Dutch House. Ms Haygreen was still in a state of nerves, which had kept Ms Hodson on her toes trying to calm her ever since they heard the news. Mr Markhall was trying without success to while away the hours of night with another chess problem. Dr Bright was working out in his head his timetable of travel for the next fortnight, when he would be acting as locum over in the West Riding, as he persisted in calling it. The Brothers Lloyd, unable to sleep, had made themselves mugs of cocoa and were drinking them in the kitchen, conversing in whispers. Ms Wilmet, in an unusual act of consideration, was listening on earphones to the *Siegfried Idyll* by Wagner. Normally she would have put it on her hi-fi system at full blast, whatever time of night it was, if she wanted to revel in the full sound of the music. Mr Spicer was drinking water and puzzling how to get cool. He never used his shower (modern invention, what was wrong with a weekly bath?) and although he wondered whether to take off his thick flannelette pyjamas, felt it would hardly be decent to go to bed with nothing on. He looked at himself in the bathroom mirror. His eyes were red with prolonged weeping.

In the attic flats of the Dutch House Ms Haygreen and Ms Hodson had been talking until the early hours. After a short sleep, Ms Hodson had called to see whether Ms Haygreen was awake and how she was feeling. It was obvious at once that Ms Haygreen was far from well.

'You must ring the Centre and tell them you are not coming in,' Ms Hodson said.

'I can't do that. They are expecting me. I have a class at ten.'

'Blow the class. Let someone else take it. Let them skip it and do something else for once. It isn't as though they are working through a syllabus.'

'That's not the point. They look forward to my classes, they will be disappointed.'

Ms Haygreen sat up in bed and blew her nose. Ms Hodson, who had brought in a cup of tea and turned the radio on, looked at her in concern, but felt she had done all she could.

'Life has to go on,' Ms Haygreen said.

'Well, we know that. I am teaching all day. It is just as bad for me. Everyone else in the Dutch House is upset too. All right – all right – I know it is different for us, I am only making the point that you are not alone in being upset, but since you do feel so strongly, you should give in gracefully and stay at home.'

Ms Haygreen swung her legs out of bed and contemplated her toes. 'I'm getting up now. Clear out, there's a dear,' she said ungratefully.

Ms Hodson had to prepare for her day's teaching, so she went. Half an hour later she returned to Ms Haygreen's flat and said, 'I'm off now,' and by nine o'clock she was parking her car at the school where she taught Art, taking her things from the car, and crossing the car-park to the front door. Thank goodness no one would have heard yet about Mrs Honor's death. Tomorrow would be much more of an ordeal. Her stomach was tight and she felt faintly sick, but she knew that the moment she stood up in front of her first class, everything would vanish away except trying to get over to them the essence of perceiving and then ordering the visual world around them and conveying it onto paper by way of marks, splashes, lines, lumps and any variant of those that might seem to them appropriate.

Ms Haygreen had longer to come to terms with the outside world and at ten she wavered her way up the drive to the Resource Centre where she taught handicrafts to mentally challenged young adults and also older people. Her old dears this morning loved the business of tying cloth up into little knobs and boiling it in vats of dye. They hadn't at first, when they didn't know what the end product was and it seemed pointless. But now they all had bright scarves which they had tie-dyed a fortnight ago they were keen to try again and see what came out this time. She couldn't lose herself in her work as Ms Hodson did. Most of her time was spent persuading and cajoling. It was different when she was working with textiles on her own at home, producing really first-class elegant results, then she could lose herself completely.

When the vet arrived at his surgery the next morning he found Adam Bransby sitting on the step waiting for him.

'You could have rung the bell,' he said.

'I didn't suppose there was anyone here.' Adam got up and dusted the seat of his jeans. Together the two went through to a room filled with wire cages, and in one of them was the heap of discoloured fur which was Blue Moon. He was still sedated. The young assistant vet who slept on the premises joined them.

A pup in one of the other cages started to whine at the exciting advent of humans and their voices, and a Jack Russell was yapping. A large black cat wearing a bandage looked agitated and tried to eat the threads it had torn loose from the fabric.

The vet examined the Peke gently. 'Having survived the night and had fluids his circulation should be better and the effects of shock less,' he remarked. 'I will operate after surgery.'

Adam said, 'I know you will do all you can.'

'You can stay in here if you like, and talk to him, it won't do any harm.'

Adam sat on the hard chair by the cage, murmuring soothing things. Towards the end of the time he saw a flicker of response from Blue Moon. First the upper visible ear twitched, then the tail moved once, slightly.

During the operation Adam sat in the waiting room and tried to interest himself in the centuries-old magazines.

'I'm quite pleased with him,' the vet said later. 'He's survived. We've fastened the broken jaw with stainless steel wire and the left leg has been pinned above the elbow. Both legs are now in plaster for breaks lower down. There isn't much one can do for the ribs except strap them up. I'm pretty sure there has been some haemorrhaging into the lungs, but that's not as serious as haemorrhaging in the abdomen would be. Luckily most of his injuries are at the front from being kicked when he went in to attack.'

'What happens now?' asked Adam.

'You go home,' the vet said. 'He's going to be groggy for two or three days and must stay here. If he survives that, you can take him.' Seeing the sudden light in Adam's eyes, he added, 'Don't count on it. It's touch and go.'

DS Joe Birch and DCI Robert Southwell had presided at a press conference that morning already. They had not mentioned Bob's theory that this was a copy-cat burglary. Apart from anything else, Birch didn't go along with that idea.

'Hunch, Bob,' he'd said. 'All you are going on is pure hunch. Where are the facts which convince you this isn't the same burglars that did the others? There aren't any. You say they were more careful before to make sure no one was in, well, this time they misjudged the situation. You say it was the first time they had worked so late at night, well, they have used all different times of day, there hasn't been any consistency in it. No. Your theory hasn't a leg to stand on, at least at present. Don't bring it to me again unless you have something pretty substantial to back it up.'

'Have I your permission to try to find something to back it up?' Bob had woken that morning more sure than ever that this was a different ball game to the other burglaries.

Joe Birch had looked at him gloomily. 'I don't suppose it is any good trying to stop you. Don't waste much manpower on it.'

'If it is a copy-cat crime, a staged burglary to cover up a murder—'

'Oh my, our imagination has been working overtime.'

'If it is . . . I want to look at all her contacts with that in mind.'

Joe Birch was growing angry, and it wasn't good for him.

'I don't want you putting this theory about and don't forget it's me that's in charge of this investigation. I don't intend to put a complete embargo on it, because on the whole I trust your experience and intelligence, Robert. What I'm saying is this, do not mention it to anyone else – have you? Have you already?'

'Only Dave Smart, just before I knocked off last night.'

'Send Dave in to see me. I want to impress on him that this line of investigation is not official policy.'

'But—'

'Yes, I said I wouldn't put a complete embargo. Let us spell it out. You are not to mention this idea to anyone unless you find proof and convince *me* with it first and get the OK, right?'

'Right.'

'Two. I will let you try to find factual support by means of your own interviews with relevant people, but it must be done in such a way that they do not suspect what you have in mind. Is that clear?'

'Sir.'

'I will be running things generally. You can go off and work on your own for the rest of the day. Let me know your results before you go tonight.'

'Yes, sir.'

When Adam arrived home, DCI Bob Southwell had finished all he wanted to discuss with Julia and was beginning to feel impatient at Adam's absence.

'He'd already left when Inspector Smart rang,' Julia was explaining for the third time when Adam walked in. 'Oh, darling, what a relief to see you. Have you had anything to eat? It's past lunch-time.'

'I'm afraid he'll have to wait until I've finished with him,' Bob said rather grimly. 'I haven't had any lunch myself.'

Julia was about to offer food, but a look at Bob's face stopped her. 'Of course,' she said swiftly. 'Perhaps a cup of tea all round.

I'll make it then take myself off into another room while you give Adam the third degree.'

Although Bob Southwell and his wife and children knew Julia well they hadn't seen Adam so often. Bob thought that he must feel his way into this interview as if the boy was a stranger.

'Shall we sit at the table?' he asked. At once the situation became more comfortable, particularly when Julia served them both with tea and then closed the door behind her. There is something about a family table where many conversations and much work takes place, which makes a friendly but businesslike atmosphere easy to achieve, particularly with a cup of tea. Bob laid down his notebook and pen, took a gulp of tea, and began.

'Your mother has taken me through finding Mrs Honor,' he said. 'You may have something to add to that – something you noticed which she didn't. We could discuss that later. She has also done her best to help on the contents of the flat. We are trying to discover whether the thieves actually made off with anything or not, and if so what. You might be able to help there too. Meanwhile, what I would like first is your account of the Dutch House itself – the routine of life here, the people in it. Try to make me understand how the place ticks, as if I lived here too.'

Adam looked both relieved and interested. 'I came here when I was five,' he said, 'and although I do remember our other house, this is home. Most of the people have been here nearly as long as we have. The only really new one is Susannah Wilmet who moved into one of the garage flats a few weeks ago. She's in her twenties I think, and teaches music.'

Something in Adam's face when he spoke of Susannah Wilmet told Bob Southwell that she was an attractive young woman and that Adam took a keen interest in girls.

Adam went on, 'Her neighbours have been grumbling like mad about the private lessons she gives in the evening. That's the Brothers Lloyd – they live in the other garage flat – they've been there ages and they're retired really. The Dutch House is like a rookery,' he said suddenly. 'I don't mean it's like a Victorian London slum. I mean a rookery with rooks – they squabble and fight, you know, and then have parliaments, and sometimes dole out punishments, and I'm sure they gossip about each other all the time.'

Bob Southwell was glad he didn't live in a rookery, but he could see that the whole set-up fascinated Adam.

'They have all been awfully kind to me,' the lad said. 'When I was a child, it must have been like having a host of uncles and aunts – not having had those I don't really know. If I fell down and cried there was always someone to rush out and pick me up, bandage me and give me a goody to stop the tears. Some of them baby-sat for me and they put up with my birthday parties and groups of friends round to play and as far as I know they never grumbled to my mother.'

'You were exceptionally lucky,' said Bob.

'Cherry's been here for ever of course. Her mother died before this part of the house was converted into flats so none of us knew her, but Cherry talks about her so much we feel we did. Next to Mum, Cherry's my favourite person. Mr Spicer next door through the wall is the gardener and odd-job man, he's getting old now but he does what he can. He's always falling out with people, but he had a special war of attrition with Mrs Honor. We tried to think it was funny but it wasn't really.'

'Not serious, I'm sure.'

'Not serious like killing people. Serious like perpetual grumbling and complaints on both sides, and both trying to outwit the other. According to Mr Spicer, Mrs Honor thought the flats were run specially for her benefit and she was entitled to all the produce in the garden – this part of the garden. It is mainly apples and pears but there's a very productive plum tree. She would sneak out at all sorts of hours and pick the fruit and he would be on the lookout and try to catch her. She picked flowers as well and herbs, and if there was anything she could do to annoy him she did it, I'm afraid. It seems sort of pathetic now she's dead.'

'You don't think he killed her,' stated Bob.

Adam gave him a startled glance. 'Oh, no!' He was quiet for a minute then said tentatively, 'It was burglars, surely – not anyone she knew.'

'That's the presumption.' Bob could have kicked himself. He didn't usually let cats out of bags. His mind was so concentrated on his own theory that he had let that sentence slip – a Freudian slip, he expected.

'Well, Cherry then Mr Spicer then us then Mrs Honor – reading the ground floor from left to right as you stand in the road that's how it is. Upstairs here in the Victorian wing there's three flats on the first floor, Mrs Robinson over Mr Spicer – she's a widow, her husband died two years ago, he was one of those hen-pecked men. She has three grown-up children. They used to play with me when they were young, but they're all married now. She's away at the moment staying with her daughter because she broke her ankle but this is going to bring her back again like a bird of prey.'

'You don't like Mrs Robinson?'

'I quite like her. She's a bit on the fussy side – fussy clothes and hair and fussy flat. She's dark and little and fat and always slimming. She's all right.'

With this neutral reaction Bob was content. Mrs Robinson didn't sound like a killer, though one never knew.

'Her entrance is different to ours – you'll realize that, Mr Southwell – it's smaller than our hallway here, because it only serves the two flats, hers above and Mr Spicer's below. Above us we have Doctor Bright, he's a medical doctor, retired – a lot of people here are retired. He still does some clinics and locums. He's always busy, dashing somewhere, giving everyone good advice. He does have a wife but we hardly ever see her. She flies abroad for her health every winter because she gets chronic bronchitis and when she is in England she stays with her sisters in the south – she has a lot of them strategically placed in holiday resorts. She'd like the doctor to be with her but she couldn't drag him away from York and all his friends, so they sold their big house and took the flat for him.'

Bob thought the doctor didn't sound too likely to be a homicidal maniac either.

'And above Mrs Honor?'

'Oh well, that's Oddsocks.'

Bob lifted his eyebrows and Adam laughed for the first time since he and his mother went out to check if Mrs Honor was all right, twenty-four hours earlier, though it felt like a lot more.

'Mr Markhall his name is really. I doubt if Oddsocks has ever been married, he's such a fusspot. Once years ago when I was a little boy I noticed he was wearing odd socks and he told me he had another pair like that at home. He does sometimes go in for these dry remarks that are intended as humour. It was actually most unusual for him to wear anything that wasn't regimented and organized, there must have been a special reason for it.'

'Fussy like Mrs Robinson?'

'Oh no, not a bit. She's fussy like tying back her curtains with bows of ribbon and having those gathered-up sheer blinds like tart's knickers.'

'And he's fussy like?'

'He's fussy like rinsing out the milk bottle with water so as not to waste the milk that clings to the glass, and putting the rinsings in the saucepan when he's making coffee. It makes it rather watery sometimes, if you like your coffee made with milk. He's a retired architect. Everything in his flat is in straight lines. He drills his books into battalions, troops and companies and sorts them according to size and colour as well as subject.'

'And the first floor in the garage flats? They are garages at the bottom, I know.'

'Well, we've talked about them. The two Lloyd brothers and Susannah Wilmet who teaches music.'

'What do, or did, the Lloyds do?'

'They used to be in partnership running an ironmonger's, I think. The youngest, Lancelot, was trained as an accountant and still does some people's accounts for them.'

'Lancelot?'

'I call him Lance.'

'And his brother?'

'Oh, he's Gawain.'

'Yes, he would be, of course. So that's it, is it?'

'No, there's the attic flats. Didn't you realize we had some?'

'I don't think I did.'

'They're at the top of this block. Because they lose a lot of height with the sloping roofs John Trim made only two up there. The access is through our hallway and up past Doctor Bright and Oddsocks. The top flight of stairs is sideways on, not back to front, to make the attic flats' floorspace even. Up there are Miss Haygreen and Miss Hodson. They always say Ms, actually. They are teachers and usually they're friends. You can always tell if they've had a row because whoever is in a huff closes their front door. So if both doors are open they're friends, and if they're both shut they're enemies. If one's open and one's shut we're in a half-way situation.'

'Of the gentlemen, three are bachelors, one a widower – didn't your mother tell me Mr Spicer is – and one has a semi-detached wife.'

'You never know these days, they could all have been married one time or another.' Adam sounded apologetic.

'And of the ladies, four spinsters, three widows. Mrs Honor had no children, your mother says. She had you, and Mrs Robinson had three, two boys and a girl, all now married.'

'Yes, that's it.'

'And all been here donkeys' years except Miss Wilmet.'

'And Mrs Honor of course,' added Adam.

'She hadn't been here long?'

'Well, no. She came after her husband died, about four years ago it would be.'

'I remember now, Miss Ducket-Penrose told me that.'

Adam went on to give Bob Southwell a number of racy anecdotes about the dwellers in the Dutch House, which were amusing but on the whole, Bob decided, not very relevant. It was good to hear the boy laugh, though, after what he'd been through. Bob knew how he would feel if, in a few years' time, his Paul or Susan were subjected to such an experience.

'The ornaments and so on in Mrs Honor's flat,' he said at last. 'Let's see what you can tell me about those and then we'll call it a day. Did she have many visitors?'

'Not as a rule,' Adam answered, 'but lately, since the main house was opened at Spring Bank Holiday, she and Cherry have grown quite pally with Taff Walker, the antique dealer. He's been to Mrs Honor's a few times for afternoon tea. She's been trying to sound him out on the value of her things. As far as I know he hasn't taken anything away to value or anything like that.'

Julia came in then.

'Finished?' she asked.

'I'm taking mi laddo next door to help us with the *objets d'art*.'

'Bob, I'm due at a conference in Nottingham next weekend, a Friday to Sunday. Is it all right if I go? Adam is going off too, with a friend, to a concert in Edinburgh.'

'Carry on by all means. Leave us a telephone number, though, or somewhere you can both be contacted, in case, but we are not likely to need you.'

Bob and Adam stood in the middle of Mrs Honor's sitting room – in fact the main living room of the flat. DI Smart was present to take notes. A piece of black plastic covered the area where the owner's body had lain. A good many of the ornaments had been removed by the police, so the place looked rather bare. The pretty French Empire ormolu desk between the door into the dining area and the patio doors had none of its usual impedimenta.

Adam described the items which usually stood on its surface and Dave Smart listed them. Adam turned very slowly round the room, describing items as he went.

'An oriental bowl on top of the television,' he said, 'celadon glaze, a very simple lovely shape, on a carved ebony stand – well, I think it was ebony. It was black and wooden, anyway. On that little mantelshelf over the electric fire, her Dresden china, shepherd and shepherdess and small vases of china flowers. Very awkward to dust or wash but she liked looking after them. On the bookcase, her collection of netsuke.'

The bookcase was a pleasant one of oak, some four feet six high, with leaded glass panes in the two doors. The polished top had previously borne a scattering of tiny exquisite objects, all of old ivory, beautifully detailed.

'There was a worried-looking mythical figure with a hat on and a little round bag on his hunched-up shoulder. There was a cross-legged figure, not a Buddha, but perhaps a god. He was about two inches high. The one with the bag on his shoulder was long and thin and wouldn't stand up. He measured about three inches. Oh, there were about two dozen of them. My favourite was a mouse eating a fruit, he was half inside it. A lot of them were animals. I can make you a list, given a bit of time to think.'

Bob Southwell looked at his watch. 'I think I ought to go, Adam. You can do this every bit as well alone with Mr Smart. Try to remember all the netsuke, they are very expensive and collectable and a temptation to anyone dishonest. Don't forget the other rooms. And now there's a thing, did she have any silver?'

'Oh yes, any amount of it.'

'See what you can remember of that.'

With a cheery and reassuring wave the DCI was on his way.

The autopsy report had arrived. It was much as expected. The only unusual thing was that the blunt instrument with which the injuries had been inflicted was of a highly characteristic nature. Not an axe or a brick, nor yet a hammer or a baseball bat. Roundish, or oval, perhaps egg-shaped was the nearest approximation to it, Brian suggested. Not however a smooth egg shape, but with projections. The projection most clearly indicated by the damage to the head was beaklike. Then also it must have had something with which it could be held and wielded.

'What do you make of that, sir?' Bob asked DS Joe Birch. They were together in the DS's office. Joe was taking life and work as easily as he could, after his slight heart attack some months before. His DCIs were doing a great deal of work which he would normally have done himself.

DS Birch read through the report carefully. 'I would have thought a weight in a sock, a metal or marble egg, perhaps, if it hadn't been for this mention of projections. Hard to envisage, isn't it. Now, her flat was full of small decorative objects. One of those, do you think? A paperweight from her desk, for instance?'

'It could be. Yes.'

'Something snatched up in the heat of the moment when they heard her coming.'

'I think you're right, sir. Thank you.'

'Smart is investigating what is missing, I believe.'

'Yes, sir.'

'Let me know,' finished DS Birch, leaning back in his chair and remembering he ought to be taking his next heart tablet.

'About my own investigation . . .' Bob sounded tentative.

'Go on, then.'

'I think you have to be an unusual sort of person to choose to live in the Dutch House.'

'You can say that again.' DS Birch had been there, and talked to a few people, that very afternoon. 'Intellectual lot. I can see why you think one of them might have murdered her. The sort who would murder for an idea, nothing as common as money.'

'You don't think my theory so far fetched after all? I hadn't actually pinpointed the *residents*, only postulated that it was not the usual burglars, and that it was a copy-cat crime.'

'The trouble is, Robert, that when the other burglaries began we didn't know, naturally enough, that it was going to be a series. You know what the manpower situation is. What do we do? Prioritize. What is low priority? Your average house break-in. So have we any forensic evidence for the previous occurrences? No, we have not, any more than we would have if they were car thefts. So we have nothing to compare this one with, forensically speaking. You may be right. Having seen the weird lot that live there, I would believe anything of them.'

'My checking is official, then?'

'Let us say, keep it quiet. Carry on as you have done today. Check into them all a bit, yes. Won't hurt to eliminate them.'

'Boss!' called Dave Smart as Southwell walked through the detectives' office at Clifford Street. 'Boss! Come here a minute.'

Dave was looking down at the report made by the uniformed constables who had been on guard duty the previous night at Mrs Honor's flat.

'Look at this.' He read it aloud. '"At two in the morning the milkman came round and delivered a pint of milk, which was paid for by PC Green. He said that he delivered every night at that time."'

'Do we have his name and who he works for?'

'Yes. He's self-employed, actually. You wouldn't get an employee to behave like that.'

'Get him in. Now. I'll interview him myself. We could do with an official statement. Find out which postmen normally deliver, as well, Dave. Who else would regularly be calling? I want to get a feel of the daily round, the atmosphere of the community. Meter readers. What are the arrangements for our regular policing of the area – is there a PC who knows it particularly well? Who cleans the windows? Apart from general queries, we can ask them if they saw anything or anyone unexpected. Someone hanging around aimlessly, or looking unfamiliar. The residents are being asked that already.'

8

For DS Birch, DCI Southwell and their team the next few days passed in the sort of relentless routine detective work which takes time to show results. In the Dutch House complex everyone was quiet and subdued, and there was much less social life than usual. While Mrs Honor's body lay unburied even their normal cheery greetings seemed out of place. The week wore slowly away.

That weekend Julia was going to her conference at Nottingham, and Adam would be in Edinburgh for the concert. Julia did not expect to see her son after Friday morning so she went to his room on the Thursday night to have a chat. He had already opened the windows and closed the curtains, darkening the room as much as possible and making the most of what air movement there was.

'Is that you, Mother?' he called. She tiptoed in.

'You're in bed early, pet.'

'It's so darned hot.' His voice sounded strained.

'You haven't told me how you found Blue Moon.'

Adam had been to the vet's during the evening, while Julia was packing.

'Alive, taking a little nourishment.'

'Well, that's good! Now I am going to get you a big glass of home-made lemonade with ice and mint leaves and that will cool you off and you'll be able to sleep. Have you thrown off the duvet? That's good. A sheet will be enough for anyone tonight, I would think.'

Julia brought the drink and knew that Adam was relaxing and growing sleepy. Before she was ready to turn off her own light, she could hear soft regular breathing coming from his room.

Early on Friday morning the Intelligence Officer appeared in DCI Southwell's office.

'Come to report, sir,' he said.

Something in his tone made Bob feel hopeful. He hadn't really expected anything from the search through back records, having looked at the basic files himself, but the Intelligence Officer had been searching through all the other stuff, the notebooks, the printouts, the ephemera, anything and everything still surviving.

'Yes?'

The man hesitated, then said, 'There are discrepancies. As you know, sir, we didn't do full reports on these break-ins at first, but as the series went on obviously we were taking it more seriously. There have been some in other police areas, too.'

'I didn't realize that.'

'It was in consulting our adjoining areas that I found out that while most of the detail corresponds, they had recorded that the antiques were wrapped and packed in the owner's underwear.'

'You're joking!'

'No.'

'That really adds insult to injury,' said Dave Smart, who was in the room and couldn't help hearing.

'Soft things, underpants and vests. I have checked with the officers involved on our cases, and they remember that earlier episodes on our patch were the same. But in the Dutch House incident, the villains seem to have taken tissue paper and bubble plastic along with them.'

'Yes.' Bob Southwell was staring at the Intelligence Officer. It was the first time he himself had been on the scene of one of these burglaries, so the different appearance of the packing material had not occurred to him. 'The newspaper reports said they'd taken their own packing, didn't they?'

'They took their own cardboard boxes each time. The newspapers weren't more specific than the general statement that the thieves had packed the items carefully while on the premises, using their own packing, but we didn't tell them about the underpants and vests.'

Bob turned to Dave Smart. 'Dave, did all that packing go for forensic examination?'

'No, sir. Most of it is with our Exhibits Officer. It has been fingerprinted, of course.'

'Go along yourself, this is too important to trust to anyone else. Look over the packing materials and the boxes for the slightest detail which might help us. You come along with me to the DS,' he added to the Intelligence Officer.

A few minutes later, DS Joe Birch was agreeing that Southwell's hunch had been right, and the whole basis of the inquiry had changed.

'So we are on more familiar territory, Bob,' he said. 'Back to the old grind of "who benefits from the crime?", "who was the last to see the victim?", relatives, friends, neighbours, motive, opportunity. At the same time, we must not lose sight of the fact that the thieves might just have changed their *modus operandi*, and decided the vests and pants were a nuisance.'

'Yes, sir.'

'She was a quarrelsome old thing, wasn't she?'

'Does seem to have been.'

'Likely to get at people? Blackmail them?'

'Possible, I suppose. She seemed to gain power over people and events, struggle for mastery, even in tiny matters where she was obviously in the wrong. She was a very strong personality.'

'Family?'

'None, apparently, nearer than an ancient brother-in-law.'

'Look for nieces and nephews. *Who benefits*, don't forget. That's usually the family.'

'Right.'

'*Last to see the victim.* Go through the neighbours with a fine-tooth comb. Anyone who has visited her. Wasn't there talk of an antique dealer? The very man. With a stalwart assistant who does the driving? Why doesn't the owner drive himself, we ask? I would say the antique dealer should be the prime suspect, Bob. Since antiques have actually been stolen, it points straight to him. You are preparing lists of the missing articles, I hope.'

'I'll interview him immediately, and yes, the lists are being prepared.'

'Didn't you say there was a vendetta with the gardener? Does the murder have anything to do with the fact that she was a heroine in the war? Bob, I want to know what everyone in the Dutch House has for breakfast and who they sleep with.'

'I'll do my best, sir.'

'Don't let the media get hold of this. It is vital that they go on thinking it is just one of the series of antique thefts. Lull the murderer into a sense of security.'

The incident room was the busiest it had been since Mrs Honor's body was discovered. Leave was cancelled. Overtime was authorized. Urgency was in the very air of the police station.

Unfortunately DS Birch's prime suspect, the antique dealer, was unavailable according to the Selby police, who found his shop closed, so other inquiries were to be made first.

Bob decided to go to the Dutch House to interview the residents. In the garage block the old harness room on the ground floor had been turned into a community room, and here he established himself with a tape recorder, a pile of files, a radio telephone and DI Dave Smart. There were a number of blue plastic stacking chairs in one corner and an old neglected table-tennis table pushed up against the wall.

One of the young detective constables had compiled lists of the information collected so far on each person who had been mentioned in the case.

'There's no doubt about one thing, Dave,' Bob remarked. 'The gardener bloke, Spicer. He comes out from this as next to a fascist. This remark he's said to have made when they had a group of disabled people going round the Dutch House, you've read it, I know. What a ghastly thing to say! He sounds, from his other opinions quoted here, as if he's somewhere to the right of Genghis Khan.'

'No love lost between him and the victim.'

'Antagonism in fact. I think we'll see him first and get him out of the way.'

'Or in jug,' commented Dave.

When Mr Spicer appeared they sized him up as a possible murderer. Physically he was the wiry, skinny type who go on for ever, dying in their nineties while mowing the grass or turning the compost heap. Definitely capable of the attack. They knew him to be irascible, and he looked it, also self-willed and obstinate. But there was something else, which surprised them both, and that was the look of shock and, yes, sorrow, on his grim face.

'Sit down, Mr Spicer,' said Bob Southwell. 'We have already

spoken to you several times since Mrs Honor's tragic death. At present we are trying to find out who was near her flat during the evening the crime took place. You have stated that you had done your normal security round before going to bed. At what time exactly would you be passing through the hallway of flats 3 to 8?'

'About ten.'

'You go to bed early?'

'I needs my rest.'

Then the two policemen began a barrage of questions, taking the older man through his evidence again and again, catching up contradictions, goading him to give himself away. One question, which was general, and merely because it was puzzling the police, was, why was the hallway not locked during the night?

'The milkman comes, doesn't he?' replied Spicer. 'And there's visitors to the flats, and sometimes the residents come in at all hours of the night.'

'They could have keys,' said Southwell.

'There's still the milkman.'

A little later he almost shouted, 'You are asking me things as if you think I done it. I wouldn't hurt the old lady. Life is boring without her, like eating beef without mustard. I wasn't the only one who was round the hallway, there was your friend,' looking at Bob Southwell.

'My friend?'

'The bloke you drink with. You don't own the pub, you know. There's other people go in it besides you.'

'Do you mean Tom Churchyard?'

'Big bloke, wears a grey tweed suit.'

'You saw him . . . when exactly?'

'The night Mrs Honor was murdered, the night you are on about. I was coming in from the garden through the door at the back of the hall of 3 to 8 as he was going out of the front.'

'You didn't get a proper look, then, could have been anyone.'

'I saw him well enough to know who it was.'

Spicer had said nothing to incriminate himself, and the police had no reason to hold him. They let him go, thanking him for helping with their inquiries.

'He is out of the frame, then,' said Dave.

'Looks like it, and my friend Tom is on the suspect list. We

97

will have to give him a proper interview and get to the bottom of this.'

Tom Churchyard and Julia Bransby met as if by chance on one of the platforms of York railway station early the following morning.

'Hello, Tom, fancy seeing you here,' Julia greeted him quietly. 'Where are you off to?' It would have been too obvious if, when she first saw him in the foyer, she had called across to him.

'Nottingham, actually.'

'You're not, are you? I'm travelling in the same direction.'

'Good! I'll have someone to talk to.'

'Are you buying a paper? I'm getting the *Independent*.'

Tom bought the *Yorkshire Post*, so that they could swap.

They were lucky. There was an empty carriage – or almost empty. All they could see were the backs of a few heads. Tom found himself in a state of nervous excitement. Dare they kiss in a public place like a railway carriage? Everything seemed to be tinged with a special, weighty significance, even outside circumstances like the pattern on the upholstery they sat on.

They settled down. The train started. They kissed tentatively, a mere brushing of lips. That first little caress was followed by a bashful interlude during which they bought coffee from the refreshment trolley as it made its own journey down the long linked corridors of the moving train. Such simple actions served to unite them. Their movements in adding milk and in Tom's case sugar to the drink, seemed to synchronize. Drinking, disposing of the packaging neatly, seemed to them like the movements in a ballet. To an unbiased observer it might have looked like the movements of a ritual mating dance of some species of large and unthreatened bird. When at last they left the train they were both in a state of bliss which seemed to them to leave a glow of gold on the walls they passed and the stairs they climbed on their way out of the station.

They found a pleasant little café for lunch, with a secluded table (not secluded enough, thought Tom and Julia). Later Julia discovered that a journey on a bus, standing on the lower deck and worrying in case they got off at the wrong stop, could have the magic quality of a fairytale.

When they arrived at the university they asked directions of one of the porters and he took them to the room Julia was to use during the weekend, carrying her case for her. The porter made it obvious he was curious about their relationship. He seemed reluctant to leave, even after Julia tipped him. He began to tell her about his son, who was at another university. She replied with a few remarks about Adam. Tom tried not to shuffle. Julia attempted to seem polite and interested. The porter cast greedy glances from one to the other of them, and from second to second put off his departure. When at last he could avoid it no longer, the man went.

After the door closed, they stood waiting.

'Do you think he's really gone?' asked Tom in a whisper.

'I think so. Yes, he has.' Julia indicated the wide picture window. They could see the porter walking on the grass, returning to his office. As he passed he looked up curiously at their window. They realized that people outside gave the impression of being very close to them. Students were drifting past in ones and twos. Whenever they thought the spread of grass would be empty, another figure would slouch by. Tom and Julia felt as though they were in a goldfish bowl.

'I had better unpack,' said Julia. She put clothes in wardrobe and drawers and her sponge-bag in the bathroom. She slipped her nightdress into the bed and guessed that all kinds of erotic images were forming in Tom's imagination.

He cleared his throat. 'It's a bit public in here, isn't it?' he asked, coming close to her.

They sat down on the edge of the bed.

'I suppose we could close the curtains,' she said as his hands found hers.

'Wouldn't it look very obvious?'

Of course it would – one curtained window in the early afternoon in the middle of that blank wall of glass which the dormitory block presented to the wide lawn outside.

Tom sighed. 'I only have a few minutes anyway, and don't you have a lecture to prepare?'

'I only need to check that I've got everything. Pure nerves, it was all checked and re-checked last night.'

'"Viking textiles, their manufacture and conservation", isn't that your subject?'

'Yes. I am sure you would find it utterly boring.'

'I don't think I would.' Tom's eyes told her she could lecture on Double Entry Book-keeping and he would sit there entranced for hours.

She laughed and took his wrist in her hand, tilting it to look at his watch. 'How long can you stay?' she asked, a sudden breathiness in her voice taking her by surprise.

'It's a pity I have that meeting of M.R.S. tonight,' he whispered in her ear.

'It was nice of you to come down with me, Tom, particularly on the day of the Medieval Reconstruction Society monthly meeting. When it turned out that one of your members had committed murder, I thought that would be the end of the group altogether, but you and Canon Grindal pulled it through.'

'George Grindal was a tower of strength.'

'He was amazing last autumn when the Dean died.'

'Amazing.'

They took advantage of a few seconds when the grass outside was empty to lean back on the bed. Combined with twitching the curtain a foot or so, they felt protected enough to indulge in little kisses, caresses, whispers, ear nibblings and so on for fifteen magical minutes. Had the porter returned his worst suspicions would have been justified.

'You had better go,' Julia whispered at last. 'You've got that meeting, and I must socialize, that's partly what they are paying me for.'

Tom swore about his meeting.

No one was looking, so they tidied themselves in front of the inadequate mirror, bumping into one another and nearly becoming involved again.

When they looked back on that plain, severe, little student bedroom in the days to come, it seemed in memory to have been filled with a flutter of translucent wings. In it their relationship had moved into a new zone of intimacy.

The police had been waiting to interview Tom Churchyard. DCI Southwell did not believe that his friend and neighbour was responsible for – or even party to – the violent death of an old lady, but a mental distance came in his mind, a withdrawal, which separated his official self from the warm friend Tom knew. All day Friday they could not locate Tom, but the following morning early on Bob saw him through the window, pruning one of the flowering shrubs which made a pleasant informal barrier between their two back gardens. Bob could not help remembering that they had first met across that same hedge, when the Southwell family moved to York. He remembered Tom's bravery and mistaken loyalty during those first weeks, when, still new to the place and the job, his own task had been to find a murderer.

'Tom,' he said, strolling out into his own back garden as soon as he had dressed, 'Tom, we were looking for you yesterday. We need to interview you in connection with this murder at the Dutch House.'

Tom looked at him in surprise, and got up from the grass. He had been kneeling to reach under the shrub to uproot an obstinate weed.

'Interview me in connection with the murder?'

'Not very well phrased,' Bob apologized. 'Some evidence has come up we need to examine.'

'When do you need me?'

'Now, if you can. You aren't at work today?'

'A slack period has come up.'

'Then can you come along now?'

Tom dusted his hands on his trousers and said, 'If you like.'

Once in the police station Tom found to his surprise that they were to talk in an interview room with a tape recorder running and DI Dave Smart present. His neighbour and friend sat across the table, putting the initial information on the tape.

'Tom,' Bob said then, and his voice was neutral, calm. 'We have evidence that you were in the hallway of flats 3 to 8 at the Dutch House complex, late in the evening, on the day of the murder of Mrs Honor in flat 4. The time is put at approximately 10 p.m. This is about the time that Mrs Honor died. You will realize that we need to eliminate you from our inquiries, and we also need your evidence about anything you saw or heard on that occasion. First, why were you in the hallway that evening?'

During the few seconds' pause, Bob felt anxiety rising. In spite of the tight official hold he was keeping on himself, his personal feelings were threatening to break through. He felt like shouting,

'Tell us you are innocent, Tom, for heaven's sake, man, get on with it!'

Tom said at last, 'I was restless that night and although I was tired I didn't think I would sleep if I went to bed so early, it was too dark to garden and I wasn't in the mood for music. A stroll seemed the best idea. Then I remembered that I had written a note to Mrs Bransby asking her to give the M.R.S. society a lecture as part of our next year's programme. Once before I slipped a note in her door instead of posting it, so the letter went in my pocket in case I walked that way.'

Bob had his eyes fixed on his friend. He was not happy about the way Tom was telling this. He was hiding something.

'This was at what time?' he asked abruptly.

'I can't tell you that exactly. It must have been half-past nine, or even earlier, when I left Ouse Avenue.'

'Did you go straight to the Dutch House?'

Tom knew now how a criminal felt when he stepped into a trap. 'No, I walked by the river. It is very pleasant in the late evening and the night-time.'

'How long did you walk by the river?'

'I don't know. Until I got tired of it. Then I was near Clifton Bridge and decided to go to the Dutch House and if it was possible drop my letter in at Mrs Bransby's before going home.'

'Why do you say, "If it was possible"? What would have made it impossible?'

'I thought they might lock the outer door of the hallway and I couldn't remember if there was a letter-box in it. There isn't, actually. I looked when I got there and there isn't one. At first I thought the outer door was locked, then I tried it, and it wasn't, so I went in, put the letter in the door of number 3, and left. That's it.'

'As you were there, why didn't you knock and give it to Mrs Bransby personally?'

'It seemed a bit late to go unannounced and knock on her door. The letter wasn't urgent.'

'Urgent enough for you to deliver it in person.'

Tom found his desire to keep his relationship with Julia private for the time being was creating quite a problem for him. They had agreed on it, though, made a pact. He couldn't break that agreement without consulting Julia.

'I was saving the society the cost of a stamp,' he said.

Both detectives looked as though that was a very thin reason for his behaviour. Tom shifted uncomfortably in his chair.

'You were seen leaving the hallway,' Bob said heavily. 'You have admitted that you were there. We will of course check your evidence regarding the letter, by asking Mrs Bransby and her son about it.'

'They weren't bound to notice it until morning.' Tom was growing more uncomfortable by the minute.

'You can leave us to check that. I must ask you not to approach them until we have interviewed them about this.'

'Isn't all this a bit heavy-handed?' Tom sounded agitated. 'I wasn't the only person in the hallway at that time, you know.'

'Yes? Can you elaborate on that?'

'There was the person who told you I was there, for one.'

'We have interviewed that person already.'

'Is that the man who was going up the stairs when I arrived?'

'No,' and Bob and Dave looked interested.

'There was a young man going upstairs when I came in at the front door. He was a stranger to me, but I don't know all the inhabitants of the flats.'

'Describe him if you can.'

'I only glanced at him. He did seem a bit shy of being noticed. In his twenties, I would say. Slim, athletic judging by the way he was springing up the stairs. Carrying an airline bag, by the look of it. I can't tell you more than that, really.'

'You saw this young man as you entered the hallway?'

'Yes. I fiddled about a bit as I told you at the outside door, then went in and at once heard footsteps going up the stairs, caught a glimpse of him moving quickly up the flight.'

'Did he stop at the doors of the flats on the first floor?'

Tom sounded doubtful. 'I don't think so. As I looked up at him he turned round and looked down at me, and then went on rushing upstairs.' He struggled hard to remember. 'At a guess, he went up to the top floor.'

Where the inhabitants are two middle-aged ladies, thought Dave and Bob. What business had he up there at that time of night?

Dave Smart put both their thoughts into words. 'Could have been looking for somewhere to hide,' he said.

'Did he come down again?' asked Bob.

'Not while I was there.'

Both detectives felt very dubious about Tom's account of his visit to the Dutch House, but there didn't seem to be anything else they could ask him at that moment. If he was lying, that would become apparent as they went on with the interviews.

'Come on,' said Bob after the interview was formally over. 'I'll run you back as you don't have your bicycle.' His attitude was more friendly than it had been earlier. As they made the journey Tom was very silent. It had been a shattering morning. He quite saw that the incident had to be followed up, but the change in Bob from friend to policeman was very disturbing.

Julia's absence was unfortunate, too. He could not consult her until Monday, it would be hopeless ringing the campus.

Bob was also severely hampered by the absence of Julia and Adam. He wanted very much to clear up this visit of Tom Churchyard's to the Dutch House on that fateful night. At least they had another sighting out of the interview, the young man going up the stairs. Reminding himself that the burglars had broken in through the patio doors, not from the hallway, Bob tried not to place too much importance on this new evidence.

It was later in the morning that Bob found out about the regular use of the community room for meetings of the residents. He was talking to the younger of the Lloyd brothers. The community room was stuffy and both policemen wandered outside to drink their coffee. They sat on the grass and in this informal and unimpressive position Lance Lloyd found them when he went out to do a bit of shopping. He stopped to have a word.

'Will you be finished with the common by Sunday night? Tomorrow night?' he asked after the preliminary greetings.

'No idea,' said Bob. 'Is it wanted for something?'

'Only for our regular monthly meeting.'

'Religious?' hazarded Bob.

'Contractual,' replied Lance Lloyd. 'It is a legal stipulation that the housing association members in the flats have a regular monthly meeting to discuss problems and in fact, run the place. We have a committee.'

'What is on the agenda this time?'

'Mrs Honor's death has upset everyone very much and there are problems arising from it, as well as the normal things. We're all partners to a certain extent. Our obligations overlap. For example, we share the cost of the gardens, paying equal amounts to Mr Spicer. Cherry has a separate arrangement, her garden needs more upkeep, and she still owns Spicer's flat. We have obligations about upkeep of the outside of the Victorian wing and the stable block, and the drives and footpaths. If there are problems amongst us we try to settle them. This damned noise of Miss Wilmet's music lessons and piano practice will be up for discussion.' He sounded grim. 'If one of the flats is for sale, we need to be sure that the incoming person will fit in – there are certain conditions.'

'You don't seem to have chosen very well with Miss Wilmet.'

'No ... she seemed tremendously suitable, and in most ways she is. If the partition between the two flats was sound-proof there wouldn't be a problem.'

'So the owners' meeting is tomorrow night, Sunday?'

'Yes, and my brother Gawain is the chairman.'

'I'd better ask him to put me on the agenda.'

'If I could suggest ...'

'Yes?'

'If you want to speak to us as a group, you should be first. Clearing up her death is the most important thing. We all feel so miserable. The atmosphere of the place is tremendously sad and it is usually such a happy place. And the other items might take up a lot of time. You won't want to sit through them. If we have our noses rubbed in reality by you first, it will put things in proportion. We might be able to get Miss Wilmet to agree to pay equal shares for sound-proofing. We might bear in mind our latter ends and see our quarrels for the solvable things they are.'

Bob Southwell smiled to see himself and his grim realities cast in the role of troubleshooter to a bunch of pampered middle-class housing association members. 'Always glad to be useful,' he said.

9

When Lance Lloyd had gone, Bob decided to move back for the time being to the incident room in the police station. He would continue interviewing at the Dutch House after the meeting. There were plenty of other things to do and he wanted to be somewhere else. The gloomy atmosphere was getting to him.

On his return, early Sunday evening, he found the blue plastic chairs on tubular metal legs had been unstacked and spread across the floor. In front of them stood a sturdy plain table. Seated behind it were Gawain Lloyd and DS Joe Birch, and Bob went over to join them.

'Are you doing the honours or am I?' Bob asked his chief, who looked unwell and ought to have been at home in Bob's opinion.

'You can, Robert. I've been listening to the tapes of the interviews so far and wanted to see some of the characters involved now I know a bit more about them. Where's this Churchyard chap?'

'He won't be here this evening,' said Bob. 'He doesn't live here.'

'In this, as in every investigation,' said his boss, 'don't forget all suspects lie,' and Joe looked at him as if handing down a tablet of stone. 'And they are all found out. *All found out*,' he repeated slowly.

'Thank you, sir. I will remember.'

By now the expected people had begun to arrive, talk, move chairs about, and finally settle themselves. The atmosphere was very subdued.

'Before we begin, Detective Chief Inspector Southwell would like to discuss something with us,' Gawain Lloyd introduced him. 'We all know about the terrible happening of Thursday night last week, and I'm sure that everyone would like to help Mr Southwell and Detective Superintendent Birch here, as much as we can. Before we begin, could we all stand for two minutes' silence in memory of our friend and neighbour, Mrs Honor.'

They stood. Two minutes can seem a long time. They all had their own memories of Mrs Honor to fill it.

When they were seated again, Bob cleared his throat and looked round at the assembly.

Neither Adam nor Cherry were there. Adam because he was not an owner, Cherry because she was not concerned with most of the problems confronted by an owners' meeting. As she had the fixed idea they were her tenants it would not have occurred to her to be present anyway.

In the front row were Mrs Robinson, with her ankle in plaster, Ms Haygreen in a trouser suit with hand-dyed accessories, and Ms Hodson in a handwoven tweed skirt and linen blouse. The line was completed by Dr Bright, his quiff of energetic white hair bouncing on his head. On the second row were Julia, neat and quiet, Lancelot Lloyd, pink-faced and round in face as in body, Mr Spicer, tall, weatherbeaten, sinewy and stringy, Mr Markhall, looking gentlemanly and precise, and at the end of the row Miss Susannah Wilmet, looking beautiful and intense.

'I will be brief,' Bob began. 'There is no need to go over the details of Mrs Honor's death, or to tell you that this was one of a series of burglaries which have been taking place in York recently. There is something very cold-blooded about thieves who go complete with packing materials to take the favourite and most valuable possessions of their victims. But Mrs Honor was the first person to be attacked during such a burglary – attacked so severely that she died as a result. Now this took place, as you know, when the heatwave was really getting going. Most of you would have had your windows open and it is possible that one of you saw or heard something which might tell us more about the assailants. You may have heard or seen a car or van, probably quite late in the evening, almost at bedtime. That might be very helpful to us. But I particularly wish to ask you who you saw visiting Mrs Honor's flat, either that day or in the previous weeks. You all know one another very well and will notice any strangers, or strange cars or vans parked on the drives. Frequent visitors you would recognize and probably know who they were. I would like to know about everyone who went to see Mrs Honor.'

There was complete silence.

Bob decided to break it by saying, 'I have been told that she

107

had struck up a new friendship, with an antique dealer, Mr Taffinder Walker, usually known as Taff Walker, who has been visiting Miss Ducket-Penrose at the main house.'

Somehow this seemed to unlock their tongues.

All at once several people said they had indeed seen Mr Walker, and that so-called chauffeur of his, Duncan.

'And why should an able-bodied young man need a driver of all things?' asked Dr Bright.

'Most unwise', said Mrs Robinson, 'to invite people like that into her flat and show them all her antiques. But she loved talking about them, as if other people didn't have nice things too. When I talked about the nice things I had she never showed any interest at all, but we were all supposed to be fascinated by her very superior items.'

There was a dead silence at this. Shocked faces were turned towards Mrs Robinson. Then they remembered that she had not been at home that Thursday night, and could not be expected to react in the same way as everyone else.

'Much better to patronize modern craftsmen and artists,' said Ms Hodson, who, in any spare time she had from teaching, painted in oils, decorated china and stuck pressed flowers onto lampshades.

'Mr Walker must have been round there half a dozen times,' put in Mr Spicer, hardy, forthright and not in awe of the police. 'That there Duncan used to hang about outside, looking as if he wondered what other people had that he could steal.'

'I don't think we ought to jump to conclusions,' Bob Southwell said, loud and clear. 'Mr Walker, as far as I know, is a perfectly honest antique dealer.'

'That's a contradiction in terms, if you don't mind me saying so, Chief Inspector,' said Ms Hodson, with feeling.

'Apart from Mr Walker . . .' Bob nudged the discussion firmly onward.

'Then there were the Frenchmen,' said Mr Markhall.

'Frenchmen?'

'A couple of Frenchmen at different times earlier in the week.'

'Do you mind telling me how you knew they were Frenchmen?'

'They looked very French,' said Ms Haygreen.

Bob wondered if they had been wearing berets and carrying strings of onions. 'In what way did they look French?'

'Dark.' Ms Haygreen's voice sank and deepened.

'Olive skin and dark hair, short and stocky. Wearing dark-blue suits. Quite old. One of them had white hair and I'm sure the other one dyed his. At least as old as Mrs Honor herself if not older. First one of them came, and then the other, different days,' said Mr Markhall.

'Oh, I know who they'd be,' broke in Gawain Lloyd. 'Number Four Group.'

'I beg your pardon?' said Bob, wondering what sort of subversive organization this was.

'Number Four Group Bomber Command. Oh, you must know all about them, Mr Southwell.'

'I haven't been in York long,' Bob said cautiously. He guessed this was something to do with the war. 'I was transferred from Harrogate on promotion fairly recently.'

'I barely remember, being only a child at the time,' said Gawain, who was sixty-eight and had done his two years' army service when the war had just ended.

DS Birch put in, 'I believe Number Four Group Bomber Command had their headquarters in Heslington Hall, where the university is now.'

Lancelot Lloyd said, 'They had sixteen squadrons in the group. We were fascinated as boys. I learned the outlines of the different planes and had some binoculars to look out of the bedroom window and identify them. York was ringed with airfields.'

Gawain had a sudden inrush of memory. 'Three-four-six and three-four-seven Squadrons were Free French.'

'That's right,' chipped in Dr Bright, 'and they were based at Elvington, where the Yorkshire Air Museum is now.'

'And this explains the Frenchmen?'

'Yes.' Lancelot took up the baton once more. 'They have kept up the links with people who knew them then. Every year they used to invite Mr and Mrs Honor to a grand dinner.'

'I understood', said Bob cautiously, 'that Mr Honor died before Mrs Honor came here.'

'She was always talking about it. There were some marvellous stories. Adam loved listening to them,' said Julia's quiet voice, coming in and calming the excited male atmosphere which was developing.

Mr Markhall, who liked putting people right, added, 'But she went on seeing the French when they came over, even after her husband died, because she helped the French Resistance, it was very hush-hush. This year I saw in the paper that they weren't having a big dinner so I suppose one or two of them dropped in to see her instead.'

'They have some kind of organization?'

'They call it Bombadier Lourds.' This was Gawain Lloyd once more.

Bob felt this information opened a whole new range of possibilities which would have to be looked into. He was unable to make much more progress, because no other mysterious visitors or even ordinary ones had been noted going to Mrs Honor's flat. At last, when everyone's information about the Frenchmen and Taff Walker had been repeated several times, he decided to call it a day, and with a request that if any of them remembered anything else, however small and apparently trivial, they would let him know at once, he left them to their discussions. DS Birch left with him.

As they walked to their cars, Mr Markhall came running to catch up with them.

'I must tell you', he gasped, 'that on the night of the murder I looked out of my bedroom window about ten-past ten, it is at the front of the block, and saw Mrs Bransby outside. I saw her quite clearly – we have those security lamps, you know. She was standing still and then started to walk about. After a few minutes she went back inside. Very odd, wasn't it? I don't want to tell tales but thought you ought to know.'

'We have four groups of possible suspects,' Bob Southwell remarked to Dave Smart on the Monday morning. 'One; the people who committed the other burglaries. Two; the other occupants of the flats, and we are getting to know them individually now.'

'What about Mrs Bransby, being outside that night?'

'I think there is an obvious explanation for that, but don't worry, I have her lined up for interview. The only one definitely

110

out of it is Mrs Robinson, who was at her daughter's with a broken ankle.'

'She has three grown-up children, though, hasn't she, boss?'

'You're suggesting there is a Robinson Gang? Possible, I suppose. Three; the antique dealer, his driver cum handyman, or a pal of either of them. Four; a Frenchman, for reasons I can't even guess at, because Mrs Honor was by way of being a war heroine, not a *persona non grata*.'

'You would think so.'

'Send someone along to Elvington Aerodrome, Dave. Better still, go yourself. They have a museum there. Have a general chat to them about the Bombadier Lourds Association, who sound very respectable and I don't imagine are mixed up in this for a moment, but we ought, I think, to locate the people who visited Mrs Honor. Check times and places and find out, if you can, whether the French Resistance could possibly have any bearing on this.'

'Right, boss.'

Everyone on the case had plenty of work. After glancing round the office, Bob told them, 'I'm going over to see our friendly neighbourhood antique dealer, Taff Walker. Sergeant Diamond, I'd like you to come with me.'

Diamond, a pleasant, solid officer who had been a sergeant so long he had given up hope of rising further, looked gratified and, with a dab at the papers on his desk to tidy them, came out to Bob's side. Other heads had lifted and various people smiled or nodded.

Taffinder Walker's shop was in a town not many miles from York, and Bob and Sergeant Diamond were lucky enough to find him there.

'I'm often out,' Walker told Bob, who asked all the questions. Diamond made notes.

Walker went on, 'No point in a place like this in staying open eight hours a day six days a week. Market days and Saturdays I'm always here. Other days I'm open if I'm about and not if I'm not.'

Bob thought this a charmingly casual way to run a shop.

'Most of my business is done outside these premises,' Walker went on to tell him.

'That is as I supposed,' Bob said. 'I gather you do valuations for people and so on.'

The old, low two-storeyed shop was on an excruciatingly busy road and the three men walked through into the room at the back. Bob noticed that the stock seemed good, although he wasn't an antiques expert. There was a well-polished mahogany chest of drawers with two white formalized dogs standing on it, who looked eastern in origin and probably represented mythical beasts. In profile their open mouths were crescent shaped and well furnished with teeth. There was a pine dresser of interesting design, loaded with pottery of the old country type, which in Bob's childhood abounded in cottages and farmhouses, but which nowadays was rapidly moving upmarket. There were chairs, similarly of a country type, and an old chest with linenfold panels. A few paintings on the walls looked as if they would be interesting if you knew about that sort of thing, and a length of embroidered cloth negligently draped across the chest reminded Bob of Julia Bransby and he thought he must remember to tell her about it. Then he recalled Mr Markhall's evidence against her . . .

The back room was small and obviously used as an office. Walker waved the two policemen to chairs and took one himself, after carefully closing the door on a large area of workshop space where the driver, Duncan, was doing something to an old table. Walker left the door to the shop a few inches open.

'Handy chap,' Bob said, referring to Duncan.

'Who? Oh!' Walker laughed. 'Yes. I don't know what I'd do without him.'

'You don't drive yourself, then?' Bob was determined to clear up the reason for this apparently able man needing to be driven about.

'I did, of course. Always enjoyed driving.'

'Until?'

'Oh, I didn't get disqualified or anything, at least not in the way you mean. Can I give you gentlemen tea or coffee, Inspector? I'm sorry, I don't think I caught your names.'

'Southwell.' Bob had given their names and ranks when he first arrived at the shop. 'Thanks, but we had coffee only half an hour ago.'

'I'll have one, if you don't mind. You are sure you won't join me?'

There was a kettle and coffee-making equipment in the corner and Walker fussed a little over making his drink. When he had it in his hand and was seated again Bob took him back to the previous topic of discussion.

'You were going to tell me why you don't drive, Mr Walker.'

Taking a deep breath, Walker said 'I don't publicize it but there's no reason why you shouldn't know. The fact is that I was seriously ill three years ago, and although I'm perfectly well now, I've been left with slight epilepsy. It isn't troublesome but I'm not allowed to drive.'

'I see.'

'Apart from the driving, Duncan is very useful. He can go out knocking, if you know what I mean by that.'

'Knocking on doors asking if people have anything they would like to sell?'

'That's right. He isn't an expert in antiques but he's picking it up well. He can distinguish things which would interest me from things which wouldn't, and that's what matters. If he finds a house which seems promising, I go along myself.'

'Like the Dutch House?'

Taff Walker looked up abruptly from his mug of coffee, straight into Bob Southwell's eyes.

'I thought that was why you had come.'

Analysing his reactions to Taff Walker at this point, Bob found them not unfavourable. The chap was tall, dark and good-looking in a way which would certainly appeal to ladies and his manner was frank, even friendly. There was something about him which would make most people feel that they could trust him. As far as Bob could tell, Walker replied to his questions truthfully.

'You thought that was why I had come?'

'I saw in the paper that Mrs Honor had been murdered in the course of a burglary of her antiques. She wouldn't have made a secret of it that I had called on her several times to advise her about values, and as I'm in the trade you were bound to want to see me.'

'That's about it,' agreed Bob.

113

'Am I right in thinking that she was murdered a week last Thursday? That's the impression the paper gave.'

'That is correct.'

'I was over in the Lake District. A four-day course in the History of Art was taking place at a rather nice hotel and I was asked to lecture on antique furniture of various periods. Duncan and I drove over on the Thursday morning with the car absolutely crammed with stuff and I'd arranged with friends in the trade in that area to borrow from their stock. The idea was that this was to be a hands-on experience for the members of the course, with real examples they could touch and examine.'

'Sounds good, but was it worth your while?'

'Definitely. It doesn't do any harm to become known as a lecturer, the fee was good, and I sold nearly all the stock I took, as well as most of the pieces I borrowed. Apart from anything else, I enjoyed it.'

'You were there from when to when?'

'We left here on Thursday morning, having loaded up on Wednesday night. The yard here locks up so the goods were quite safe. Thursday afternoon, after unloading my own stuff, we spent visiting friends who had offered pieces on loan and taking those to the hotel. You can imagine Dunc and I were both about shattered by the evening. We were ready to relax. I had a bath before dinner. Duncan went off with his pals. For the rest of the evening and for the next three days I was fully occupied, didn't set foot outside the hotel. It was only on my return here that I heard about the murder.'

'You do realize, Mr Walker, that in a case like this we have to ask all the victim's friends and neighbours what they were doing, and take statements, which they sign, about their movements. This is purely routine and helps us eliminate those who are not involved.'

'That's us,' interposed Taff Walker.

'Certainly. So you won't mind signing a written statement, now, while we are here?'

'Not in the least.'

'And your driver, Duncan, as well?'

'Understood.'

'You also understand that we may check what you tell us?'

Walker hesitated. No one likes the idea of the police going

114

round checking their movements. But after a moment, he said, 'I understand that.' Bob noted his hesitation.

'There is also your epilepsy. May I have the name of your doctor?'

At this Walker did look as if he were going to rebel, but he thought better of it and gave the name.

'I will be checking your statement about the epilepsy, Mr Walker, both with your doctor and with DVLC at Swansea.'

Walker shrugged. 'It's not a secret,' he said again. 'I don't advertise it, that's all.'

'You said it was a four-day course, Mr Walker?'

'The members of the society which ran it had arrived on Wednesday night. They spent all day Thursday visiting local museums and being lectured to about the contents. We weren't involved until Friday.'

'If you'll give me the name and address of the organizer . . .'

'Of course.' Mentally, Taff Walker saw his chance of becoming a regular lecturer on antiques going down the tubes. He got up, rummaged in the desk, and produced a brochure. 'You can keep that,' he said, passing it over. 'I've got several.'

'What was your assistant doing while you were lecturing?'

'He was needed to help move furniture in and out. When I showed slides he worked the projector. Oh, he was kept pretty busy. He might even have listened and learned something.'

'Off duty?'

'He went with a group of other youngsters, drinking I expect. He's entitled to free time, like anyone else, Chief Inspector.'

'We'll take a statement from Duncan now, if that's convenient,' said Bob. Taffinder Walker could hardly say that it was not convenient. He showed the two policemen through to the work-shop, introduced them to Duncan, who had his sleeves rolled up and was rubbing the table down with fine wet-and-dry sand-paper, and left them to it.

Some time later Bob Southwell and Diamond were ready to go.

'By the way,' Bob said to Walker when they passed through the office again, 'when you saw Mrs Honor's antiques, what opinion did you form? Were they valuable or did she only think they were?'

'Oh, they were very nice pieces.' By now Walker was escorting

115

them across the shop to the street door. 'Valuable certainly. I would have liked to have the disposal of them, but she was only playing at wanting to part. She really wanted to hang on to them. It satisfied her to be told a value, they went up in her own estimation.'

'And you did not charge her for this service? I thought estimates were usually charged for.'

'Certainly. I have a standard charge. But an estimate on a purely friendly basis with nothing in writing I don't charge for. There often turns out to be something in it for me in the end.'

'You mean a recommendation to a friend who is serious in wanting to dispose, something like that?'

'Exactly. Or they change their mind about selling, when they know the value, particularly if something is worth a lot and they need the money.'

It occurred to Bob that Taffinder Walker was the ideal person to list Mrs Honor's antique possessions for him. If he wasn't honest, there would be Adam's list, compiled with DI Dave Smart, and Julia's list, to compare against Walker's and spot discrepancies. With the door open and traffic roaring within inches of his ear, Bob turned back and shouted a request across the two feet which separated him from Taff Walker, in answer to which Walker nodded and smiled and mimed 'Right away', or 'Straight away', Bob couldn't be too sure which.

The shop had been shady and cool but the heat and noise and fumes of the road hit Bob in the face like a blow. He thought longingly of his own garden back in York, with a pitcher of Linda's home-made lemonade on the garden table, Susan and Paul and the kitten playing in the tent on the lawn, Linda and himself sitting at ease in the hammock or on the garden chairs, the shadows stealing across the grass. It was a seductive picture but he was not going to be able to walk into the frame for goodness knows how long, had to be thinking instead of murders and motives, and why the heck was he a policeman anyway?

The car was parked round the corner and was as hot as an oven when the two men reached it. Bob wished there had been a friendly tree to park under, so that the moving leaves would have kept the car cool and shadowed for him. With both windows wound down he edged the car into the stream of traffic

116

and headed back for York and the incident room, which would be, if not as cool as his garden, at least much more pleasant than this bare road and its heavy load of metal boxes grinding along among petrol fumes. Sergeant Diamond, on the other hand, was sorry that the little expedition was nearly over.

'Look, Terry,' said Bob as they drove, 'I'd like you to go over to the Lake District and check all this out. Visit all the hotel staff and all the members of that weekend course and get statements. We need to know how much truth there is in the statements from these two characters. Take the others over the weekend minute by minute, but obviously concentrating on the times last Thursday when our friends Walker and Duncan might have been away from the hotel – driving back here to do a murder, for instance. You might have to do quite a bit of travelling. Don't worry. Find everyone. I'm not saying we suspect Walker particularly, but any sudden friendship like that is suspicious, occurring just before a murder, especially with an antique dealer when it was antiques that were the target of the burglary. Not that Walker has a bad reputation – he has a very good one.'

'I'll do my best, boss,' said Terry Diamond, tremendously pleased.

Dave Smart returned a quarter of an hour after his superior officer. By then Bob was in the incident room writing up his interview with Taffinder Walker. He looked up as Dave's massive shape came in at the door.

'Leave it open, for heaven's sake, Dave,' he said as Dave was about to close the door carefully after him. 'At least there's a bit of through draught.'

Not in the best of moods, thought Dave. A trifle agitated with the heat, as if it didn't affect all of us.

'Well, how did you get on?'

'Not too bad, boss. It's an interesting museum.'

'I didn't send you to spend your hours on duty looking at the Yorkshire Air Museum.'

'No, boss. I was getting background information.'

'What did you find out about these Frenchmen?'

'They come over every year, but at different times. There

might be an anniversary to celebrate or something of that nature which decides the date. They have gone back now, after this year's visit.'

'That's helpful.' Bob sounded unduly sarcastic, Dave thought.

'I have a full list of those who attended.'

'Give it here,' said Bob succinctly, reaching out his hand. 'Hmmm. Enough of them, weren't there?'

'Quite a few.'

'An address to contact them in France?'

Dave produced it silently.

'You'd better do it, then. Through Interpol I suppose, though let's hope they're a bit quicker than they usually are. Get it through their thick heads that we need to eliminate these people as quickly as possible because this is a murder inquiry. Or to keep them in the frame, of course, if they look suspicious.'

'A general inquiry, saying that after the recent sad death of Mrs Honor we would be very grateful if those members of the group who were courteous enough to contact her would tell us the time and duration of their visits?'

'In a word, yes,' said Bob, then bent his head again to his task. Dave took himself off to a quiet corner.

About that time Tom Churchyard was ringing Julia Bransby. He didn't care a hoot about the police prohibition on contact between them.

'Julia, would you like to have a run out in my car?' he asked, rather diffidently.

'Tom, that would be lovely.'

'Why not this afternoon?'

'Are you off work?'

'Yes. I had some leave owing. Even British Telecom engineers have free time. I want to take you out of that place for a few hours, into the country.'

'There's Adam.' She sounded doubtful, then paused. 'Look, Tom, I'll have a word with Adam. He will probably be fine. Can I ring you back in ten minutes?'

'I'll be waiting.'

Julia had taken the call on the extension in her bedroom cum workroom. She was still struggling with her working drawings for an embroidery design based on the water trough. She hurried to Adam's bedroom, where he was sitting at his desk.

'Look, Adam, I've got the chance of a run out into the country this afternoon with the telephone engineer, Tom Churchyard – you remember him—'

'I can't remember him, I've never met him,' said Adam.

'You know who I'm talking about. Now I would like to go, but will you be all right? I don't know where we are going or how long I will be.'

'Yes, Mum. I'll be going to see Blue Moon. I can feed myself. Don't worry.'

'All right, darling. You are a dear. I'll be off, then.' She scurried back to her own room and after accepting the invitation she changed into different clothes, combed her hair, and put on a little make-up. By the time Tom drove up to the front door of the flats she was ready and waiting.

Tom's car, which normally lived a pampered life in his garage, was a Rolls Royce 20/25 sports saloon built in 1932. Julia stood and looked at it in amazement. Tom climbed out and came to stand beside her, looking alternately at her and the car with profound satisfaction.

'I can see why you don't run over to Leeds on business with her,' Julia said at last. 'She's immaculate. She's lovely. I feel very privileged.'

'I thought you'd like her.'

'No one could help liking her. She's feminine then? Do you always call your car "her"?'

'I suppose I do.'

'Has she a pet name, as well?' asked Julia.

'I haven't quite got that far. I call her "the car".'

'She ought to have a name – Rita – Ophelia – Marguerita—'

'Madame, Mopsy, Mistress Masham ... no, I'll stick to "the car".'

The car had a cream and black body. The wings, bonnet, and parts above the waistline were black, the lower parts cream. Julia felt this was a little illogical, all the bits most likely to be soiled by mud or grit from the road being paler than the more protected upper parts, but she did not voice her opinion to Tom.

'The coachbuilder was James Young,' volunteered Tom.

'Oh.'

119

'Would you like to get in?'

Tom held the door open and Julia climbed in and sank onto the brown leather upholstery.

'Where are we going?' she asked.

'Round and about – down the river, I thought, towards Selby, though not as far, unless you want to go into the town. We could branch off and explore the villages in that part of the world—'

'Are they worth exploring?'

'I take it that question was rhetorical. You must know that area as well as I do, all this travelling about you do to country houses and churches.' Tom gave her a fond look, as though she were being deliberately and femininely naïve.

'I know it a bit, but it isn't the territory I'm usually asked to visit.'

'Once I went on a weekend course studying vernacular architecture. We were measuring houses in Cawood and Wistow. You'd be surprised how unchanged and interesting some of the houses in those villages are. It was fascinating. I'd like to do more of it.'

'Why don't you?' Julia asked idly, enjoying the strange sensation of driving along a road in a 1932 Rolls Royce. She began to know what the phrase 'the cynosure of all eyes' meant. Other motorists and all the pedestrians they passed were riveted by the sight of them. The pedestrians stood as if bewitched and frankly stared. The drivers approaching them did a double take. Those behind hung on their tail as if mesmerized, and when they did overtake did it slowly with only one eye on the way ahead.

'I think we're a danger on the road,' she said after a few minutes.

'Oh, you get used to them staring,' replied Tom. 'We can do sixty-five, you know. We don't have to meander along. But this is a thirty miles per hour zone.'

Soon they were out of the city and heading south along the flat land of the Vale of York – valley being too exaggerated a term for the lush meadows, the brick-built houses, the trees and hedgerows. There was an unchanged feel, as though the last century had never happened, as if this was an interwoven community of a different nature altogether to the fragile, intellectual community of the Dutch House. When they were exploring the villages of Cawood and Wistow, Tom pointed out to Julia the houses that had been studied on his Vernacular Architecture weekend, and the lodge of Wolsey's palace which the Landmark Trust had rescued and converted into a holiday home.

It was a good deal later, when the hurly-burly of Clifford Street outside had calmed down after the evening rush hour, that in the incident room Bob appeared at Dave's elbow with a couple of mugs of tea. Many of the staff had gone home – there was no longer enough urgent work to justify overtime. Bob planted one of the mugs in front of Dave and went to sit on the windowsill with the other in his hand, looking down into the road.

'Feeling better, boss?' asked Dave.

'A bit.'

'Made any progress?'

'Taffinder Walker and his sidekick went to the Lake District early on Thursday morning and were lecturing and assisting at a residential study course until Sunday night, when they came back. There were some forty members of the course. I've sent Terry Diamond up to check it all out with them and with hotel staff.'

'So that knocks out one of your four possibilities.'

'It may do.'

'We aren't making much progress with the other burglary cases, apparently.'

'Nope. Dave, how about the stuff in Mrs Honor's flat? Do we know yet if anything was taken away after all?'

'Some stuff certainly was. Table silver—'

'You mean cutlery?'

'Cutlery and flatware, Bob. Cutlery is knives and flatware is forks and spoons.'

'Oh well, we don't all have an aunty in Sheffield, do we? Cutlery and flatware, then, that's gone, it's pretty certain, is it?'

'All there is in the flat is the very utilitarian stuff in the kitchen drawer, no dining-room supply at all, and Adam says she always used the silver for the table. It was old and heavy, with a crest. Various ages, but everything with the same crest. An eagle's leg erased – that's a fancy word which seems to mean cut off – with the motto, "Ad finem fidelis." Apart from that, the silver teapot, the hot-water jug which she used for coffee, and the milk jug and sugar basin. Again with the same crest. All gone. Adam said she was very proud of her silver and used it all the time. The Dresden china has also gone. The celadon bowl with the carved stand is among the packed things.'

'What about the netsuke?'

'So far no joy on those.'

'They've gone, then?'

'It looks like it.'

'Motive, Dave . . .?'

'Plain theft, surely. Pure bad luck that she interrupted them.'

'I still think there is more to it than that. Another purpose. Her death probably. And apart from the antique dealer, who may be in the clear, all the suspects could have done it. When did you say the Frenchmen returned to their homeland?'

'The day of the murder – Thursday. In the afternoon.'

'There you are, you see. One of them could have missed the plane, or bus or whatever, and done it for a reason we can't even begin to guess at, to do with her wartime record. Any of the other inhabitants of the Dutch House could have done it for some reason, again, which we cannot guess. The burglars might have acted out of character. We haven't begun to reach a solution and I can't see what we can do next.'

'I've sent the general message through Interpol.'

'It's a pity about the antique dealer. He looked such a good prospect. But he might still be involved, one way or another.'

'What did you say his first name was?'

'Taffinder, Taff for short. One of the old Dutch or Walloon names, he told me, from a settlement in England in the seventeenth century. He said that the families in the area he comes from had a tradition of calling the sons by the maiden names of the mothers, or the surname of an ancestor.'

'I'm surely glad they didn't do that in my family,' said Dave Smart fervently.

'What was your mother's maiden name, then, Dave?'

But Dave had seen the sparkle back in his chief's eye. 'I'd rather not say, sir,' he replied coldly.

After exploring the villages, Tom and Julia in the beautiful car ran into Bishop's Wood, and were enveloped by the greenness and coolness of long grass and underbrush under thick ancient trees. Tom drove the length of the car off the road and stopped. Everything was utterly quiet and peaceful. Julia felt strain and sadness melt out of her. When his arms went round her she fell into them gratefully and let joy enfold her spirit. They kissed as expertly and long as if their bodies were having a conversation, exchanging thoughts and sensations. They knew one another a little better at each encounter, and liked one another more. It was time out of mind in the green wood, and they would have been hard put to it to say how long they spent there.

'It is a pity the car isn't one of those modern jobs,' said the Rolls' owner ungratefully, 'where you can get in the back seat and the windows steam up so that no one can make out what's going on. We're very limited like this.'

'Oh, this isn't enough for you, isn't it?' teased Julia, her head on his shoulder.

'Of course, every time I want more,' Tom admitted. 'It's funny, isn't it. We drive along as decorous as anything as if butter wouldn't melt in our mouths and as soon as the opportunity offers we're away in our own world and on a completely different journey altogether.'

'Soon,' she said gently and stroked Tom's cheek. 'We could take refuge among the trees, I suppose.'

'You wouldn't be very comfortable. I'd rather our first time was one to remember, with everything perfect. Besides, if we were in our own world the car would be left at the mercy of anyone who happened to come past.'

'Oh, she means more to you, then, than . . .?'

'No, of course not, but it would take the gilt off the gingerbread if she were vandalized. I'll tell you what, let's go to a decent hotel for dinner. You did say Adam would be all right?'

'Would the car be all right in a hotel car-park?'

Tom rubbed his nose affectionately into her cheek. 'She'll be all right at one hotel I know of. I can put her in a garage. We go there sometimes with the Vintage and Classic Car Club.'

'You planned to take me there?'

'I thought perhaps we might.'

'Come on then.' Julia sat up and stroked her hair smooth again. 'I've suddenly realized I'm hungry. We'd better see what we can organize for that perfect occasion,' and she smiled

123

saucily sideways at him. 'I've already bought a lacy black nightdress.'

'You haven't, have you?' and Tom, making an immense effort to control himself, started the car engine and, seeming to take no notice of Julia because he daren't, just then, steered them onto the road again and towards the hotel where he had already booked a table.

They had a delightful, romantic, candlelit dinner and Tom returned Julia to the Dutch House in a state of mind so uplifted that she doubted if she would be able to sleep for a week.

10

The next morning Julia had coffee with Cherry Ducket-Penrose in the little pine-panelled cabinet room. Adam was swotting again until the time came for him to visit the vet's and Blue Moon. The two women could hardly believe that so many days had passed since Mrs Honor's death. Cherry's eyes still brimmed with tears when she remembered her friend, and Julia felt a physical chill whenever small daily things reminded her.

'What's happening?' Cherry asked now, and Julia knew that she meant about Mrs Honor and her flat.

'The police have contacted her solicitors and they came and took away her bankbook and other securities. The flat is locked up, ultra locked up. Extra locks have been put on. It has all been very efficiently and quickly done. I had a word with the solicitors about the dog, they've no objection to us keeping it if it survives. The solicitor was rather nice. He said there was no one else who would claim it and he was sure that until probate was obtained Mrs Honor would have wanted to pay any expenses involved in its care. Not that I minded the expense in the least, but it shows he's a sympathetic and caring man. Everyone has been wonderful, really. The police have been kind and considerate and the vet has been marvellous.'

Cherry put a saucer down for Oberon. Titania appeared and shrieked her displeasure at being left out of the good things. Cherry took the saucer from her own cup and filled it with milk.

Julia looked the other way. The china they were using was old Worcester and although Julia did not know its value she could see that it was hand-painted and charming and was certainly antique. Cherry was not always careful where she put her feet.

'The cats ought to have their own dishes, you know, Cherry,' she could not help saying.

'This is only old stuff,' Cherry replied. 'I'm not spending good money on buying them expensive new china. If this is good enough for me it's good enough for them. I think we've got mice.'

'Where?'

'I heard a rustling in the bedroom above. It was too hot to sleep last night. The cats don't go upstairs but I think they will have to.'

'I know you are short of money, Cherry dear, but if you still have dresses of your mother's and don't mind parting with them, they would probably make enough to pay for cleaning the house up ready for your opening, and a few stainless-steel dishes for the cats.'

Cherry knew that she needed Julia if she was going to open the house. She said nothing for a while. Going along with Mrs Honor's ideas – so forcefully expressed – had resulted in tragedy – not resulted, exactly – but tragedy had occurred. It might be wise to humour Julia. Let her discover for herself that the dresses were absolutely worthless.

'If mice got in and nibbled the dresses the value could be destroyed,' Julia persisted.

'You can come up with me, then, and we'll see where the mice are,' promised Cherry, and Julia could hardly believe it. 'Oberon and Titania had better come too.'

The two Siamese followed the women up the gracious curving stair and Cherry unlocked the door of an imposing but appalling bedroom. The smell of dust and mice and the closeness of ancient unchanged air wrapped round them. Julia made her way through clutter to the window and struggled with the stiff catch before throwing it open. Gusts of scented breeze blew in from the garden and out through the door onto the landing so that within minutes the whole place was fresher and Julia felt she could look around.

Cherry had pulled at a drawer and stood looking down into it.

'They've been making nests and having babies,' she said regretfully.

Going over to her Julia could see a mass of shredded paper in the front corner of the drawer. 'What have they used?' she said sharply, reaching out and lifting the shreds. 'I don't believe it. Cherry, my dear, the mice have been chewing up old five pound notes, those big white ones we used to use.'

'So they have.'

'Did you know they were there?'

'Not really. I haven't been up here for years. Mummy always liked to keep money in the house. They are out of date, now, you know.'

Julia felt like clutching her forehead. Oberon and Titania were busy tracking down the exciting smells of mouse. Running downstairs Julia fetched a plastic carrier-bag from the pocket of her coat, and once back in the bedroom she began to push the shredded notes into it. 'Where do you bank?' she asked Cherry. 'Do you know the manager? I'll go to see him and ask if anything can be done about these – if you'll let me.'

Cherry didn't seem to mind one way or the other, and mentioned the name of her bank manager. 'You wanted to see the dresses,' she reminded her guest. 'Mummy always put clothes she'd finished wearing in this chest of drawers or in that wardrobe.'

'I'll have a quick recce.'

The beaded twenties dress shown in the large oil painting of Mrs Ducket-Penrose lay in one of the drawers, together with two others equally elaborate and lovely. The drawers fitted beautifully and opened like silk. Julia realized that either the top drawer had been left partly open or the mice had chewed their way in from the back. These things at least had been safe from them and protected from light. She lifted out mounds of exquisite old garments and laid them on the dusty bed. There was a deeply fringed Chinese silk coat in blue with gold and orange patterns and the fringe space-dyed in several colours finishing with orange, folded with a feather fan in the same shades and a pair of orange silk evening pumps, perhaps from the thirties. There was an underskirt of thick firm silk with a stepped hem dropping to touch the floor at the back, deeply edged with lace, meant to go under a lace dress, possibly even a wedding dress.

There were model evening gowns from the famous Hull dressmaker, Mrs Clapham, who was the favourite of the court ladies of the time of Edward the Seventh.

'I expect those were my grandmother's,' Cherry remarked. She was looking on with interest. 'The dresses with beads were Mother's, although I never remember her wearing them. That coat and fan were Mother's. She used the coat sometimes if we went to the theatre.'

Julia felt worried in case Cherry was going to take the same attitude to these clothes that she did to the trivial embroidery done by her mother or the crude Berlin woolwork perpetrated by her grandmother. But luckily clothes did not seem to hold the same sacred quality for her. She did not realize the superb craftsmanship embodied in these garments, or the beauty of the materials of which they were fashioned.

'Could you bear to part with them?' Julia asked carefully.

'They wouldn't fit me,' Cherry said sadly, with an extra inch of cigarette ash falling onto the shelf of her bosom as she waggled her lip while talking. 'What would you do with them?'

'Sell them. Museums or private collectors would be thrilled.'

'I would have given them to Oxfam if I'd thought about it,' Cherry said with interest. 'They send things they can't sell to be made into shoddy, you know. Recycling, they call it.'

'These aren't suitable for that.'

'If we leave them they will only be eaten by the mice,' Cherry said indifferently. 'Look, Oberon's caught one.'

Oberon had caught more than one, so that Titania rushed to help as little mice exploded in all directions from under the wardrobe.

'I'll fetch something to put these in. I'll be back soon.' Julia was hardly noticed as she left to fetch her largest suitcase and a few big plastic carrier-bags for the overflow from the chest of drawers. She was going to have the time of her life, sorting them out, gloating over them, estimating their value from catalogues of Christie's, London, and Phillips, Leeds, and then carefully marketing them, and she hadn't yet even opened the door of the wardrobe. To a textile specialist this was bonanza and heaven. And she would, having done that, be able to lever Cherry into spending the money on things that desperately needed doing.

Mrs Honor was not forgotten. Julia could not look out of her window and fail to see her neighbour, or go out of her front door and confront the sealed door of number 4, without that involuntary sad shiver. The feeling was overlaid, not gone. But far from Julia on that morning of subdued joy were the kind of thoughts that were passing through DCI Bob Southwell's mind.

At the police station the team of detectives were badly needing a breakthrough in the Honor murder case. The information had come from Interpol and it was of no help at all. The organization of Bombadier Lourds sent their deepest regrets and sympathy, and the dates and times when two of their number had called to pay their respects to Mrs Honor, and it was obvious that the whole group had left England before the murder had taken place.

'There may still be something in the theory of a French involvement,' Dave said.

'It's possible, but I don't see it at the moment.'

'You did have the theory, sir, that her wartime activities might be relevant.'

'They might be.'

It was obvious by Bob Southwell's downcast face that he had given up the idea.

'What else is happening?' he asked, looking round the incident room. The team was now much depleted. Records of interviews had been written up, information had been filed and typed into computers, the reports from forensic examination were coming through but so far they had not provided any leads. The burglars had worn gloves. Fibres found were of common types of fabric and popular colours, as worn by fifty per cent of the population.

'This is going to be one of those dreadful cases where we get nowhere and years later the murderer is still at large,' said Bob.

'I've set young James Jester to work on the records of the antiques,' Dave Smart told him. 'He's through in the other office where the art reference books and files are.'

'I'll go and see how he's getting on.'

James Jester was startled and embarrassed to find his chief at his elbow.

'Well, James? You look immersed in that file. Found anything?'

'Well, no, sir, that is, something is puzzling me, sir.'

'What?'

'There's this china, sir.' Laid out on the desk-top were photographs of the missing Dresden china. The set of prints had been found in the 'secret' drawer of Mrs Honor's dressing-table, together with some more photographs of her valuables. The other items shown were all still in the flat; from the photos, only the Dresden pieces had been stolen.

'Yes?'

'I've been looking up the marks and the colours and designs and they are genuine Dresden of a good period, sir, very valuable.'

'Didn't we know that already?'

'Yes, but Mr Smart said go over everything and check everything.'

'Quite right. Go on.'

'Then I looked in the list of stolen antiques, sir, that have been reported nationally. It was interesting and I got out the back copies. Five years ago a group consisting of shepherd and shepherdess and a number of vases of flowers were stolen in a robbery in the Midlands. Their marks are given and a description of the pieces. What is puzzling me is, what are the distinguishing points between that lot and these of Mrs Honor's, because I can't find anything that is different.'

Bob Southwell gave the lad a sharp glance.

'If you can't find anything different, might that not mean that they are the same? They wouldn't make one model of each, they'd make hundreds, I suppose, at least.'

'Yes, I see that, sir, but what I mean is, the group that was stolen consisted of the same items as Mrs Honor's, exactly. Each must have been manufactured in hundreds, as you say, but would two unconnected people have collected exactly the same group of items? These pieces belonged to the murdered lady, and the other group were stolen property.'

Bob took the list of previously stolen pieces from James and bent over the desk, where a description by Taffinder Walker of the recently stolen pieces rested beside the photographs. Carefully he checked off the features of the two groups of china.

'They are identical,' he said at last.

'That's it exactly, sir.'

129

'Mrs Honor was in possession of stolen property.'

'There must be some way of telling the two lots apart, sir. That's what I was trying to find.'

'Blow me,' remarked DCI Southwell. 'Now did she know, that's the point? Did she buy them not aware that they were stolen? Or did she know? Now then.'

James stood looking at him, unsure what answer to make to this.

'James, you're involved in this bit of research. Go on with it. Get onto the relevant police force and obtain copies of their files on the robbery in which this Dresden china was stolen, five years ago.'

James had come to the conclusion that he had been a bit thick. He should have seen for himself that this group must be the group stolen before. He felt relieved that the DCI was leaving him on the case at all, in a position of trust.

'Yes, sir,' he said.

'Let me know the result as soon as you have it. And, did you send the list of the stolen property to *Trace* magazine?'

'Yes, sir.'

Bob went to take another look for himself at the reports of some of the interviews. He picked up the one made from the notes Sergeant Diamond had made on the occasion of the owners' meeting at the Dutch House. Moodily he flicked it over. Everyone had seen the two Frenchmen come to Mrs Honor's flat. Some had seen the two together, some apart. Here, wait a minute, Bob thought to himself. He went over it again. Yes. In the rush of the inquiry he had not noticed that the owners' reports did not exactly tally. In his mind's eye he saw again the meeting with the two rows of audience. He saw himself asking for information. He heard again the excitement when someone mentioned the Frenchmen, and how almost immediately they seemed to have become 'the two Frenchmen', but now he was wondering if there had not been three.

If so, the third may not have been connected with the other two at all. The two could have been perfectly innocent, paying a call on the widow of their dead comrade, who had herself taken part in one of the most dangerous forms of anti-Nazi activity. The other one – or even two, dare he stretch his imagination to encompass four Frenchmen – had been not innocent but part of

130

a chain or a conspiracy. His imagination must be running away with him. Look again. Dr Bright had seen two Frenchmen, they had been together. He had seen them both approaching and leaving Mrs Honor's flat. The description tallied with the description Interpol had sent of the two men who had visited Mrs Honor. Mr Markhall had seen one Frenchman at one time and his description was too vague to be of use. The person he saw could well have been an English tradesman. Julia had seen one Frenchman once, and the description tallied with one of the men seen by Dr Bright. Ms Haygreen had seen two Frenchmen together, obviously those seen by Dr Bright, and one 'Frenchman' on his own, who may have been the man seen by Mr Markhall. Ms Hodson had seen two Frenchmen approaching separately and two leaving separately, she thought, but her description was so different to everyone else's that she was almost certainly carried away by the general enthusiasm and had probably not seen anything at all.

Bob wondered if the Continent was entirely denuded of Frenchmen as they seemed to be to-ing and fro-ing a great deal in Britain.

Under cover of the visit of the highly respectable Bombadier Lourds, had some other traveller, of dubious reputation, used them as an umbrella? He imagined a man attaching himself to the end of the group as they passed through customs, getting on the same airport bus, even alighting at the same destination and going to the same hotel, always quite safe because it was assumed that he was a member of the party ahead of him.

Bob decided to ask for a check with HM Customs of all other passengers on the ship or ferry or aircraft which had brought the French party over and back again. The extra, supernumerary member might not have gone back, as the rest had so clearly done. The official party would not have noticed his absence as they had probably not noticed his presence. He could have remained in England for another day and murdered Mrs Honor, or, the whole thing might be a mare's nest. 'I might be wasting my time and mental effort when there are other leads to follow,' thought Bob Southwell. Hadn't he already decided once that the French connection was a complete red herring?

Southwell rose from his chair and went in search of DI Dave Smart.

'Doing anything, Dave?'

'Of course, boss. Catching up with paperwork.'

'Fancy a run out?'

'Don't mind. It's stuffy in here. I opened the windows but all that does is let the flies in.'

'We'll take an official car, we're in pursuit of an inquiry. Let's get out of the city for a bit.'

Wondering what on earth his DCI was up to, Dave Smart agreed.

'I want to have a look at Elvington airfield, from which exiled Frenchmen flew bomber sorties,' Bob said when they were both in a car. 'You've been there before.'

They drove up the Hull Road, round the vast new roundabout over the A64 dual-carriageway bypass, and turned left then right towards Elvington. At once they had the sensation of being in the deep country. The road wound from side to side and the trees and fields on either side were soothing and peaceful.

Dave said, 'This makes a change.'

'I feel restless. If I can only get a bit farther with this case, Dave . . . In cool weather a hot bath sometimes works wonders for the thought processes but who wants a hot bath when the thermometer is stuck at eighty Fahrenheit?'

They were quiet as Bob steered the car rapidly towards the airfield at Elvington. Their route ran through the characteristic calm flat rural scene of the true Vale of York. The sky above was the unchanging blue which Bob for one had grown tired of seeing. The houses and cottages they passed were brick-built, the fields still surrounded by hedges. They turned right and reached the entrance to the Yorkshire Air Museum.

'Do we really want to go in here?' asked Bob, stopping the car short of the place where tickets were sold. 'What I want is a straight, plain, ordinary walk. Aren't there any runways we can walk on?'

'There's the longest runway in Britain – at least someone told me it was – nearly two miles.'

'Lead me to it.'

They backed, and a few yards farther saw the notices: WAR DEPARTMENT ONLY. PRIVATE. KEEP OUT.

'No walk,' said Bob grimly.

'Oh, I don't know. A friend of mine walks his dog in these

parts,' replied Dave. 'Drive on a bit. I think I can remember where he goes.'

At last they found their way onto the long runway and began to walk down it. On either side was flat grass and then small scrubby trees and bushes, the kind which spring up anywhere when cultivation stops and nature has a chance to make a comeback. Perfectly flat and dull grey, the runway stretched ruler straight in front of them.

'Does anyone use it?' asked Bob idly. 'This is new territory for me.'

'I don't know. I don't know much about it. I did hear that Church Fenton want it kept open as an emergency facility. It was built by the Americans for the use of their biggest aircraft but the university objected to it being put into regular use because it would disturb the students' studies.'

'For someone who doesn't know much about it you're very informative,' Bob remarked.

'Do my best, boss,' replied Dave.

For twenty-five minutes the two men walked silently along the runway, side by side. Each was vaguely thinking about the murder of Mrs Honor, and consciously enjoying open air and movement. They seemed to be far from roads and the birds could be heard to sing. A few clouds now moved slowly across the wide sky.

At last Bob came to a halt, and sighed. 'It's tempting to go right to the end but I think we'll turn back,' he said.

They walked a little more slowly as if reluctant to return. Bob had learned to love his adopted city, crowded in its medieval street pattern, but for once it was a relief to be away from it, to escape from the pressure of people and the weight of history.

This runway, which had been made for the constant use of heavy aircraft not many years ago, then abandoned almost unused, was history so fresh that it was still being made, impersonal, raw, unmarked by human personality. When the two men turned to go back, their angle to the sun changed and now stems of grass stood illumined, the distant larger trees had a different aspect and the warmth of the sun fell on a different part of their bodies. Dave deviated and walked on the grass, kicking at thistles. Bob still kept to the runway but now on its edge instead of striding down the middle.

A brighter gleam on the dull surface caught his eye. Bending, he picked up something made of metal.

Dave turned round, realizing that his chief was no longer alongside him.

'What have you found?' he asked.

For answer Bob held out the bit of metal. It was a spoon. Dave took it and turned it over in his fingers and said nothing.

'Now I ask you, Dave,' Bob said in a voice full of suppressed excitement, 'how did that come to be here?'

'How did any spoon come to be here, or how did this particular spoon come to be here, do you mean?'

'You are onto it, aren't you? I can't believe this.'

Dave looked blank. To him a spoon was a spoon was a spoon, but Bob had not been studying antiques for nothing during the last week or two.

'It's silver,' he said now, 'and with lying out here in the weather it has oxidized or tarnished or whatever so that it is almost the colour of the runway. But look at the hallmarks, Dave. If those aren't Georgian then I'm a Dutchman.'

'Pure English through and through you are, boss.'

Bob took the spoon back.

'Assay mark, the lion passant. Duty mark, the sovereign's head – head of George the Third, Farmer George.' He pointed to the part of the die stamp with the king's head. 'City of origin – Sheffield, because that's a crown, Dave. Year letter – I think that's a K. It would need to be looked up.' He passed the spoon over, hallmarks upward.

'I'd go along with your diagnosis, Bob, surely would.'

Bob Southwell looked curiously at his DI. 'You look serious, Dave, almost sorry. Aren't you excited? Don't you see what this means?'

The big, broad, red-faced man stood looking down at the spoon, now in his hand. 'I see, all right.' He turned the spoon over. 'You've noticed that, Bob?' Dave had his own, different bit of expertise to contribute. He knew nothing about hallmarks but he knew something about the contents of Mrs Honor's flat.

On the end of the handle was a tiny, beautifully engraved crest of part of an eagle, and the motto, 'ad finem fidelis'.

'Yes, of course.'

'But you didn't spend hour after hour taking down the details

134

people could remember of the things stolen from Mrs Honor's flat at the Dutch House. You might not recall all the fine points. Her table silver was engraved with the family crest and motto, and it was the eagle's leg erased – cut off, if you remember, Bob – and "ad finem fidelis". This is part of the loot. It was for this and a few other such trivial bits and pieces that a brave old lady lost her life. Faithful to the end. Wasn't she in occupied France for a while, helping shot-down airmen escape? She had to be prepared to withstand anything in the case of capture – she had to be prepared to be faithful to the end.'

'She didn't cower under the bed when she heard burglars – she went to confront them.'

'That's it, exactly, boss. I know what you mean. I know it is exciting to find this and it opens up a whole new ball game, but I can't help it, it makes me sad. Here we are in the sun and air and . . .'

'Come on, Dave,' Bob said impatiently. 'You're getting morbid. In our job we can't afford to be. Now we have arrived at a different point in the inquiry and it has nothing to do with those young French lads, or the girl who once helped their cause.'

Dave Smart looked puzzled. He could follow his boss's train of thought so far, but not all the way.

Bob sounded excited, impatient. He went on talking. 'The spoon was here – here. Can't you see the significance? You'd think with all the care they took packing things that nothing could drop out unnoticed, but it must have done, while they were putting the stuff into the aeroplane, Dave, God damn it.'

Bob knew he had a breakthrough. He could feel it in front of him, almost tangible, like the surface of something large, spherical, light, composed of light, the new much wider knowledge of the case, the overall perspective which would lead him inevitably to the murderer. He wasn't in full possession of it yet. There were other facts to discover and connections, connections between a teaspoon on an airfield and the Dutch House, for he knew now instinctively but with great certainty that all the threads were centred there, amongst that group of people.

'Come on, Dave,' he said again, striding off purposefully with the spoon held so firmly in his fist that it would not have been surprising if he had bent it, strong thick old silver that it was. 'We have work to do at last. First thing, call off the search for people who might have travelled under cover of the Bombadier Lourds. They have nothing to do with the case and there was no one travelling with them. Get in touch with the controllers of air traffic. If I know anything about it, this will have been an unauthorized flight, but there may be some trace of the aircraft. A light aircraft, almost certainly a private plane. How fast dare I drive on this road back?'

Julia sat on the edge of her bed looking at the piles of historic costumes she had brought from Cherry's. She had already been to the bank, seen the sympathetic manager, and left the remnants of the ten pound notes with him. He had promised to find out if anything could be done in the exceptional circumstances. Cherry was obviously a very popular customer of his; an understanding and affectionate smile came to his face when she was mentioned.

There was a ring at the doorbell.

'Mrs Robinson!' exclaimed Julia. 'Do come in. You might be interested. There are all these lovely clothes . . .'

She hardly got the words out before Mrs Robinson was in the bedroom, ooohing and aaahing, touching with predatory fingers.

'If only we wore clothes like this nowadays! May I?' she said all in a breath, picking up the Chinese coat and putting it on in front of the looking-glass without waiting for permission.

'That's the only thing that will fit you,' Julia said firmly, pushing the other clothes into a heap. 'I thought you might like to *look*, but they are too delicate to try on.'

'I bet you've had a go, though,' said her neighbour, posturing in front of her reflection before taking off the coat and returning it to the bed.

She was absolutely right. Julia had yielded to temptation and tried everything on. Being small and slim, and very careful, she had had a delirious time. She had been completely absorbed and completely happy. At last she had decided to her own satisfaction how to dispose of the garments to the best advantage and separated them into groups accordingly, ready to offer them either to certain museums, or to a few specialist shops she knew well, where the proprietors were friends and would, she believed, give her as much as could be obtained in a saleroom and a good deal quicker.

'If clothes like this were still made, of this quality and beauty, they would cost the earth and you and I wouldn't be able to afford them anyway,' said Julia now.

'What are you going to do with them?' Mrs Robinson's eyes were bright with interest. 'This is the most interesting thing that has happened since . . .' She stopped herself abruptly. 'Do tell me what your plans are for these lovely pieces.'

They had a very enjoyable time discussing the future of the clothes, over a cup of tea, before Mrs Robinson came to the real reason for her visit, which was to bring Julia up to date with the marvellous and thrilling news of her grown-up children, the 'Robinson Gang' as Bob Southwell had jokingly christened them.

For several hours that afternoon Julia was able to forget everything else, the murder, the little Peke, Adam's exam, even Tom Churchyard – though a glow in the bottom of her mind never quite went away.

Then she prepared a meal. The heat was still continuing as if England had turned into the South of France, so she made a cold cucumber soup followed by cold meat and salad and early strawberries and cream.

Full of satisfaction, she thought she would go and report her progress with the clothes to Cherry Ducket-Penrose. On entering the main Dutch House – the residents normally tapped at Cherry's front door and then walked in – she heard an odd sort of scratchy noise. Peeping into Cherry's favourite little room, she found it empty. There was no doubt, the sound came from the drawing room. Listening intently as she crossed the hall once more, and pausing before further opening the door into the drawing room, which was standing a few inches open already, she still could not decide the cause of the mysterious sequence of small sounds.

There was no point in delay. Pushing open the door and edging round it uncertainly, she found herself up against some tall steps on top of which Cherry was teetering to and fro, with a pot of paint in her hand. Dipping her finger into the paint, Cherry dabbed it onto the mouldings of the cornice, then repeated the action, producing a number of quiet little noises overlaid with her panting breath. She looked very insecure up there.

'Cherry, what on earth are you doing?'

137

Cherry grabbed the top of the steps to stop herself falling. 'What you told me to do,' she said breathlessly.

'My dear, I know better than to try to tell you to do anything.'

'Nonsense, Julia, you're a great one for ordering me about. Didn't you say, when you were in this room the other day, that the cornice needed regilding?'

'Yes, I did, but . . .'

'Well, I had an estimate and it costs an absolute fortune, my child.'

'I know craftsmen repairing the cornice and real gilding will be terribly expensive. Believe me, Cherry, it was only a remark off the cuff. I knew it was an impractical suggestion when there is so much else to be put in order.'

'But you said it, you know. So I thought, I'll paint it myself, and I went to Woolworth's, and there is this really very good gold paint, so I bought some, you see.'

'Cherry – you're not—'

I can't believe it, Julia thought. I just can't believe that my dear friend is up there dabbing on with her finger ordinary gold-coloured metallic paint over gilding of pure gold leaf.

'I decided to paint it myself, but the brush wasn't much good so I'm using my finger. It's surprising how one can get on when one uses one's powers of invention.'

'Cherry . . . Believe me, it would be better not to paint it . . . Really . . . Do leave it, dear . . . If ever you can afford it, then have it done properly but until then it would really be better not . . .'

'Do you think so? But I can't waste this paint. It's expensive.'

'I'll buy it from you,' said Julia in desperation. 'Adam can use it for painting models or something, a notice for you, perhaps. Come down, Cherry, before you fall off this step-ladder and land yourself in hospital.'

By this point in the afternoon Ms Hodson, Ms Haygreen and Miss Susannah Wilmet were all home from their teaching jobs, Ms Haygreen at the Resource Centre and the other two at different schools in the city. Mrs Robinson telephoned all of them and told them what a delightful time she had had with Julia, and that if they wanted to see the beautiful old clothes they ought to go round straight away because Julia was setting about disposing of them without delay.

Susannah Wilmet was struck by the thought that something among the clothing might be rather stunning to wear when giving a solo concert performance and rang immediately. When Julia heard the dulcet tones she did not realize at first who was speaking. Susannah's voice was only like this when she wanted something. It was the voice the Brothers Lloyd had liked so much before their new neighbour moved in.

'Of course, you are welcome to visit,' Julia said helplessly. It was lucky that the evening meal was prepared and cold, and Adam not in yet. She was not really pleased, and even less so when she saw the way Susannah handled precious old fabrics. Her heart lurched as she tactfully rescued a silk georgette dress and jacket, pale grey with leaves in darker grey and tiny yellow flowers, trimmed with small sections of white fur, from Susannah's grasp.

'They couldn't stand up to the strain of being worn by a concert performer,' she assured Susannah. 'If you feel inspired by any particular garment, I have a friend who might copy it for you in strong new materials.'

At that moment she heard Adam coming in at the front door, and without thanks, Susannah left the bedroom and began to talk to the young man, her interest in the clothes apparently forgotten.

Luckily she went fairly soon, and the mother and son were able to eat their meal.

'You won't believe what Cherry was doing this afternoon,' she said to Adam. 'Only painting – with her finger, mark you – painting over a cornice gilded with pure gold, and using ordinary gold-coloured metallic paint from Woolworth's for the purpose . . .'

The Bransbys had just finished eating when Ms Hodson and Ms Haygreen arrived.

'I hope we are not too early,' Ms Hodson said, when Julia opened the front door to them. 'Mrs Robinson told us you were allowing people to see some marvellous clothes you got from dear Cherry. Is it all right for us to come?'

'Of course, do come in.' As Julia stepped aside for them, she reflected that there was something to be said for Mrs Honor's

139

insistence on telephone calls first when visiting, even amongst the community themselves.

'Oh, how entrancing,' Ms Hodson said. She was the more vocal of the two. Julia had noticed how subdued Ms Haygreen had become since the murder. Even within Julia's flat, she kept glancing over in the direction of Mrs Honor's home.

'Such fabrics,' Ms Haygreen murmured in her turn. 'How well silk takes dye. Nothing to touch it for depth and glow of colour.'

'I do so agree,' said Julia.

'One would love to paint someone actually wearing these garments,' enthused Ms Hodson.

'Unfortunately I can't keep them long enough for that,' Julia replied quickly. 'I have persuaded Cherry to let me sell them to finance essential work in advance of opening the Dutch House again, and I intend to start marketing them tomorrow.'

'Are they very valuable?' asked the ladies.

'Not all of them, of course, and the most valuable are probably only worth in the low hundreds, we haven't found intact eighteenth-century gear, nothing here is older than late nineteenth century, but luckily well preserved.'

'Not like *some* things in the main house,' added Ms Hodson.

'Exactly.'

'And you may be allowed to look further and find even greater treasures.'

'It is possible. There is a wardrobe I am going to be allowed to explore.' Then Julia thought she had spoken very unwisely. Now all the female residents would expect to be in on any discoveries she made in the wardrobe. More time-wasting visits ahead.

As the two ladies left Julia's flat and climbed the stairs back to their own apartments, Ms Haygreen said fretfully, 'I wish you hadn't persuaded me to go there.'

'We have to seem normal,' replied her friend.

'Normal! They are going to find out about me! Us!'

'Nonsense. We have covered our tracks.'

It was going to be too hot to sleep, again, thought Julia. She lay with her windows open – an invitation to any passing burglar as

140

she lived on the ground floor – and the light summer curtains hung straight.

She was turning restlessly, trying to find a cool bit of pillow, when the telephone rang next to the bed. Reaching out a hand she hoiked it to her ear and said 'Yes?'

'I'm so glad you're awake too,' murmured Tom.

'Thomas Churchyard, what do you mean by ringing me in the middle of the night?' she murmured back at him.

'I can't sleep for thinking of you.'

'And me of you, my darling.'

'Am I? Am I really your darling?'

'Of course. Don't you know by now?'

'I thought there was a strong possibility,' whispered Tom. 'Let's spend a night together soon.'

She was silent for a long while – long enough for him to feel that he might have offended her – then she murmured back, 'Yes, but how do we manage it?'

'If you can get away for a night . . .'

'On what pretext?'

'. . . I will take you back to that hotel we had dinner at the other day.'

'That would be lovely, Tom. When I went up to the ladies' room I peeped in some of the bedrooms and they really are gorgeous.'

'That's fixed, then.'

'No it isn't! How can I spend a night away again, at the moment and in the present circumstances?'

'I don't know,' said Tom, suddenly sounding rather defeated.

'I'll think of something,' she reassured him, and after a few more minutes' substitute pillow talk he rang off, and she dropped into sleep with a lingering smile.

11

Adam was sitting the first part of his philosophy examination on the Wednesday morning. Before he left for school the phone rang. It was the vet.

'If you like you can take Blue Moon home today,' he said.

'Whoopee! Mum, listen to this! What time? Oh ... I've an exam this morning.'

'Come during surgery this evening, then. Or, if you like, I'll bring him round on my way home. I need to show you and your mother how to feed him.'

Julia had taken the phone from her excited son. 'That is very good of you,' she said. 'We do appreciate it. Do we need anything special? I'd better buy it today if we do. Adam was talking about a syringe.'

'I can let you have a couple the right size.'

'Oh, thanks.'

After she replaced the phone, Julia said, 'He is being awfully kind, that man.'

'He's the best,' said Adam fervently. 'I'm wondering whether to become a vet.'

'Off you go, darling. This news should put you in such a good mood you'll walk the paper.'

'Mum – you'd better contact the police—'

'What for?'

'It would be best to have Blue Moon's own bed and plate and whatnot if we can.'

Julia cringed inside at the thought of going into Mrs Honor's flat again, but she fought this down and said calmly, 'Of course. I'll see to it this morning.'

It was every bit as bad as she thought it would be. DI Smart came with the keys in answer to her request. She had to obtain clearance from Mrs Honor's solicitors as well, and the man there wanted to talk about the case and the police inquiry, which was the last thing Julia wanted, but she told him all she could. Then with Dave Smart she went into the flat, and he supervised her as she collected the dog-bed and its blankets, the lead, the water bowl, the two special dishes and the pooper-scooper.

'Do you think I've forgotten anything?' she said doubtfully.

'I don't think so.'

'It's horrid being in here, it positively is.'

'You're doing a good job, Mrs Bransby.'

Once back in her own flat, she wondered where it was best to put the dog-bed, and at last decided it had better be in the main living room. It would be easy enough to move it into Adam's bedroom at night, if required. She filled the water bowl, although she was not sure whether the little dog could drink yet. The feeding dishes went in the cupboard under the sink. The lead on a hook near the front door. If he needed special food she could moped to a 12-hour supermarket, she supposed.

When Tom rang, unable to wait until evening to talk again about their first night together, she felt that it was never going to happen at all. 'I won't be able to leave him,' she said rather pathetically, and the 'him' meant not only Adam but also Blue Moon. 'I'll be really stuck. I don't want to seem to desert Adam in the middle of exams, either.'

Tom sounded miserable. 'We're not getting any younger,' he said.

That brought a spark of spirit back to Julia. 'Speak for yourself,' she retorted. 'Since we went to Oakwell Hall I feel younger every day. We'll be back in our teens soon if we're not careful.'

They both laughed and felt better.

'Something will turn up,' Tom said. 'Until tonight, then. I'll ring about eleven.'

'Till then.'

Julia had the rest of the day to organize the disposal of the clothes she had so far taken from Cherry, and she had several towns and museums to drive to. There was not going to be a minute to spare, she decided. The day was a great success. She made some outright sales to shop owners she knew well and various museums were putting acquisition proposals to their committees. It was all so promising that she had a word with Cherry's bank manager on the telephone and he agreed to make a short-term loan. When she called on Cherry and gave her the good news, the response surprised her.

'I'll be able to buy the donkeys, then,' said Cherry.

'What donkeys?'

'I promised myself that if any unexpected money turned up I would give a home to some of those ill-treated donkeys you read about. Two, I thought, to keep each other company.'

'Do you have to *buy* them? Aren't they free to good homes?'

'A donation at least, I would think.'

Julia said nothing, because she was sure there would be

enough money to cover the donkeys as well as a fair bit of cleaning.

Meanwhile, the police had turned up a good deal of background information about the various inhabitants of the Dutch House. It was spread out on a table and a group of officers were standing around, looking at the notes and discussing the case. Present were DS Birch and DCI Robert Southwell, DI Dave Smart and DC James Jester.

'This Markhall seems a shady character,' said Birch, who didn't remember the man.

'You wouldn't think so to talk to him. Butter wouldn't melt in his mouth. Very precise and just so. Spends a lot of his time on chess problems.'

'Retired early, and look what the newspaper index check turned up.'

York is lucky, perhaps unique, in having in its reference library an index to items in the local papers which referred to York people – or at least, those living in York, which is not the same thing. Any native of the place considers anyone not born in the city to be an incomer, not one of us, 'not a York person' – the ultimate indictment in some circles.

The newspaper index was arranged in alphabetical order of surname and all one had to do after finding a reference was to request the newspaper of the relevant date. These turned up, all too often, on microfilm.

'*Had* to retire, by the look of it,' went on DS Birch. 'Did you get all this stuff from the newspaper index, James?'

'No, sir. First I rang up the Architects Registration Council of the United Kingdom. They told me the details about his career, where he studied, and all that.'

'Then the newspaper index put you onto this scandal, the fiddles about awarding the contracts, the structures built with materials below the specified standard, the inferences of bribery, corruption, and unprofessional conduct.'

'That's right, sir.'

'I see the Royal Institute of British Architects ran an inquiry into the matter. They will have a file on it, I suppose.'

'I didn't approach them, sir. It was a good report in the newspaper. There is something else, sir, about Mr Markhall.'

'Yes? Go on, lad! Don't keep us in suspense. This isn't a strip-tease.'

'In Mrs Bransby's statement she said that on the evening of the murder, she saw Mr Markhall at Mrs Honor's door, bent over like a walking-stick as she put it, then knocking.'

'Thanks for reminding us, James,' said Bob Southwell. 'The flats were like Piccadilly Circus that night. Somewhere we have a timetable of the comings and goings. Earlier in the evening there had been a row, raised voices. We don't yet know who was involved. Mrs Bransby heard it, that was why she looked out and saw Mr Markhall. His explanation was that he had been disturbed by the noise and come down from his flat to complain.'

'Then later when he was looking out of his window he saw Mrs Bransby wandering about,' said DS Birch, who had been riffling through the papers on the table.

'I have to ask her about that,' said Bob Southwell. 'But with respect, aren't we wandering from the point? The point was that Mr Markhall was disgraced in his profession and forced to retire, Mrs Honor might have known of the fact and in some way this information, which no one else seems to have known, might have brought about her death. The relationship between them doesn't seem to have been all that good, and that evening he was the only person known to have sought admission to number 4.'

'I told you, Mum, that I'd stay and work in the library this afternoon,' said Adam, later that day.

'So you did. Was it a decent lunch at school?'

'It was OK. I didn't go into the library, though. I sat on the grass with Pete and we talked. Neither of us felt like working.'

Julia remembered sitting on the grass and talking with her friends at school and wondered why one never did that when one had grown up.

'How was the exam?'

'All right. I'll tell you what I did. When I wanted to put my own ideas about something, I wrote, "According to Klopstock, so and so . . ."'

'Who was Klopstock?' asked Julia.

'Oh, he was some old German or something, the point is, his name's familiar but no one can remember why, so they think I'm really quoting someone when it is me all the time – you see?'

'Yes, dear. Do you think it was wise?'

'Oh, yes, perfectly all right. No one will bother checking. They'll just think I'm jolly clever, as Cherry says.' Noticing the dog-bed, he asked, 'When's Blue Moon coming?'

There was a knock on the door.

'Now, by the sound of it,' said Julia.

The vet took some minutes to explain to them how to look after the little dog, then left. As she saw him out, Julia thought with relief of Mrs Honor's solicitor's offer to pay the costs until probate, and hoped probate would not take place until the animal was quite better.

One person who was not pleased to see Blue Moon back at the Dutch House was Mr Spicer. Cats and dogs were anathema to him. Cats scratched up his seedbeds and newly planted seedlings and dogs did things all over the grass.

'He's back then,' he said gruffly to Adam, noticing Blue Moon's first visit to the grass at the back of the flats. 'At least he's better than them damn cats.'

'You can't mean Oberon and Titania? But they're lovely!'

'Lovely is as lovely does,' Spicer said darkly. He put out a cautious hand and stroked the little dog's head. 'Have you heard Miss Ducket-Penrose is getting two donkeys? We'll have to put up with them on this grass, there's nowhere else. Well, I can't stand here all day. This won't give the old woman a ninepence.'

'Where are you going?' asked Adam.

'To tidy up a bit outside Mrs Honor's,' was the unexpected reply. 'Those climbers of hers haven't been pruned for a twelve-month. She liked everything in a tangle, but I don't.'

'I rather like her tangle of climbers,' Adam said afterwards, as the Bransbys went back into their flat.

'Well, so do I, Adam, but we aren't all alike, you know. Most people will prefer them clipped back a bit. It seems a pity to do it when they are such a mass of flower, but that's Mr Spicer for you. I expect he wants to take the opportunity of pruning them while the flat is empty and no one can stop him.'

After a little while Julia thought she would go to see how the old gardener was getting on. She took a basket with her. Sure enough, the ground was a mass of flowers which had been ruthlessly severed from the climbers.

'I may as well have these,' she said. 'We haven't any flowers in the house at present.'

'You can take them for me.'

So Julia began to put them in her basket. There were several types of roses, and some clematis. As she laid them lengthways she was planning how to arrange them and what containers to use. Mr Spicer went on with his task. He was getting down to the bones of the plants and soon would be able to sort out the worst of the tangle. In among the clematis was an old bird's nest, tipping precariously to one side.

'That's a rather nice bird's nest,' said Julia. 'Can I have it, Mr Spicer? I have a friend who is a flower arranger and she likes to use things like that.'

'It's a bit stuck, like.' The gnarled old hands struggled to free the nest from the twisting clematis. 'There's something heavy in it that's got wedged at the back.'

'Oh, I hope it isn't a dead bird.'

'No, it's something metal. By, it is heavy. I'll just get it wriggled out of these old stalks. It's a big thing, Mrs Bransby.'

Julia had put down her basket and now she reached up her hands. With a grunt of relief Mr Spicer dropped nest and metal object into them, and with such a rush that the unexpected weight almost made her drop the lot. She gasped. 'What on earth?'

'Big lump of metal of some kind.'

Julia knew what it was. She was familiar enough with the bust of de Gaulle to which Mrs Honor had given pride of place on her pretty desk. It had always looked incongruous there. Now it looked even more incongruous, half in and half out of a bird's nest and wrapped firmly round with strands of clematis. How had it managed to be so tangled up in a such a short time? As she unwrapped it Julia began to have a horrid suspicion. The whole head of de Gaulle was covered with some kind of dark painty stuff. And a white hair or two. She dropped it as if it had stung her. Turning abruptly away from the blank curtained patio door, Julia sat down sharply on Mrs Honor's paving stones. Somehow in front of Mr Spicer – even though he had his back to her and was taking no notice – she could not break down. She took several deep breaths and put her head between her knees. Then she scrambled to her feet, picked up the basket and, using her handkerchief, put the bust and the bird's nest, still wound up together, into it on top of the flowers and walked fairly steadily to her own tiny bit of garden.

There she put down her basket again and went into the house without it. Picking up the phone she dialled the police station and asked for DCI Southwell. Fortunately he was there.

'Bob, it's Julia. Mr Spicer is pruning Mrs Honor's climbers.'

There she stopped.

'Did you ring up to tell me that?' asked Bob, rather puzzled. 'Do you want me to stop him?'

'Oh, no, nothing like that. Hidden in the tangle he found her bust of de Gaulle. It was one of the things we noticed was missing from her flat. I think someone must have thrown it there, Bob. It landed in a bird's nest among a tangle of twigs and tipped the nest over backwards and got wedged. No one could have seen it. If Mr Spicer hadn't been moved to prune, it could have stayed there for months, years even.'

'He shouldn't be pruning them at this time of year.'

'No, of course he shouldn't.'

'I'm glad one of the missing items has turned up.'

'It isn't only that, Bob. You don't understand. I'm not explaining myself very well. It looks to me as if this bust has had something like blood on it, and there is at least one hair, if not two.'

'Have you touched this?' asked Bob Southwell as he bent over the basket full of flowers and bird's nest and the bronze bust of de Gaulle.

'Yes, before I realized. So has Mr Spicer. He had to, to get it out of the clematis.'

'Anyway they were wearing gloves so it probably wouldn't have any fingerprints. A handy weapon. The base has been gripped, you see. It would fit well into the palm of a hand. Then the base of the shoulders would fit under the fist – like so' – curving his hand round in the air – 'with the head projecting, and could be brought down with force – like this . . .' Bob had forgotten Julia was there, in his reconstruction of the crime. 'Then out of the patio door and hurl it into the mass of foliage – it might well have crashed straight through, but it didn't, catching in the nest – then away . . .'

'I'm sure you are right,' Julia said faintly. 'Adam, I think a cup of tea is indicated for your mother. Well laced with brandy, please dear.' She sat down hastily and put her hands to her face.

'Oh, I'm sorry, Julia,' said Bob.

'It's quite all right. You policemen must get used to this sort of thing. I'm not, that's all,' came her muffled voice.

Bob sat down and wondered what he could say to help her recover. 'I went to see Mr Taffinder Walker,' he remarked, conversationally. 'Have you been to his shop?'

'I have walked past it,' muttered Julia.

'There was a piece of embroidered fabric draped across an old chest, it gave a very rich effect, very attractive. I thought I must remember to tell you about it.'

Adam came with a cup of tea and a bottle of brandy. He put down the tea and measured a decent dollop of the spirit into it. 'Mumsy,' he said.

Julia's head came up slowly and she sipped the tea. 'Thank you, Adam. And you too, Bob. I'm always pleased to hear about interesting things I might otherwise have missed. Did you decide that Taff Walker had murdered Mrs Honor?'

'He was in the Lake District at the time.'

'So that was a dead end, then.'

'It looks like it. Perhaps it's someone nearer home.' Bob spoke jokily, still trying to distract her.

'Nearer home? Possibly even in the Dutch House?'

'We mustn't rule anything out.' Now Bob felt uncomfortable. He tried to rescue the situation. 'We suspect everyone, you know we must do, Julia, until we actually catch the guilty party. In fact there is something I need to ask you about your own movements.'

12

This was a further shock for Julia, as if she hadn't had enough already. The realization that she was a suspect entered her head for the first time.

'What do you want to know about my movements?' she asked, a blush rising to her cheeks.

'On the night of the murder you were seen outside the flats, wandering about, apparently, quite late at night.'

Fortunately Julia had been primed by Tom about the police curiosity as to his own presence.

'There is no mystery about that,' she said firmly, and explained.

Bob Southwell had been jotting down notes. 'What time was all this?' he asked.

'What time?' Julia had to think about that one. Eventually she said, 'About ten o'clock,' hoping that it was right.

'Who saw me, anyway?' She was feeling nettled, even though she had often commented herself on the fact that she could do nothing without constant observation from the other residents.

'I can't tell you that,' Bob said. 'How is the little dog?' For the first time he noticed Blue Moon lying in his basket.

'He's doing very well.'

Bob went over to bend down and speak to the dog. 'Tell us who did it, eh, little fella?' he said to him. Straightening and turning back to Julia and Adam, he asked, 'How is everyone bearing up?'

'Not too badly,' said Adam.

Bob noticed a book lying on the coffee table. He picked it up. 'Linda would be interested in this,' he said. It was on *Opus Anglicanum*, meaning English Work, the embroidery of the Middle Ages which was famous throughout Europe. 'She loves anything medieval.'

'It is Ms Haygreen's,' Julia said, relieved to be talking about ordinary matters. 'I don't happen to have a copy of it and there is a section I wanted to refer to, so she kindly lent it to me.'

Bob looked at the flyleaf. 'It isn't her name,' he commented.

'Really? She probably bought it second-hand. It's been out of print for ages and costs the earth.'

'Was Mrs Honor friendly with the two ladies?' asked Bob.

'In a formal way,' replied Julia.

'And you two? Did you spend time socially together?'

'With Mrs Honor or with Misses Haygreen and Hodson?' asked Julia.

'Either.'

'The ladies upstairs tend to be wrapped up in their own affairs, although they are friendly. You know we had quite a lot of, as it were, neighbourly, or communal, life with Mrs Honor.'

'While Mother was away in Manchester she came and spent the Saturday evening with me,' replied Adam. 'We played Scrabble. Except at one point she said she wanted to fetch a handkerchief, and went out. I wasn't sure if she was tired of playing so after a minute I followed her. I was going to call and ask whether to put the board away or if she wanted another game. Something made me turn my head and look up the stairs, and I saw her on the landing, listening for all she was worth to the conversation from the Brights' flat. Mrs Bright was home at the time. Mrs Honor's ear was pressed to their door. I've only just remembered that, it seemed very out of character. I came back in here and waited for Mrs Honor, we did have another game, but she seemed to be having a struggle to concentrate. I had forgotten about that little incident until just now.'

'Interesting,' said Bob, and prepared to go. He put down the book on embroidery and picked up the bust of de Gaulle, which was now in a clear plastic evidence bag. 'I'll have this sent for forensic examination. Look after yourselves.' He closed the door gently behind him.

'Does he really suspect the people here?' asked Adam. 'Should we follow them about and ask leading questions?'

'Certainly not, Adam, don't be ridiculous.'

Adam sat down across the table from her. 'I'm a bit worried about you, Mumsy. All this fainting and stuff. It isn't like you.'

'I didn't faint.'

'You almost did. I think you ought to get right away for a bit and have a change of scene.'

'Tom Churchyard asked me if I'd like to go somewhere one

151

weekend but I said I couldn't possibly leave you and Blue Moon.'

'Pete wants to come and help look after the dog. You know he's applying for a course in veterinary medicine.'

'I might have known there were something behind your solicitude, Adam. You want me out of the way so that you can have Peter to stay. He could always sleep on the fold-up bed, you know, as he has before. There's no need for me to go anywhere.'

'We're both beginning to find those fold-up beds pretty uncomfortable now. They aren't really long enough or wide enough. And if you've been asked off on a jaunt . . .'

'But would the dog be all right, in the care of you two hooligans?'

'We'd enjoy looking after him.'

'All right, then. I'll ring Tom and see what his plans are for this weekend. Not long since it was you that couldn't stand the idea of coming back to this flat, Adam, now you're OK and it's me that's the problem.'

As Bob Southwell drove back into town and to the police station on Clifford Street he thought about the murder at the Dutch House and felt convinced that an international traffic in stolen antiques lay at the back of the whole thing. It wasn't a field he knew much about, and the traffic would be continuing. There might well be another in the series of burglaries. If there was, the investigation would be so thorough that nothing, but nothing, could be missed.

The main Dutch House itself was an obvious target for antique thieves, and that worried him. Cherry Ducket-Penrose was trusting and seemed to have no understanding of values – or, no, that wasn't true. She had her own system of values and they weren't the same as those of the antique trade. Her values were much like those of many middle-aged ladies in suburban semis or terrace houses. She valued the embroidery her mother had stitched and the sketches her mother had drawn, and she valued her home, not because of its age or its architecture or its beauty, but because her family had always lived there. Family and the love of its members were what her life was about. There was nothing wrong with that – probably it was what made the world go round and kept the stability of society. Unfortunately it left her wide open to be preyed on by those who had no perception of property as belonging to other people, but thought they had the right to take anything they wanted and sell it to gain money for themselves.

Julia rang Tom to tell him she could go away for the weekend, and it seemed too good to be true. He stammered and fell over his words. Yes, this weekend was fine – it was so fine he couldn't describe it – yes, he'd call for her in the car. Would she really like to go to the place where they'd had dinner? She would? Great, it meant that taking the car presented no problem. When? Saturday afternoon, and perhaps they'd better come back Sunday afternoon. Right. Whatever she said. He agreed fervently that she needed a break from the Dutch House.

When they rang off Julia sat on the edge of her bed looking pensive. She was sure that Adam hadn't meant that she was to go off for a naughty weekend. He would think of his mother sightseeing in some country town well-provided with ruined priories, derelict castles, an interesting unspoiled town centre with enticing shops including one full of antique clothes and another with exciting new threads and yarns. Certainly that kind of venue would be right up her street. Instead she was going with Tom to an isolated hotel, elegant and with super food, where they would set the seal on their relationship but not do any sightseeing at all.

She pulled herself together. There were several clear days before Saturday and in them she could do something to help Cherry, whose date for opening the house for the rest of July and the whole of August was approaching very fast. So far all Julia had done to help her was to take some photographs to be made into postcards, place advertisements in the York leaflet *What's On* and in the *Yorkshire Evening Press* and the *Yorkshire Post* for the appropriate dates.

She had also hired a cleaning firm who were experts in treating stonework to come and scour the flagged floor of the basement kitchens and storeplaces and then seal the surface, since the old kitchens were included in the visitor route.

With Adam, she was to spend this evening clearing as much as they could, piling things on the stout stone shelves and in the fixed cupboards. All that was to remain in situ was to be the great heavy kitchen table which must have been assembled where it stood, because it could never have been taken in through the door.

The other big thing she wanted to see done in the way of professional cleaning was the drawing-room floor. The wood surround was a dreadful mess and the carpet was so grubby and faded that no one could see the pattern. Julia fetched the cordless telephone and the Yellow Pages. She was sure the carpet was not only old but also valuable, so found a specialist firm who could call for it on Monday and clean it, and she then found someone to clean the whole wooden floor and repolish the surround. Julia believed that if a floor was clean the whole room looked better immediately. Dusting down cobwebs could be done by anybody, and usually cleaning started at the top of a house not in the basement, but this was not usual cleaning and this was the way she had decided to tackle it. She was being very selective in the targets for expenditure, knowing how little cash there was to play with. The stone-cleaning outfit were going to come back after the drawing-room floor had been done, to tackle the marble floor of the hall and passageway, and then that was going to be that.

So before the Saturday when she and Tom were to go off together Julia put in two days dragging the furnishings of the Dutch House drawing room upstairs and piling them in a disused corridor, with the help of Cherry and Mr Spicer, while down below the stone-cleaners were creating noise and dust. When at last Julia sat down on the Friday night she was exhausted but triumphant.

They arrived at the hotel at half-past three and first of all sat in a secluded corner looking out at the view as they shared a pot of tea and a few delicate triangular sandwiches. Then, hardly daring to look at one another, they went upstairs and discovered that they had a long time to fill in before eight o'clock dinner.

'Whatever shall we do for nearly four hours?' Tom said in mock puzzlement, before they had moved into one another's arms and used the first part of their time in leisurely embraces and even more leisurely undressings. They had all the time in the world, so why rush something so longed for? When they were both undressed Tom fell to his knees and put his arms round her waist, his cheek on her body, and gave a long sigh of pure delight. She laid her hands on his shoulders and looked down, pleased but nonplussed, at his mop of hair. How was she supposed to respond to this? She felt protective in those moments instead of passionate and crossed her wrists behind his head, her hands spread on his back, and held him close.

They slid into bed and lay touching from head to toe. Both of them commented afterwards on the strangeness of this space in time. It may have been two minutes, it may have been twenty, certainly for what seemed endless, a time outside time, they had simply lain there holding each other, without kissing or moving. For both of them there was the extraordinary sensation of being recharged with life by the contact. They were revived as a thirsty plant is revived by the blessing of rain. They interchanged some kind of spiritual nourishment. They were re-created.

At last they left this ethereal plane. One of them moved a little, there was a tiny kiss, a small caress, and their first lovemaking began.

When Julia returned to the Dutch House late on the Sunday afternoon she was in an uplifted and transfigured state. She could not help remembering Spring Bank Holiday Monday, when she had still been full of doubt and hesitation about Tom. Her fulfilment now showed in her face and her step.

As she opened her own front door she thought at first that the flat was empty, but moving from the tiny entrance hall into the sitting room she saw her son and his friend Pete kneeling by the dog basket where she supposed the little Peke was lying.

'I'm back!' she said jauntily.

Adam turned his head and looked at her over his shoulder. 'Hi, Mum. You're looking much better. We're just doing the afternoon feed, we won't be long.'

Peter turned his head and said briefly, 'Hi, Mrs Bransby.'

Both heads went down again and the delicate manipulations of feeding the dog with a syringe went on. Julia shrugged her shoulders and went into the kitchen. There were some dirty pots in the sink but the place looked quite good considering. She put on the kettle automatically and began to sort out a meal, thanking progress for the boons of the deep-freeze and the microwave. It was some time before the two lads appeared looking pleased with themselves.

'You're staying for a meal, Peter?' asked Julia.

'Thanks, Mrs Bransby, but I must go home straight afterwards. Thank you very much for letting me use your bedroom. I was very comfortable.'

'Yes, it's a nice comfy bed.'

Peter began to tell her about the veterinary course he would be joining in the autumn. He was a year ahead of Adam, who was not going to university for another fourteen months. This was an easy conversation for Julia, who only needed to nod and smile. Later, after Peter had gone, Adam announced that he ought to do some revision and vanished into his bedroom until it was time to feed the dog again and, after an hour's television, go off to bed.

Julia drew a sigh of relief. She would have to tell Adam some taradiddle about her own weekend, but she was pleased to have time first to calm down. When the moment did come, on the following day, she made a few remarks about Tom's interest in vernacular architecture and the houses he had helped to record on his weekend course – none of which she had mentioned to Adam before – which served very nicely to pass the subject over.

Adam only had his General Studies exams to come and seemed to think that Monday was a free day, so she asked him to help her at Cherry's and he agreed cheerfully. They saw to Blue Moon and then went round with buckets, whiting, a blue bag, some lumps of lard and a couple of large brushes. Before the stone flags were cleaned Julia had brushed down the cobwebs and dust from the ceilings and walls of the kitchens and store places with a large aggressive broom. Now, they covered the newly cleaned floors with plastic left by the workmen, and mixed the old-fashioned whitewash. There were already layers of old whitewash. To strip it off would have been a horrendous task, and the result out of keeping with the character of the place.

So she and Adam sloshed and brushed on the grey coating which dried to a most sparkling white. They covered the area quickly, with breaks to go home and see to the dog, and other breaks for the sandwiches and coffee Cherry brought down for them. By the end of the day they had finished.

'We're going to be as stiff as posts tomorrow.' Adam stretched his arms luxuriously after stripping off the overalls Julia had borrowed from the Lloyd brothers. Gawain's fitted him nicely and Julia had been wearing Lancelot's. She put both sets into the washer straight away.

'I'm going to be busy all week,' Julia remarked. 'When the floor has had its second coat of sealer we can put out the most decorative and interesting of the kitchenalia to make the place worth seeing. The carpet cleaners took the drawing-room carpet this morning and they're bringing it back on Thursday. Tomorrow we've the men doing the wooden floor of the drawing room, they're expecting to finish in a couple of days and I hope they do. It's amazing how mechanical aids speed things up. There isn't time or money to do it by hand. We can only do our best.'

'You're marvellous, Mum,' said Adam, giving her a hug before all his attention was diverted to the dog.

It was Thursday afternoon when the drawing-room carpet came back. For once Julia was glad that there was an economic recession because the firms she had contacted for Cherry were pleased to have the work and did things straight away. Julia was sure that in normal times she could have whistled for them for weeks. The other residents were fascinated by what was happening. On Friday night Cherry rang round and invited them to view the result and they trooped over *en masse*.

Julia and Cherry had prepared flasks full of coffee in advance. Cherry's tiny kitchen area, at one end of the old basement kitchens, was back in use. At some time Mrs Ducket-Penrose had installed an electric stove and a two-yard run of fitted units with sink and fridge, and then they had stopped using the rest of the vast kitchens.

Now on the enormous old kitchen table lay plates of quickly prepared refreshments, biscuits, potato crisps, and sausage rolls. The servants' pottery had been brought out of the cupboard where Julia had discovered it, washed, and was ready for use.

Susannah Wilmet and her neighbours the Brothers Lloyd walked over together, the first to arrive. They had agreed to investigate sound-proofing on a mutual basis and were now quite friendly.

'We needn't wait, I'm sure,' said Cherry, who was feeling very hungry. 'Everyone will be over in a minute. Lancelot, do have a sausage roll.'

It was strange how quickly the basement took on a festive atmosphere. All the windows were open and the warm evening air, loaded with the scents of the garden, drifted in to the cool kitchens. The floors were gleaming and clean. The walls and ceilings sparkled white. Suddenly the irregularities, the ups and downs of the stone flags, the bulges in the walls, the arches here and there into further parts, the doors cutting off the stairs down into the wine cellar, the vast old cooking ranges now rusty and in need of blackleading, the wooden kneading tubs and meat safes and whitewood kitchen chairs, took on a surprising air of romance and a kind of sturdy beauty.

Flat kitchen candlesticks with plain candles stood ready at various points to provide a flickering light if people stayed long enough to need it. Now through the shadows of these basement rooms the residents drifted, formed into chattering groups, went back to the table for more coffee or more refreshments, congratulated Cherry, Julia and Adam, volunteered their services in any possible way to help with the coming grand opening, and in general were more pleasant and sociable than Julia ever remembered seeing them. You could tell that they were all thinking of Mrs Honor. There was a Mrs Honor shaped space amongst them, but they were calmer about her death than before.

Julia had been very upset by Bob Southwell's hints that everyone in the Dutch House was a murder suspect. She couldn't get the idea out of her mind, during this party, and looked at everyone with that in mind.

Mr Spicer, the gardener and odd-job man, had the slightly uncomfortable air of staff hobnobbing with bosses, but he was lashing into the refreshments and seemed to be chatting to everyone. He had promised that he would clean all the windows before the opening and that he would guide people round the gardens. Julia knew now that he was genuinely sorry about Mrs Honor's death.

Mrs Robinson wore a fussy cocktail dress and was crooking her little finger in the air as she carried her coffee cup from one group to another. She told everyone how even to look at a biscuit would cause her to gain a pound in weight. Barely coming up to Mr Markhall's shoulder, she explained the progress of her broken ankle to him, then cornered Lancelot Lloyd, the accountant, to discuss an investment. Passing with a plate of sausage rolls, Julia tried to see her in the role of murderess, and failed utterly.

Dr Bright had, as locum, coped with a lengthy clinic that afternoon and was less bouncy than usual. His light, open quiff of hair was trembling a little in the cross currents of breeze from the gardens.

'What a pity your wife isn't here,' Julia remarked to him.

'Yes, indeed. She is at Bournemouth at the moment with her sister Mary. She would have found this very interesting, very interesting indeed. I have promised Cherry that I will take a turn at guide duty when she opens the house. My wife would have been delighted to help, had she been here.'

He began to drink his coffee. Julia, who didn't much care for Mrs Bright, would gladly have cast her in the role of murderess. She passed on to have a word with Oddsocks – Mr Markhall. The thought flicked across Julia's mind that it was very strange indeed that he had not heard the murder. There must have been sounds, cries for help. Sound carries upward, she felt sure. He now gave her his usual courteous and formal greetings.

'A delightful occasion, Mrs Bransby. And due to you, I believe. These kitchens are really most interesting. I have volunteered to be the guide down here, if Cherry will trust me with that task, when she is open. During the quiet times I will enjoy looking at the brickwork.'

'I'm afraid the detail is obscured by the centuries of whitewash.'

'True, true, but one can see enough, you know, to piece it together in one's mind.'

Susannah Wilmet's appearance was dramatic as usual, and she was looking over the various men in the room with a thirsty aspect. Julia found it hard to gain her attention.

'How is your programme for the concert going? Do tell me what you are going to wear?' she said, knowing either subject

159

was almost guaranteed, with Susannah, to prevail over the interests of sex.

'Brahms', said Susannah, fixing her with a glowing glance, 'is *neglected* these days. I intend to resurrect him.'

'I didn't know he wrote much piano music.'

Susannah snorted, indicating that what Julia knew about music could be written on the back of a postage stamp.

'And as for *wearing*,' Susannah went on, 'that little dressmaker you told me of is *creating* something for me in black lace. Over black taffeta. Very *flowing*. I had thought of *scarlet*,' she went on dreamily, 'but *black* has always been my colour.'

'It will be magnificent,' said Julia, thinking that there were times when Susannah was distinctly not safe to be near. All that emotional energy. With a parting smile, she moved on to Gawain Lloyd. 'Can I tempt you to another sausage roll?' she asked him.

'You could tempt me to anything, my dear,' he responded gallantly, and took one. 'Though, really, I am gaining the avoirdupois.' He patted his midriff, which had certainly expanded over the years.

'I hope you will advise Cherry on the legal aspect of opening one's home,' Julia said earnestly. 'Didn't I hear that you trained as a solicitor?'

He smiled in reply. 'However did you hear that? In the end it wasn't my career, as you know. I have advised her – she must look into the insurance position before the opening. I'm inclined to believe that she has hardly any. Incidentally, thank you, my dear, for the return of the overalls. They have not been so clean for ages, and you certainly put them to good use down here.'

'One advantage of whitewash over plastic emulsion', said Julia, 'is that it does come off when one washes clothes. You like the result, then?'

'It is very good. You can come and slosh paint around in our flat any time you like.'

She turned smilingly away from him and reflected on his suitability for the role of murderer. It seemed at that moment impossible that any of these pleasant, cultured people would be capable of a crime so gross, so uncontrolled. She carried her plate of sausage rolls onward to Ms Haygreen and Ms Hodson.

The two ladies were obviously good friends this evening. Ms

160

Hodson, startling in trousers and top of brilliant emerald, had newly dyed her hair to match and combed it into a pale green aureole around her head. Ms Haygreen had put her short and stalwart person into Bermuda shorts of homespun linen and a shirt of tie-dyed silk she had coloured herself in her Burco boiler and cut out and stitched on her dining table. The result was interesting and harmonious – in fact the shirt was beautiful. Julia asked her what dyes she had used and they had an animated conversation to which Ms Hodson stood aloof. She was herself more interested in Fine Art, as she explained when there was a gap in the conversation, than the Crafts, although the Crafts had their own interest, of course she could see that.

'Your pressed flowers, though, Ms Hodson, are they not craft rather than art?' asked Julia.

'My dear, haven't I asked you many times to call me Vernal? You know I can't call you Julia if you insist on being so formal with me. And the only craft involved in my flowers is the actual pressing. Once they are pressed they become as paints, and one paints a picture with them, do you not agree?'

Julia smiled and let it pass. Could either Ms Haygreen or Ms Hodson have committed murder? She had seen them very heated indeed, when they had fallen out with one another. Tonight their tempers were well under control or she herself would never have got away with suggesting that Ms Hodson's pressed flowers partook somewhat of the tincture of craft. On some days she would have been metaphorically annihilated for such a sugges-tion. And as for calling her Vernal, there were often times when one would not dare call her any such thing.

Ms Haygreen was always easier, as it behoved a mere prac-titioner of the crafts to be, but even so one did not always dare to address her as Whimsey, the unfortunate name given her by her parents. Before she escaped back to the table to refill her plate of sausage rolls, Julia learned that Ms Hodson was to be the guide in the drawing room – 'I shall stand near that lovely painting, my dear' – and Ms Haygreen in the dining room, where she would be able to discuss the beautiful carving on the William and Mary walnut chairs with the passing crowd of visitors.

Julia passed Adam, who was circulating with a large Thermos full of coffee, filling up the cups, and they winked at one another.

'Found the murderer, yet, Mum?' he whispered in her ear.

'Shush!' she reproved him. 'I can't believe it of any of them. It's out of the question.'

13

The team of detectives was studying the occupants of the Dutch House from a more practical aspect, money, with the possibility of blackmail in their minds.

They had established that Mr Markhall had been well pensioned off by his firm after the scandal, and lived frugally. There seemed little reason to consider him as murderer, apart from propinquity, and being – as far as was known – the last to see Mrs Honor.

'Julia Bransby,' Bob Southwell said. 'As you know she is my wife's friend. When her husband died there was a good insurance, a pension, and she became owner of her house – one of those mortgage protection policies.'

'Worth killing the husband for?' speculated DS Birch.

'He died of TB,' Bob explained. 'Anyway, she sold their house and bought the flat outright. There was money to invest and to top it up she developed her design and conservation business.'

'Another one with no apparent motive, except propinquity again,' said DS Birch.

'We aren't excluding anyone at all, yet, are we? Friend or no friend,' said Bob.

'What about the two ladies on the top floor?'

'It is odd about them. You haven't turned much up, have you, constable?'

The raw new detective constable who had been given the job swallowed nervously and said that he hadn't. There had been a little in the newspapers, various activities they had been involved in, but nothing before they came to the Dutch House, at the time that Ms Joan Hodson took up her teaching post. Ms Jean Haygreen had begun her job a little later. He had contacted the colleges they were said to have attended, without result, no students of those names were on the records.

'I could hardly approach the places they teach and ask for their CVs,' he said, 'and they weren't asked about their backgrounds in our interviews.'

'We could ask them now,' said DS Birch, 'but they are hardly under suspicion.'

'Why not?' asked Dave Smart diffidently. 'There was that young man seen going up the stairs . . .'

'More likely going to the doctor's flat.'

'We can't take anyone out of the frame.'

'Anyway, the ladies should both be earning reasonable salaries, there shouldn't be a money problem.'

Bob suddenly remembered something. He remembered picking up a book – a big, heavy, beautifully produced old book, from Julia Bransby's coffee table. She said Ms Haygreen had lent it to her, but that wasn't the name inside. For that matter, he wasn't sure about their Christian names. Looking at the notes in front of the group of police, he saw that they had given their names as Ms Joan W. Haygreen and Ms Jean V. Hodson. He struggled to recall the name written on the flyleaf of the book on *Opus Anglicanum*. 'She must have bought it second-hand,' Julia had said, but that was an assumption. Hydebound! That was it. W. Hydebound.

'Smith,' he said, 'go out, now, never mind the York Reference Library's own newspaper index, ask them for the index to *The Times*. See if you can find any mention of this name,' and he wrote it down on a scrap of paper. 'Be quick.'

'What about Miss Ducket-Penrose?' asked DS Birch.

'I would be very surprised if she was involved,' said Bob. 'But of course, one never knows. I hear that she lives on a trust fund her grandfather left her. It is not enough to keep up a historic building. That is why she has leased the lesser parts to the housing association and why she wants to open the main house to the public.'

'Mrs Robinson seems to be in the clear. Her husband was a prosperous and well-known businessman in spite of a reputation for being henpecked. On retirement he sold out his partnership in a firm of insurance brokers and the family retired to York with a substantial sum to invest as well as his considerable pension. He died of perfectly natural causes and since then his widow appears to have lived within her means. As for Doctor Bright, wasn't he at a lecture that night?'

'So he said. But surely, a doctor . . .'

'They sold a big valuable York centre house when he retired from practice, and he does locums. His wife's lifestyle seems to be expensive. I think we ought to investigate further, specifically into his wife's affairs. Is there anyone who knew her when she was living all the time in York? This flipping to and fro from the Continent could bear examination.'

'What about that gardener chappie?' someone asked.

'Mr Spicer has a pension and lives on that, his flat is provided by Miss Ducket-Penrose in return for his gardening and odd-jobbing. He has no bank account and probably keeps his money under the mattress. As far as we can trace, he's never been in debt, likewise never in funds. And if there's one characteristic we are looking for, it is large, sporadic amounts of money.' Bob Southwell was quite positive about that.

'We haven't much about the Lloyd brothers and Miss Wilmet,' said Dave Smart.

'Ah, but we have something,' put in DS Birch. 'Here in the notes. The Lloyds went bankrupt. Now do the other tenants know that? I doubt it. If we are thinking about blackmail . . . and what about Miss Wilmet . . .'

Probably all the men in the force who had contacted Susannah Wilmet had been having daydreams in which she figured, scantily dressed. One smouldering glance was enough to launch a fleet of fantasies.

'She seems to have been taken up, befriended, by Mrs Honor in a big way. Where's the motive?'

'If we knew the motive we'd know the criminal,' said someone, stating the obvious.

'This investigation in depth into the residents seems to be yielding food for thought,' said DS Birch. 'Carry on with it, Mr Southwell.'

Tom Churchyard and Julia had confined themselves to telephone calls during that week. Every night Julia had unplugged the sitting-room telephone, plugged it in at her bedside, taken the cordless phone as well, and enjoyed a whispered conversation with Tom without worrying that Adam might overhear. Now the weekend was coming they wanted to be together but Tom had to work. He was in charge of a big duct-laying project down a major access road involving the construction of a number of new joint boxes and the traffic disruption was going to be horrendous. He would be on site from dawn to dusk.

'It can't be helped,' Julia reassured him. She thought he would have preferred her to fuss. Men didn't really appreciate reasonable women. Of course she was longing to see him. She was still glowing as a result of the previous weekend. But her success at the Dutch House was also important to her and she was anxious to organize the drawing room.

While the room was empty, Mrs Robinson had swept down the ceiling and walls with soft brushes and dusters, much to Julia's astonishment. The broken ankle seemed to be holding up amazingly well under the strain of constantly climbing stepladders. The wooden floor had been cleaned professionally and the edges polished. When the carpet returned from cleaning on the Thursday, the men laid it in its previous position. Now Julia spent Saturday morning, with a little help from her friends, in carrying downstairs the drawing-room furnishings. The last things she had taken up were the painted chairs and matching occasional furniture, which were of a different style to the heavy mahogany pieces. She stood them around in the positions she had marked on a rough plan of the room. She was bending over one of the chairs checking the condition of its silk-upholstered seat when the pleasant tenor voice of Taffinder Walker came from behind to startle her.

'You have wrought a transformation,' he said in a tone of warm praise.

Julia jumped and turned round. 'I didn't hear you come in,' she said defensively. He might have been in the Lake District at the time of the murder but she refused to be won over by Taff Walker's charm. In her mind he was still chief suspect.

'Miss Ducket-Penrose let me in and told me that you were so busy she daren't disturb you. She is putting on the kettle for a cup of coffee.'

'That will be very nice.' Julia realized how dry her throat had become. Before she brought each piece of furniture downstairs she had gone over it with a duster and used her small hand-vacuum on the stronger upholstery, but much of the dust seemed to have flown upwards and been breathed in. Or was her difficulty in speaking ... because she found this man attractive? It made her feel despicable even to consider such a thing, when she was in love with Tom.

She stood and looked round the room, which was still very bare. The carpet had come up beautifully. It was now cream with delicate wreaths of flowers in pastel shades. The wooden boards of the surround were lighter in colour than they had been, waxed and gleaming. The curtains were still down from the windows, which Mr Spicer had been washing that morning both inside and out. The whole room was full of sunshine. Mrs Robinson had washed the fire surround of coloured marbles. She had used a mild cream abrasive on parts of it, and steel wool on the fender. The painted furniture stood about, sparse, but adding to the feeling of lightness and grace.

'Yes, it's quite charming,' Taff Walker said in a tone of great satisfaction. 'What a pity you have to put the rest of the stuff back in. But inevitable, of course.'

Julia felt as though scales had dropped from her eyes. She had been concentrating so hard on what she was doing that she had not taken time to realize the effect created.

'I only wish I knew more about architecture and furniture. Of course one absorbs the general style and so on,' she said. 'I can see what you mean – it does look pretty, and all in keeping. The other furniture is very different in character.'

'But of course.'

'Tell me about the room,' Julia heard herself asking. 'It seems to speak to you, and it doesn't to me.'

'Really?' He gave her an incredulous look, then, seeing that she meant what she was saying, he began, almost dreamily. 'It wouldn't be at all like this when it was first built. The planks of the floor are original but they would be bare. The fireplace would be the same style as the one in Miss Ducket-Penrose's cabinet room.'

'The one with all the little shelves for china?'

'Similar. The furniture would be solid and heavy, covered with marquetry in the Dutch style. The settler families were not short of a bob or two, and they clung to the fashions of their homelands. If there was a carpet it would be a fine quality near-eastern one, covering a table. There would be an early musical

166

instrument, and oil paintings on the walls, portraits, flower pieces, landskips, of the kind popular in the Netherlands in the seventeenth century.'

'Not at all like this,' Julia objected.

'No. It probably stayed in that first state for a century or two, until a new bride entering the family was indulged by a complete revamp of the room.'

'And then?'

'Then it probably looked much as it does at the moment. The fireplace is in keeping. The curtains would be yellow silk.'

'As they still are, what's left of them,' said Julia.

Taff Walker nodded, and went on, 'The carpet is of course an Aubusson. The graceful painted furniture would stand a long way apart much as it does at the moment. All was lightness, gaiety, grace and charm. There may have been an early piano. Delicate embroidery would be carried out in this room. Pretty, trivial songs would be sung. Small handmade books with elegant letterpress would be read aloud.'

'The curtains are dropping to pieces,' Julia said. 'I wish I could envisage the room's various stages as you do.'

Taff Walker threw her a humorous glance from the corner of his eye. 'It changed again, of course,' he went on. 'Not a complete revamp but a gradual accretion of fashionable items as one decade succeeded another. A great heavy elaborate harp. A prie-dieu embroidered in beads by one of the ladies. Several pairs of footstools, similarly embroidered. Large heavy brass fire irons in quantity, in addition to that graceful polished steel fender. A dozen or so small tables, intricately made and increasingly heavy in wood and outline, all for different purposes. A bearskin rug or two. The delicate watercolours were no doubt moved to the bedrooms and replaced by heavy gilt frames round meaningless dark paintings. A few great mahogany Chesterfields, *chaise-longues* and armchairs. As you found it.'

'You make me feel sorry that it can't be left as it is now.'

Julia hardly got out the words before Cherry's head appeared round the door and she invited them to take coffee with her. After a glance round, she added critically, 'Cold and bare, isn't it?'

'Nothing can be cold on a day like today, Cherry.'

'I must say the carpet has come up very well,' her hostess replied. 'I had no idea it was so pretty. You make me feel you were right, Julia – at least to a certain extent,' she added.

'How much more do you propose to do?' asked Taff Walker, when they were seated.

'Very little. The hall floor, that's the last. And dusting down the rest of the cobwebs. Miss Ducket-Penrose is opening in a week.'

'Don't forget,' Taff said caressingly to Cherry Ducket-Penrose, 'whatever I can do, whatever information I can give, you have only to ask.'

'We ought to compile some notes for the guides, and perhaps an information sheet for the visitors,' Julia cut in quickly.

'I'll do that,' said Cherry, her cigarette waggling and dropping its load of ash onto her bosom.

'I would be delighted to help.' Taff Walker smiled at Cherry with such charm that Julia hoped he would choke on it.

She finished bringing down the furniture later that morning. Against her will, she accepted Taff Walker's help in carrying the large heavy pieces. It saved her going to fetch Adam. Mr Spicer helped too, and Cherry and Mrs Robinson.

Julia agreed that it was a pity that the elegant room they had known briefly was submerged under the tide of later additions, but that is the way old houses are. Stripping away accretions often produced an unreal perfection, whereas the clutter at least gave the feeling of growth through the generations.

Once the heavy pieces were in place she told the antique dealer that they could manage without him. When he had left she knew that she had been cold to the point of rudeness, but it was too late then.

'I see you've finished,' shouted Cherry over the noise of Julia's vacuum cleaner, 'except for the curtains.'

It had been decided that on the evening of their first open day they would have a wine and cheese party in the drawing room so that all the residents had a chance to enjoy it.

'Should I organize the wine and cheese?' asked Mrs Robinson.

'They'd better eat in the dining room.' Cherry was looking at the carpet.

'We certainly don't want them spilling wine in here. They

168

could sit around here afterwards and listen to music. Should we ask Susannah Wilmet to bring equipment and discs over?'

'Dare we? Will you ask or shall I, Julia?'

'It would come better from you.'

'That girl!' said Mrs Robinson. 'I can't bear her!'

The room looked a different place, even though the gilded cornice was still crumbling away, the paintings were obscured by a century of tobacco and coal smoke, the embroideries were filthy and the curtains were dropping to bits. It was no use even thinking about mending them, it would take months, and not worth doing anyway. Julia had fetched them and was now teetering about on top of the step-ladder putting them up, ignoring the scraps of yellow silk which dropped to the floor like celestial scurf.

'Don't you want any lunch today?' asked Adam indignantly from the doorway.

'Have you prepared some? I didn't realize. Sorry. I'll be along in just a minute.'

'Let me help.'

'No, dear, you're all right. I've got the hang of it, I'm into a rhythm with these curtains. There's only one more set to do.'

'Don't be long,' said Adam, and departed.

There was no doubt that Julia was pleased with herself. She took a last look from the doorway and patted herself on the back.

She remembered how pleasant the kitchens looked. Glancing over now to the head of the basement stairs, she saw, looking at her with a grimly glare, the stag's head with its great crown of antlers, each sporting its own long tattered flag of filthy cobweb. Oh no! Julia thought to herself, making a quick exit through the front door. It's a task which will never, ever, be finished. I'll be on with it for the rest of my days. However much is done, there will always be something overlooked, something else mouldering away.

It was that afternoon that Tom phoned to say that he was taking a couple of hours off.

'Will you come and have a cup of tea with me?' he asked. 'I'd like you to see my house. You've never been there. But – darling

– a fine warm day like this the Southwells will be in their garden. Bob said he was going to cut the front hedge if he could get away from the police station for a bit. It might be silly but if they see us arriving together they will expect to be asked to join us and I want you to myself. I'm coming home in one of our British Telecom vans. Will you be near the end of my road, hop in the back, and not mind the secrecy too much?'

'Of course, Tom, you idiot,' replied his ladylove.

Bob Southwell was cutting his front hedge. He was also turning over in his mind the extra information he had been trying to absorb about antiques. He knew quite a reasonable amount about silver, it was something he longed to collect, but there seemed to be an awful lot still to learn about furniture and china – different woods, carpentry techniques, the composition, glazing, and marking of ceramics ... That British Telecom van was Tom, wasn't it? Bob waved and shouted hello.

'Hi,' Tom shouted back. 'No time to stop. Just home for a quick sandwich.'

'Have some tea with us,' invited Bob Southwell.

'Thanks, but I won't today. See you soon.' The van went on into Tom's own drive and, once hidden from his neighbours, he opened the back to let Julia out.

'This is really ridiculous,' she said, only half laughing. 'Does it matter if the Southwells know or not? They're friends after all. Anyone would think we were married to other people and having an illicit affair.'

'I know I'm being over-sensitive,' Tom answered.

Once inside, Julia asked, 'Are you really going to eat a sandwich?'

'More interesting things to do,' he answered, taking her in his arms. 'What do you think to this little hall? The carpet is nice, isn't it. It matches the colour of the kitchen floor.'

'Very nice,' she murmured against his shoulder.

'Let's go upstairs.'

Once upstairs they ran into difficulties. In the large front bedroom ('Do you like the wallpaper?' Tom asked Julia) they would be very obvious if Bob happened to look up from his hedge-clipping. In the back bedroom they could see Susan and

170

Paul arguing, one on either side of their tent on the back lawn, and Linda swinging and reading on her new garden seat. Although the canopy shielded them from her view, Tom drew back nervously from the window.

'We could close the curtains,' suggested Julia.

'They would wonder what on earth was the matter.'

They edged back into the privacy of the landing and Tom closed all the doors which opened off it.

'This is ridiculous,' Julia said softly, but that was before the two of them discovered that it was possible to make passionate love on a landing measuring eight feet by two feet six inches, and be quite deliriously happy.

Bob Southwell returned to the police station refreshed after his short session at home doing physical work. That was the trouble with police careers these days, they were too desk bound, all paperwork. There were times when he could almost wish for the feel of pavements under big boots again. And there were many times when he didn't. He knew he would miss the intellectual stimulation – when it came – the battle to outwit the criminal with brains, not brawn.

They knew now from their contacts with Interpol and the specialists in the police forces of other countries that regular consignments of antiques arrived in France, usually Normandy, by an unknown method, which they thought might be a private aircraft touching down secretly at disused airfields. There had been no reports of such a plane landing at Elvington, but that did not mean that it had not happened. Probably the gang involved used different airfields at different times. No doubt by the time the burglaries were reported to the police the stolen goods were already in the air and on their way.

Southwell felt more and more sure that the key to the puzzle was in the Dutch House, but although some of the residents could be eliminated from the list of suspects, there were too many still under suspicion. He wondered what new checks he could do to narrow the field.

Bob Southwell thought with pleasure about Ms Haygreen and Ms Hodson. One heard of such delightful and eccentric ladies but to meet these two had illumined his last weeks. The two

171

ladies would probably have the expertise to deal in antiques, but he doubted if they would have the interest. Creative spirits were usually too busy creating to think of making wealth in other ways, apart from artist forgers . . . He considered the matter. Did Ms Hodson receive stolen paintings and paint over them, so that they could be taken out of the country without suspicion? He doubted it. She prized her own work too highly. She might paint over a priceless work of art, but as for having her own painting cleaned off later – no, he was sure she would never consider that.

Ms Haygreen's textiles were good, she ought to make money from them if she made something saleable like scarves, but instead she created her memorable shirts which probably took her too many hours to be profitable.

His mind moved on to busy Dr Bright, whose wife, living amicably apart, went abroad for parts of every year. She was said to winter on the Continent for the sake of her health. Elderly and fragile, he had gathered. Anyway, doctors tended to save life rather than take it.

The police station was quiet that afternoon. Bob, leaning back on his chair and digging its rear legs into the thermo-plastic tiles on the floor to make two more deep marks, was able to relax and think over the case. Lines of inquiry were bringing results. Threads of thought could travel in directions previously barred by lack of knowledge. It would only need a little, a very little more to connect up a few of the stray ideas he had, connect them up and knot them.

Some of the evidence arrived on his desk before his thoughts had progressed any further.

Joan Whimsey Hydebound had stood trial for the murder of her husband and been acquitted. Her cousin, Jean Vernal Harris, had likewise been acquitted of being an accessory.

14

Terry Diamond arrived back from the Lake District and points north, south and east thereof, with piles of witness statements from the members of the Art and Antiques course and the staff of the hotel where it was held.

'Results in a nutshell, then, Terry?' asked Bob Southwell.

'Duncan, at least, could have driven back to York at the relevant time and taken part in the burglary and murder,' said Diamond.

'Not Walker?'

'No. It really does look as if he's in the clear, sir. The hotel kept the bar open late, they had applied for an extension. Walker was in the bar each night to the bitter end. Not drunk, doing more talking than drinking, but he was certainly there. The members of the course were queuing up to talk to him. They kept it up every night until twelve o'clock, then a group of them would adjourn to one of the bedrooms to carry on the discussions, or parties which is what they became. He has half a dozen people to vouch for him up to two in the morning on all three nights. I would have been worn out, myself, when you think he was lecturing off and on all day as well.'

'He says he enjoys these weekends,' said Bob thoughtfully.

'I don't suppose he buys any of the booze himself.'

'No, I don't suppose he does. Get back to Duncan Fraser.'

'He slept in the staff annexe, not the main block of the hotel, which is where Walker was. From the annexe it would be much easier to slip out. He didn't socialize with the guests, being only the assistant. His friends were the hotel staff. They have a common-room where they can get together. A fair proportion of the staff are casuals, some of them foreign. Over half of them are female.'

'A good time was had by all?'

'They work long hours and get very tired. I don't think there is much hanky-panky. The point is that although some of them already knew him and are his pals, the staff didn't take as much notice of Duncan as the guests did of Walker. They can vouch for him at various times and he was out with three of them boozing on Thursday, but after half-past nine no one seems to have noticed him. They thought he'd gone off with one of the girls, who all deny it, but they would, wouldn't they? It was his first night there. He says he went to bed early because he was shattered and read a bit before falling asleep. That might be the truth, but there are no witnesses. If the murder was at eleven o'clock he could have been here for it. The roads are quiet at night and I checked out the estate car, it has a heck of a good engine.'

'Would he have done the burglary on his own?' pondered Bob Southwell. 'It has the look of a two-man operation, probably the brains and the brawn. Duncan could certainly have supplied the brawn. If Taff Walker wasn't the brains, then who was? Walker knew exactly what the pickings would be. He might have tipped off someone else.' Returning his thoughts to Diamond, he clapped him on the back and said, 'You seem to have done very well, Terry. Thanks. Get those reports and statements in with the rest of the records, it will take you a couple of days by the look of the pile.'

Meanwhile Ms Haygreen and Ms Hodson – or Hydebound and Harris – were sitting in two separate interview rooms at the police station and waiting to give statements. Bob Southwell intended to keep them waiting as long as he could.

The day after the next was to be the first official Open Day for the Dutch House, from two o'clock to five.

Returning that morning from a shopping expedition into the centre of York, Julia rode her moped back along Bootham and out towards Clifton. As she drew level with the pleasant open space of Clifton Green she saw an incredible figure marching across the grass. Cherry Adelaide Honoria Ducket-Penrose, still in her wide-brimmed garden hat and with her cigarette waggling on her bottom lip, was wearing a sandwich board which proclaimed in large letters 'Tea and Cakes on sale Saturday afternoon at the Dutch House, price £1.50'.

Julia stopped so quickly that the car behind almost ran into her. She pulled her moped onto the fringe of grass at the side, between road and low white railings, jumped over the railings and confronted Cherry with an appalled look and the words, 'Cherry, whatever will you do next?'

Cherry was remarkably pleased with herself. 'They're rather good, aren't they?' She indicated the two boards. Walking round

174

her, Julia could see that the one at the back said the same thing. 'Adam has improved since he did me the sign, don't you think?'

'I might have known', said Julia, 'that if you had a hare-brained scheme my son would be mixed up in it. Must you really make a spectacle of yourself, Cherry, my dear?'

'One has to go in for self-promotion these days,' Cherry answered. 'There's a lovely bus queue over there. I'm going to walk past them, slowly.'

Leaving the green by the gap in the railings near the little brick building which had once been a booster station and was now a public convenience, she walked to the crossing then, although it was at red, she set off across the main road regardless of the traffic, which fortunately pulled up in astonishment, the drivers craning their necks to read the wording on the sandwich boards.

As Cherry reached the bus queue and began to walk by it, people asked her questions and Julia could see their heads turning as they glanced in the direction of the Dutch House. Then Cherry moved off towards the town centre and Julia, groaning aloud, went back to her moped and decided that she had better go home as quickly as possible.

She didn't say a thing to Adam. There didn't seem much point. He was obviously bursting with something to say to her.

'Mum, there's another concert me and Pete want to go to. Will you be all right on your own here tonight?'

'This is short notice, isn't it?'

'Yes,' said Adam.

'Will you be back to help with the opening tomorrow?'

'Yes, of course I will. Pete's dad says he'll take us again. It's going to be great.' Adam enlarged on the terrificness of the groups who would be playing, their extraterrestrial qualities – they were, apparently, spaced out and far gone.

'You go, dear. Blue Moon isn't much trouble now.'

'As long as you'll be all right.'

'I think I'm big enough to take care of myself,' said Julia.

As soon as Adam was out of the way, attired in the special gear he kept for these occasions, Julia went to phone Tom Churchyard, who was using a mobile while he supervised the duct-laying job, and asked him if he would like to come over that evening and spend the night.

175

'There's a free and easy invitation for you,' she teased.

'Try to stop me,' he said.

Bob Southwell took the interrogation of Ms Haygreen (or Hyde-bound) on himself, and delegated Ms Hodson (or Harris) to Dave Smart.

'You haven't been altogether frank with us, have you, Mrs Hydebound?' he asked.

She flinched and said, 'I don't know what you mean. My name is Haygreen.'

'Originally I think it was Hydebound, and you have a previous acquaintanceship with the police.'

She said nothing.

Bob took out of a folder the photocopies of the newspaper account of the trial. 'Familiar to you?' he asked, spreading them before her.

'I was judged innocent,' she said. 'You have no right to rake up these things.'

'You admit that you are Whimsey Hydebound, accused of murdering your husband?'

'I repeat, I was acquitted.'

'You have now been in the same place as a second murder?'

'My husband was not murdered,' Whimsey Haygreen said firmly, although her eyes filled with tears.

'Tell me your side of it, then,' said Bob, sitting back and fixing her with a gimlet stare.

'If you have read the reports you know that we were moun-taineering, myself, my cousin, and my husband. He was a heavy drinker and although he had been a first-class rock-climber he had grown careless and was no longer in charge of his temper. I was seen by a fellow-climber through binoculars; she thought I pushed James over the edge. She was mistaken. I reached out to adjust the belt which he had not fastened properly, but before my hands touched him he lurched forward into space.'

'On the night of Mrs Honor's murder,' Bob changed tack, 'a young man was seen mounting the stairs to your flat. Or, of course, your cousin's flat. What can you tell me about that?'

Whimsey Haygreen winced, but she had no alternative but to tell the truth.

'I had two children,' she said quietly. 'A son and a daughter. My daughter chose to believe that I was guilty. She has never spoken to me or contacted me since the trial. I feel that I have no daughter. My son believed me innocent, but he does not care to acknowledge me publicly. In other words, he keeps it quiet that I am his mother. He lives in New York. Now and then he comes to England on business, and when he does he tries to visit me. These visits mean a great deal to me as you can imagine. He came on the night Mrs Honor was murdered. The two facts are not connected. When he calls, he usually takes back with him a shirt-style blouse or two, for sale in a very exclusive New York shop. That's all.'

Dave Smart gained roughly the same information from Vernal Hodson.

They let the two women go home.

'Do you believe they are innocent?' asked Dave.

'I don't know. Do you mean of the original murder, or Mrs Honor's?'

'Either.'

'Who can say?' said Bob Southwell gloomily. 'You would see that according to the newspaper reports, Ms Haygreen had suffered years of mental and physical abuse. Her cousin is said to have helped her get rid of a brute of a man. They wouldn't want their new life ruining. If anyone had got hold of the facts and threatened to publicize them they might have been tempted to take drastic action.'

He could not help remembering how Whimsey's eyes had filled with tears but she had still faced him, doggedly, proclaiming her innocence. If the trial had been today instead of all those years ago, the women's rights movement would have been campaigning for her release, saying that she was right to kill him – if she had.

'I don't know, Dave. We must just bear these facts in mind. She has been judged already.'

When Tom arrived at Julia's door that evening he was in the state of heightened consciousness when one is unnaturally aware of everything. It was to be the first time he had been inside the flat. There was no longer a constable on duty outside Mrs

Honor's front door, so Tom was alone in the entrance area as he rang Julia's bell. He stood looking sideways through the glass exit door which led from the hallway onto the long vista of grass stretching to the group of old silver birches which, for once, were still in the breathless summer heat.

'Come in, Tom.' Julia opened her door and reached up to kiss him. He put his arms round her, returned the kiss, and glanced warily about her tiny hall.

'There's nobody here but us chickens.'

'That's nice.'

'Would you like a drink before dinner?'

'Very much.'

He followed her into the living room, where Blue Moon came over to inspect his trousers, and gave him grudging approval. They sat one on either side of the open patio door in the relaxed holiday atmosphere which comes sometimes in the unaccustomed heat of summer evenings. There was the sound of insects, which Tom did not remember noticing for years. A distant pigeon cooed. Some way off a neighbour's radio played softly. The drink in their tall glasses was partly fresh orange juice and partly spirit, decorated with leaves of mint and cubes of ice. The silence between them was so full of content it seemed a pity to break it.

'Everything's ready to eat,' Julia murmured at last. 'When you're ready.'

'Whenever you like.'

As she went through into the kitchen, Tom looked round the living room. There were fresh flowers in a lustre pot. The bookcases were long and low and pictures hung above them, a mixture of pen and ink sketches and collage or embroidery pictures. Near one armchair stood a floor-frame for embroidery with a piece of linen stretched across it and a needle stuck in the border. The floor and walls were of soft pale neutral tones, but there were many spots of bright colour from fabrics and books. Adam's possessions blended in, his row of tapes and his ghetto blaster on top of a bookcase, his academic books in one set of shelves, a stoneware pot holding a selection of pens on a small table.

Tom followed Julia into the dining and kitchen areas, which were continuous, but Julia had produced a different effect in each. At the dining end stood a Victorian oval mahogany table with chairs of the same period. The wide-open window allowed them to look out towards the graceful trees. They seemed to be eating in the open air. At the other end – where Julia had produced food as if she were a conjuror bringing rabbits out from a hat – there were the normal kinds of kitchen units and cupboards, plus fridge, cooker and washer.

There was a graciousness about it all which struck Tom particularly. That and the consciousness of design. Each glass or plate or chair had been carefully considered and chosen and while the flat was informal and homelike it was also a feast for an educated eye.

They took their time over the meal.

At last, after they had washed up together, Julia took Blue Moon onto the grass for a few minutes, then closed the windows and locked the front door. They stood in one another's arms for a long embrace before showering under cool water and getting into bed . . .

A couple of hours later they began to find the disadvantages of the heat because their skins were sticking together. They pulled apart, laughing, and lay looking at one another from opposite sides of the bed, touching only with their hands. Then Julia pulled the thin cotton sheet up over them.

They alternately drowsed and made love through the summer night, and in the morning Julia was awake first and showered and dressed while Tom was still asleep. Knowing he had to be at work early, she woke him with a mug of coffee, to a mood of such contentment as he never remembered feeling before. With a swift kiss she left him in peace to drink the coffee, after he had assured her that he would love bacon and eggs.

Propped up on all the pillows he could find, Tom lay at ease and contemplated the room. It was, above all, tranquil. The walls and ceiling were white and the carpet was pale grey – her favourite colours for clothes. The furniture looked as if it had been made specially by a modern designer and was stained black. It was all long and low. There was a white-painted fitted wardrobe taking up the whole of one wall. All this was very simple in effect although he was sure it had been expensive.

The thing though that made all the difference to the room was a very big panel of embroidery on the wall opposite, so that Tom lay looking at it, drowning in its colours. He decided at last that it was three panels, not one, hanging to touch one another. The fabrics of which it was made were blues and greens, the most subtle, silvery shades and tints of each, blending and seeming to change with the light or the angle. The three panels together made a long horizontal shape and he wondered if they represented the sea.

They ate a happy breakfast, but the whole time had been one of deep pleasure in one another's company. It was when Tom was leaning back and looking at Julia over the remains of the toast that he said, 'Do you think we could get married, darling?'

'We could, if we wanted to,' and she laughed happily and low.

'Where would we live?' he asked seriously. 'My house or here? Do you remember what my house is like? You've only been in it briefly.'

'I remember your landing carpet pretty well.'

'There wouldn't be room for me in this flat as well as you and Adam.'

'No, there wouldn't.' Julia thought about Tom's house in Ouse Avenue, and knew very certainly that nothing would drag her to live there. She couldn't imagine Adam and herself sharing that house with Tom, and it was no use, Adam would be with her for another year at least and for holidays after that. Her home was Adam's until he married, or set up on his own.

'I don't think I could live here,' Tom said, 'even if it were bigger.'

'There wouldn't be any hurry to settle that, would there?' asked Julia.

'We aren't getting any younger,' said Tom, and arrived at the nitty gritty without warning. 'If we wanted to have children I suppose we'd have to have them fairly soon.'

Julia looked across at him and for the moment was frozen with shock. Children! She was nearly thirty-nine. If he wanted children and they were to marry, she would have to have them straight away – because he had said children, not a child. She was absolutely certain that he had not meant to be cruel. He looked so blissfully happy. Obviously his vision of heaven would be her in Ouse Avenue in an apron with a baby in a pram and a toddler at her feet. She couldn't think of anything she wanted less. Ten years ago, with Tom whom she loved, it might have been an attractive idea, but not now. She was sure he had not realized what a blow his remark had been. The difference in their ages had been something to be ignored, even laughed at, but when the biological clock came into question, the stark fact was that for a woman childbearing was for a limited period and hers was nearing its end, while he could be a father any time in the next fifty years if luck was with him.

Was it unfair of nature? No, Julia was more inclined to think it a blessed release for women. For a few years they could have fun without dreading the consequences.

Tom, wrapped in his daydream, took a while to notice that she was no longer as happy as he was. 'What's the matter?' he asked at last, taking her hand and stroking it gently.

'You gave me a shock, Tom, talking about children. Are you very keen on them?'

'Oh yes,' he replied without thinking. 'I'd love children. Two at least.'

'But it's different for me, you see. I don't think I could face having another family now.'

Tom's face dropped, as hers had done earlier. No children! The joy of being married to Julia, and that would be great, but no children!

She decided there was no point in beating about the bush. 'And I don't think I'd want to live in Ouse Avenue, either.'

'You didn't like it?'

'Of course I like it, but I don't want to live there myself.'

'We could sell both places and buy a bigger one to share,' Tom said slowly.

'Buy a bigger one to not have children in?'

'We'll have to think it all over,' said Tom. After a silence, he said, 'Can we shelve it for now and enjoy this heavenly morning, what's left of it, because I must be on site in twenty minutes?'

Julia cleared the plates and brought over a large cafetière of fresh coffee.

'No matter how hot the weather is, I still need my coffee in the morning,' she said pleasantly, with love in her voice.

It was at that moment that Adam opened the front door with his own key and walked in on the scene. He stood in the doorway and looked at them.

181

'Darling!' cried Julia. 'I thought you were coming back tonight!'

'I can see that,' said Adam.

'You haven't met Tom, have you?'

Tom rose to his feet and offered his hand. 'Morning, Adam,' he said.

Adam took the hand warily, but there wasn't anything else he could do.

'Coffee, dear? Have you had breakfast?' Julia thought she probably sounded just like a mother hen but she couldn't help it.

'I'd like some coffee and I've had breakfast at Pete's.'

'What happened?'

'The concert was cancelled, wasn't it?'

'Oh no! What a disappointment. Why?'

'The lead singer was ill and one of the backing groups didn't turn up. They're arranging another concert and everyone is going to get complimentary tickets but we don't think we'll go.'

'It wouldn't be the same, I suppose,' said Tom.

'That's right.'

After a pause, in which Adam drank a very large mugful of coffee, he went on, 'We arrived back in the early hours of the morning and Pete's dad offered me a bed. It seemed sensible to stay there and not wake you up.'

'Thank you, dear, that was very thoughtful,' Julia heard herself saying, and felt the blood run up in a tide under her skin.

'I'd better collect my things,' Tom said, remembering that his razor would still be in the bathroom and his pyjamas dropped on the floor at the side of the bed. He went into the bathroom and bedroom and quickly gathered everything of his together. Julia came in and shut the door.

'It's terribly awkward, isn't it?' she said softly. 'Whatever we do won't be right in this situation.'

Tom could not have agreed more. 'Unfortunately I simply must fly,' he said. 'Can you cope?'

'Somehow,' she said, and kissed him. 'The Dutch House opens tomorrow.'

15

Tom considered.

'There is a Vintage and Veteran car rally over at Tadcaster this afternoon,' he said. 'If I can get time off work, could we all three go? Adam might find it interesting. It might be easier than if I vanish and we meet again later with this all fresh in our minds.'

'It's worth trying.'

'Put the idea to him. I'll give you a ring as soon as I've had a chance to arrange some leave. I hope that he will come.' With a light kiss on Julia's cheek, Tom left the flat.

Adam agreed to go with them to the Vintage, Veteran and Classic Car Rally. They went in the Rolls. Adam was very quiet and the expedition was not a howling success.

After the car rally, Tom invited them both to have an evening meal with him, suggesting something simple like the Pizza Hut or McDonald's.

'Why, Tom?' she asked him when they had a moment to themselves.

'Don't you feel Adam and I ought to get to know one another better?'

'I suppose so.'

'If I'm going to be his step-father?'

Julia hadn't been able to help it, she had recoiled, then realized why. She didn't want Tom to butt in to the relationship she had with Adam. How ghastly she was being! How mean! How unChristian! After a moment's silence she made herself answer warmly, 'That's a lovely thought of yours, Tom darling.'

Later, Tom and Julia wished that Adam had never been asked. It had not occurred to Julia that her precious son could be sarcastic and offensive, under the veil of the politest manners in the world. Tom was a nice, generous-hearted, intelligent bloke doing a skilled job for which he had trained long and hard. Adam was a sixth-former with more brains than were good for him, Julia decided savagely before the evening was over.

'Can't we all be friends?' she cried, half-way through the meal. 'Adam, do you have to be like this?'

'Like what, Mother?' he asked innocently.

'Let it go, Julia,' put in Tom.

They had walked down to the restaurant through the warm scented evening. As they walked back again Adam stalked ahead, refusing to be associated with the other two.

'It's hopeless,' Julia said. 'I do apologize.'

'It has been a shock for him,' Tom replied. 'Being a teenager is difficult at the best of times. We can all behave badly when our security is threatened.'

'When we're jealous, you mean.'

'That too.'

Tom was holding her arm. If it had not been for Adam, they would have been walking in a golden cloud, divinely happy. As it was, the warmth was still there, but the golden cloud was absent, and neither of them felt anything which could be called happiness.

'We will have a lot worse things to encounter than teenage sulks,' Tom said as they parted.

'If we marry you mean?' Julia almost snapped at him.

'Exactly.'

'You're right, Tom. I'm sorry if I sound cross.'

'It's strain,' he said, lightly stroking her cheek. Both of them felt they had better not kiss. They were standing outside the Dutch House and were not sure where Adam had got to, or who might be listening or looking. 'Poor Mrs Honor's murder makes it all worse. You must be over-wrought about that, even without Adam playing up.'

'Sometimes I think I shall be glad when they find out who did it, then at other times I'm afraid of what or who they might point to.'

'I know what you mean.'

'Will you ring later?' she whispered.

'Yes, love.'

The promised call took place. Julia was snuggled in her bed, whispering with her mouth under the sheet and the earpiece

184

between the side of her head and the pillow. They cooed at one another for a while, then the topic of marriage raised its head again.

'I wouldn't think of asking you to leave your job, or sell your lovely car, or move house,' Julia said, 'but you don't think it strange to ask me to have at least two children, when it would mean a complete change in my life. We fell in love and we're so happy together, but I'm not ready to start another family, and the more I think about it, the more I know I don't want to do it.'

There was silence at the other end of the line, and in a minute she went on again. 'Adam would get over his sulks, but would you two ever really get on? I think it would only be toleration at best.'

Tom for his part was thinking that to a large extent she was right. He loved his job and would hate to have to give it up, and he could see that while she had managed to work as a young widow with a five-year-old, to continue her career with two toddlers and a husband, when she was some twenty years older, would be quite a different matter.

'It isn't that I don't see your point,' he said at last.

'I know we've fallen in love and ending it would be terribly hard for both of us,' Julia whispered on, 'but the more we see of one another and the more deeply involved we are, the worse it will be. For you, Tom, there are other fish in the sea. You're a delightful, attractive man and you need a girl of about twenty-five who wants to settle down, and you'll be so happy together that you'll wonder, if you ever think of me at all, what on earth made you want to marry me.'

Tom was very indignant about this.

'Can't we go back to being friends?' she asked him.

'You ought to know by now that one can't go back. No, it wouldn't work. Every time we met we'd be longing to be in bed together,' he said bluntly. 'Anyway, I'm not giving up as easily as all that. We will talk it over again. I love you, Julia.'

'I love you too, Tom.'

On the morning of the first official open day at the Dutch House Julia was doing some washing. The weather was still so warm that everything was dry almost as soon as she hung it out on her rotary clothes line. When DCI Bob Southwell rang the bell she was about to embark on the ironing.

'Coffee?' she asked him. 'You must forgive the state of the place.'

'Coffee would be fine, thanks.' Bob stood for a few minutes gazing out of the patio door at the trees, thinking how refreshing it was to see the moving leaves. When Julia returned with coffee he sat down to drink it. 'I have had an oversight,' he said. 'Or committed it. Does one have oversights, or commit them?'

'You have made an inadvertent mistake,' said Julia.

'Got it in one.'

'Tell me, then.'

'We asked all the residents here what visitors Mrs Honor had, and you all kindly told us – about visitors from outside. We also asked when you had last seen her, on that Thursday. We have not really ascertained which of you were in the habit of visiting her, or had done so recently.'

'You mean amongst ourselves? Popping to and fro?'

'Exactly.'

'I told you that you would find my fingerprints all over, and Adam's.'

'We did, and some others.'

'Now who else went in to see her? Mrs Robinson was asked from time to time, usually at the same time as Cherry. You didn't pop in unannounced at Mrs Honor's. Not unless you were Adam, or the doctor of course. Mr Markhall up above is not very sociable. He was always grumbling about her climbers, if they grew as far as his balcony he used to snip off the ends and throw them down, she got very irritated about that.'

'And she was at odds with Mr Spicer.'

'Oh yes, she wouldn't have had him in her flat, no way.'

'What about the ladies on the top floor?'

'They didn't have much in common with her. They are always creating new things, she spent her time in the past. From time to time there was formal socializing. I was sometimes invited up there to Ms Haygreen's or Ms Hodson's with Mrs Honor, and if she invited them back I went too. To smooth the occasion.' Julia laughed. 'You didn't know I was such an emollient person, did you?'

'I'm sure you would be good at that sort of socializing.'

'Then our friends over the garages. Lancelot Lloyd did help her with her income tax forms, but I don't know that he saw her at any other time – apart from casual meetings in the garden and so on. Gawain saw more of her because when he went in his car to the supermarket he took her with him.'

'Regularly?'

'Every week. When they came back he always carried her shopping into the flat and in return she offered him a cup of tea. Every Thursday afternoon.'

'Do you mean they did this the day she died?'

'I suppose so. They always did.'

'And no one told us! Not even Adam!'

Julia looked surprised. 'It's such an everyday thing, no one would think about mentioning it.'

'Gawain Lloyd did say he had seen her in the afternoon, but not that it was a regular occurrence, or that he had taken her shopping.'

'You see we do meet all the time.' Julia sounded diffident. 'Take this morning. I've been washing and hanging the things to dry, Adam went across to the newsagents because the paper didn't come, and between us we must have seen nearly all the others. I went to collect Cherry's washing (I've persuaded her to let me dry it during the tourist season), and on the way Mrs Robinson waved to me. Mr Spicer said hello to Adam as he went, because I heard him through my bedroom window while I was stripping the bed, and I saw Doctor Bright go through the hall and out when I was bringing in the milk bottle. He stopped and we had quite a chat. Lance and Gawain walked across the grass and waved, when I was hanging out the clothes. I haven't seen Susannah Wilmet or Mr Markhall but Adam might have.'

'You mentioned earlier that the doctor went in to Mrs Honor's unannounced. Did you mean her GP or Doctor Bright?'

'Well, both.'

'Did she enjoy bad health?'

'For someone her age she was very fit, but she liked a bit of attention from medical men, and she did go on rather about her arthritis and backache. Her GP popped in if she was in pain with the arthritis and Doctor Bright, while he wouldn't attend her formally – that wouldn't be medical etiquette – gave her hints and tips. He is enthusiastic about fish oil at the moment, he's been on at all of us to take it. I know he paid Mrs Honor several visits to talk to her about fish oil.'

'None of you would take much notice of one resident calling on another?'

'I'm afraid we wouldn't. It would be seen, naturally, but not noted – if that makes sense. It was because Adam and I hadn't seen Mrs Honor out that morning with Blue Moon on the grass that we became worried. Normally one of us would glance out of the window and she would be in sight at about eight o'clock. We wouldn't consciously make a note of it, but not having seen her, we became aware that a normal daily event was missing.'

'What were you chatting to Doctor Bright about this morning?' asked Bob.

'Oh!' She paused to consider, then laughed. 'Doctor Bright asked me if I was enjoying organizing the Dutch House, and I said yes. I've longed for years to poke about in Cherry's rooms and now it has been sanctioned and approved. If it has been of benefit to her too, then that's all to the good. No normal woman could walk through the house as it was without wanting to do something about it.'

'Are you suggesting Cherry has a screw loose?' Bob Southwell cocked his head on one side like a bird as he asked her.

'She's one of the sanest people I know. Intelligent, cultured, lovable. It is only that her intelligence doesn't work in the same way as other people's. Is that what is called lateral thinking? And she is not domesticated, there are no two ways about that.'

'Right.' Bob rose to go. 'Thanks. I won't bother questioning anyone else, Julia. I think you've given me what I need.'

'Pleased to be of help.'

Once outside the door, Bob Southwell looked again at the programme he was compiling of Mrs Honor's last day. In the afternoon she went to the supermarket with Gawain Lloyd then gave him a cup of tea. Then Susannah Wilmet came across and they had a cup of tea and cakes out on the patio, with Mr Markhall throwing bits of clematis at them. Then Mrs Honor's hairdresser had arrived so Susannah had gone. The next thing known was that Mr Markhall had heard a row in her flat during the evening and come down to complain about the noise. Later still, Ms Haygreen's son had gone up the stairs as Tom Church-yard was entering to put a letter in at Julia's door, and Tom had been seen by Mr Spicer who came in from the back as Tom was leaving at the front. Later still Julia had gone out to the front to see if she could catch Tom to save her writing her reply, and Mr Markhall had seen her through his bedroom window. At about that time, the burglars had broken in through Mrs Honor's patio window, committed the murder, and of that nobody had heard or seen a thing . . .

Bob was standing outside the Victorian wing, thinking, when he saw Adam returning from a very short walk with the recovering Blue Moon. As he came nearer, Susannah Wilmet came from the garage block and walked to her bicycle which was leaning against the wall. She greeted Adam, who looked both thrilled and embarrassed, but Blue Moon did not seem so enthusiastic. He sat down behind Adam's legs, making himself small and pressing up against Adam's calves. After another word to Adam, Susannah jumped on her bicycle and went off towards town.

'He's still very nervy, isn't he?' Bob remarked about the dog, after saying 'good morning' to Adam.

Adam still had that embarrassed look on his face. 'He's a funny dog,' he answered. 'I don't know what's the matter with him lately. He used to like women better than men.'

Bob showed him the timetable he had compiled.

'Oh, Susannah was leaving then, was she?' asked Adam, pointing to one entry. 'I saw her in the hallway and wasn't sure if she was coming or going. Mrs Honor's door was partly open and Susannah was crouching down outside it, she was fastening her shoelace.'

'We have the evidence of the hairdresser that she left as he arrived. So she didn't walk directly away?'

'I don't suppose she was there more than seconds,' said Adam, wistfully. 'I spoke to her, but she snapped at me, although she is usually friendly, as she was just now. On the whole she seems to prefer older men.'

After closing the door behind Bob Southwell Julia went back to her ironing board with a puzzled expression, but forgot the episode almost at once in thinking about herself and Tom. She pondered the problem again which had arisen – children. If she

189

truly loved Tom – and she was sure that she did – would she feel like this about children? Having Adam had been a sheer joy from the start, in spite of the moments when she was tired of endless nappies or when he was teething and woke her in the night. But to start again at thirty-nine?

She had friends who had postponed the onset of age with a last baby before the menopause. She didn't feel the least desire to upset her life in that way. The more she thought about it the more her resolve hardened. But could she condemn Tom to a childless life? Could she do that to a man who longed for children, who kept posters and childish drawings on his walls left there by the family who had had the house before him? Wasn't it better to break it off before they became more involved?

Before two o'clock Julia was standing in Cherry's bedroom, the second little corner cabinet room. She could supervise all three rooms on that side, because she could see through the open doors into the bathroom and the State Bedroom beyond. There, only a narrow path ran between the piled-up boxes, newspapers and magazines tied into bundles with string.

It was an anxious time. The postcards lay on the desk in the hall, ready to be sold. The tin for the money was modestly hidden in the half-open drawer of the table. A suitable chair, from an upstairs bedroom, stood behind and was occupied by Mrs Robinson in readiness for the invasion, her left hand on the roll of admission tickets. She was wearing a see-through blouse, well frilled.

There was one matter on which Julia had unbounded admiration for and gratitude to Mrs Robinson. On the entrance table and throughout the house were cut flowers, very nicely arranged. They varied from the small, low, scented arrangement next to Mrs Robinson to the great conflagration of bright gladioli on the dining table, which changed the character of that dark and gloomy room completely. In the basement the theme had changed again, and there were moonpennies, stuck into straight-sided milk jugs. There were bunches of fresh herbs in stone jam jars near the great old kitchen ranges, and terracotta pots of cheerful geraniums on the windowsills. Julia thought nothing suited a kitchen windowsill better than a geranium, except for two geraniums.

Near her in this bedroom was a very pleasant simple bowl containing the few sweetpeas which Mrs Robinson had managed to find on the row at the bottom of Cherry Ducket-Penrose's garden.

The front door was open.

The hour of two o'clock approached.

At that moment, Bob Southwell arrived at the Dutch House with Dave Smart, Terry Diamond and four uniformed officers. Of the police, only Bob drove up to the parking area outside the Victorian wing. The uniformed officers parked their cars on the roadside, and came up on foot. Two of them went round to the other side of the flats. Bob and Dave Smart went up the stairs inside the entrance used by Julia. They knocked on the door of a flat above. Terry Diamond was waiting in the hallway below.

'Up here quick, Diamond!' shouted Dave, as the two people they had come to arrest first tried to escape past them and then put up a determined struggle. The uniformed men dashed in through the glass door from the back. Diamond charged up the stairs.

In a couple of minutes it was all over.

Dr Bright, his arms held firmly on each side, was marched down the stairs and out to one of the police cars. Immediately after him, Susannah Wilmet, spitting with fury, was marched out by Dave Smart and Diamond, and put in the other police car.

Bob locked the door of Dr Bright's flat.

'We'll come back later and search this place,' he said to the others when he arrived outside. The detectives climbed back into the cars and went away.

Two o'clock struck on Cherry's grandfather clock and she opened the front door and propped it open with a cast-iron early Victorian door-stop. Apart from Julia in the bedroom and Mrs Robinson in the hall, there was Ms Hodson in the drawing room, Ms Haygreen in the dining room, Mr Markhall in the kitchens,

Mr Spicer in the garden, Adam peripatetic, and Cherry was to supervise the refreshments. Mrs Robinson had baked a batch of buns and cut a load of sandwiches that morning. Three wrought-iron tables had been resurrected from an old barn at the bottom of Cherry's garden and white plastic chairs had been bought as cheaply as possible from the supermarket.

It did not occur to anyone to wonder where Dr Bright and Susannah Wilmet were, as they were not due to arrive until cup-of-tea time when they were to relieve the others in turn, enabling them to have a short break.

The first visitors were a novelty for almost everyone. Adam and Cherry were nonchalant – they had seen visitors before. The very first people were a family group, mother, father, a couple of grandparents and two children, altogether very symmetrical, and so pleasant and clean and tidy that Julia, usually considered the neatest of women, felt untidy beside them. Because all the doors were open, she could hear them enter at the front, buy their tickets, and go into the drawing room, where Ms Hodson awaited them. Then through the connecting door into the cabinet room where Cherry ate and lived. From there across the short corridor which led to the garden, and into the dining room. Past the foot of the stairs and the head of the flight down to the kitchen, then through the connecting door on Julia's right, across the small room she was in, across the bathroom, through the State Bedroom, and back into the hall before going on, if they wished, into the gardens or down into the kitchens.

As they came through the bedroom each one of the party nodded politely to Julia. The mother remarked that it was a nice day for it, and the grandmother asked if anyone slept in this room nowadays. Then they progressed into the bathroom, and exclaimed how rare it was to see a bathroom in an open house, and one of the children pulled at the wicker chair and revealed the loo, at which everyone laughed and the chair was hastily put back again.

Next they went into the State Bedroom. Cherry had pinned hand-written notices on all the doors and Julia had felt at the time that it was a mistake, particularly this notice, which said THE STATE BEDROOM. She was convinced of its being a mistake when she heard the visitors laugh about it, the grandmother saying, 'Well, it certainly is a State Bedroom because I've never seen a bedroom in such a state.'

This was a remark Julia was to hear many times in the course of the afternoon.

She was always to remember those first visitors. The rest came thick and fast, so that by half-past two there were visitors in every room, entering or leaving, standing to stare or rushing through as if they had a train to catch. It was pleasing that very few of them looked the type she had worried about when Cherry first suggested opening the house – there were none who looked like villains or potential burglars. But then, how was she to know what such people looked like?

As each party of visitors walked into the bathroom they exclaimed, 'Oh, a bathroom, you don't often see those in stately homes, do you?' Followed by a movement of the wicker chair and the amused or embarrassed remark, 'It's a loo,' then the pushing back of the wicker chair and their entrance into the State Bedroom. After a few seconds Julia could be sure of hearing them say, 'What's this room – the State Bedroom – well, it is in a state, isn't it?'

At half-past three Cherry arrived at Julia's elbow and hissed, 'We have run out of butter for the scones.'

'I'll get some. Can you stand here, please, Cherry?'

Julia ran for her moped and went to the shops. She was back in ten minutes and left her moped outside in case she needed it later for more urgent shopping.

A car full of visitors seemed to be picnicking inside their vehicle on Cherry's front lawn. They were tossing papers and general litter out of their window as they progressed through their meal. As Julia walked round and saw them, she also saw Adam approaching the car. She thought he was going to tell them off, but instead, without saying a word, he picked up the mess and stood absolutely silently posting it back through the half-open car window. The people in the car didn't say a word either.

Nothing else very dreadful had happened. The house and garden greeted her with their ancient beauty and seemed to be basking in the summer sun. Once she had taken off the jacket, gloves and helmet which she wore when riding, and delivered the butter to Cherry, she was at her post once more. It was time Dr Bright and Susannah Wilmet arrived to allow the other volunteers to go in turn for tea. Julia looked at her watch and wondered what was delaying them.

16

Unable to understand why Dr Bright and Susannah Wilmet had not appeared to take over from the other residents who were busy guiding at the Dutch House, Cherry decided to make tea anyway and persuade Adam to relieve. Accordingly, Julia was drinking a cup of tea on the terrace by the back steps when Taffinder Walker, the antique dealer, arrived. In minutes, Taff, Cherry and Julia were talking over the tea cups.

Cherry was telling them for the forty-second time how when her family had sugar plantations in British Guiana they had used their own sugar at the table. Taff was telling stories about his weekend in the Lakes. Julia put a word in now and then about an exhibition of modern patchwork quilts she was hoping to organize.

Mr Spicer dashed through Cherry's front door, which was still standing open to the warm air, past Mrs Robinson selling tickets to the latest tourists, over the now clean and gleaming black and white marble tiles of the hall, and on to the garden steps. The three people on the terrace looked up at him in surprise.

'The Bill are here,' Spicer gasped out. 'They are after that driver of Mr Walker's.'

'Who is Bill?' asked Cherry, who didn't have a television and was not up to date in her slang.

'The police want to arrest Duncan?' cried Julia.

'I'd better go,' said Walker. 'He was to meet me back at the car.' Taff Walker put down his cup and saucer, directing as he did so a long glance straight into Julia's eyes. She looked back at him, surprised. It was the kind of glance which tells a woman that she is desired, and at such a moment, she didn't know what to make of it. He went out with Spicer following

194

him, but only seconds later Duncan rushed down the steps from the house.

'Where's my boss?' he asked roughly.

'He went to the car,' Julia answered.

Duncan reached out a hand. 'You don't want this, do you?' he asked Cherry Ducket-Penrose, grasping the sugar basin.

'Want it?' She sounded astonished. 'What do you mean, want it? I put my sugar in it.'

'Give you a good price, lady,' he said, and slammed down a five pound note.

'That's very generous,' Cherry jerked out, 'but . . .'

'That's all right, then,' he said, tipping out the sugar and pushing the basin into the breast of his jacket, before running off.

'He's taken my sugar bowl,' said Cherry, and sat there with her mouth open.

'I'm going after him,' Julia said, and then she also ran.

Duncan had rushed through the house, then across the front grass to the estate car and found Taff Walker sitting in the passenger seat.

'Where have you been?' Taff asked irritably, as his chauffeur flung open the door, jumped into the driving seat and started the engine. 'I hear the police are after you.'

'Take too long to explain,' Duncan said breathlessly. 'Look after this, will you?' And steering the car with one hand, he used the other to withdraw the sugar bowl from his jacket and pass it to Taff Walker.

'What are you doing with this?'

'Bought it off the old lady.'

'I don't believe you, Dunc. You'd better stay and see the police.'

'No fear. And that thing will see us all right for a few months.'

'What are you talking about? For heaven's sake be careful! What's the rush?'

The long estate car was already leaving the drive and edging onto the busy road.

Julia remembered her moped. Running along the front of the building she came to Tom, in his parked Rolls, and her own parked moped. 'What are you doing here, Tom?' she gasped.

'I came hoping to have a word with you. The job is held up,

we've had to stop work over a technical difficulty so I'm free for a bit and thought you might be able to get away for a short run out. What are you doing?' asked Tom, as she stood pulling on jacket, helmet and gloves.

'The police are here arresting people.'

'I know about that, I just saw Bob, he's taken Doctor Bright and a young woman to assist with inquiries and wants Duncan, that driver of Walker's.'

'And Duncan Fraser has run off with Cherry's sugar bowl. Well, driven off. He and Taff have gone in the car. Didn't you see them?'

'And what do you think you're doing?'

'I'm going after them on the moped. You come too if you like, Tom.'

'I think I'd better,' said Tom, watching her stutter past him with her cold engine, and pause to look right at the roadside. He started the stately Rolls and by the time she set off he was already in motion following her.

Duncan turned right at the traffic lights and went towards the town centre. Well within sight of him until she was caught by the lights was Julia Bransby. Within sight of her was a Rolls Royce 20/25 sports saloon built by James Young in 1932, with a cream body and black wings, bonnet, and above-waistline paint-work. Tom Churchyard's six cylinders and maximum speed of 65 mph were of little avail to him in the typical York traffic, no more use than Taff Walker's more modern engine and greater potential speed were to him and Duncan.

When the lights changed to green (she was on the ball with traffic lights today) Julia was able to push after Walker. By now he was out of sight, but there were more sets of lights further along and she was counting on at least some of those being against him. As she zoomed quickly along the side of the slowly dragging line of cars, coaches and heavy transport of all kinds, her heart seemed to be beating in her ears. Things were coming to a halt ahead.

She had been on the inner side of the traffic lane, now she slid in between two cars as they slowed to a stop, and gained the outer edge of the lane. She hated driving in this position because she felt so vulnerable, not only to sudden jerky starts of the vehicles beside her, but to the oncoming traffic which whizzed unheedingly close, seeming to ignore the yellow-clad person riding so near to the central white line. She daren't go over it, except when an over-wide load on an articulated lorry forced her to either cross the line or be stuck behind him as he inched his way forward in the stop-start queue now that the light was green again.

Taking her life in her hands Julia crossed the centre line for the time it took her to pass the artic and drew in again in front of him with a gasp of relief. Somewhere behind her Tom had seen this manoeuvre and felt like clapping his hands over his eyes and not looking any longer. On such a lovely day visitors to York were thick, in addition to normal commercial traffic, and both lanes of the carriageway were full. Here and there a cyclist or someone on a motorbike swooped past the line of cars like a freebooter or a pirate, taking their own individual way through twentieth-century problems. Usually Julia hung modestly back and let teenagers on massive motorbikes overtake her, but not today.

She swooped and freebooted and pirated with the best of them and all the time she was gaining on Duncan and Taff Walker in the long estate car, while Tom sat helplessly immobile in his beautiful Rolls and wished for a Vincent Black Shadow motorbike.

By the time Duncan and Taff approached creamy stone-built Bootham Bar Julia was level with their back wheels. Duncan was intending to take his usual route through the Bar, along High Petergate, Minster Yard, Deangate, Goodramgate and out through Monk Bar, but in the middle of the road which led through the ancient medieval entrance to the city stood a policeman, stopping all traffic going that way.

Duncan caught sight of Julia through his rear mirror, and in the distance, he could see Tom in the Rolls some way behind. Ignoring the policeman he drove straight for the entrance through the Bar. The man leapt to one side at the last moment and as Julia followed on the heels of the estate car she could hear him shouting although she could not distinguish the words.

High Petergate was empty of all but pedestrians but it was full of those. They too jumped for the pavements as Duncan leaned on the horn and blasted a way through them, Taff beside him clutching his seat belt and the sugar basin for dear life. Julia stuck with them, muttering apologies to everyone inaudibly inside her helmet.

As Duncan and Taff reached the junction with Duncombe Place there was a complete line of policemen across the road. Duncan blared the horn again and drove on, but by now his speed had lessened.

Once more the police looked round, startled, gestured to him to stop, then jumped clear, to reveal, in the middle of the road, a tea-table spread with a white embroidered cloth, a silver teapot, silver milk jug, and matching silver sugar basin glittering in the sun, elegant china cups and saucers and tea plates and toasted teacakes, a Victoria sponge, and a plate of dainty mixed sandwiches. On one side of this surprisingly situated feast was the newly appointed Dean of the Minster, and on the opposite side the Lord Mayor wearing his chain of office. A representative of the Civic Society sat on the third side. The three men were lifting their tea cups in a kind of toast and smiling at the assembled journalists, the TV cameraman, the photographers from the local papers, and the commentator from *North News*, who were all involved in news items about the closure of Deangate to traffic. No longer would the heavy transport shake the foundations of York Minster. Peace would reign in the cathedral close, such peace that a tea-party could take place in the middle of the newly pedestrianized carriageway.

Cramming on the brakes Duncan stopped the estate car within inches of the elegant tea-table and jumped out, wondering what on earth was going on. From the passenger seat, Taff Walker got out also, still holding the sugar basin. Julia stopped beside them and jumped off her moped. Some distance behind her the policeman stationed at Bootham Bar, by now feeling distinctly nervous and unsure of himself, allowed Tom and his Rolls to pass through.

Duncan looked around him. Everywhere, it seemed, there were policemen. The TV camera was turned now in his direction and still rolling. He was defeated. Throwing in his hand, he decided to make a run for it and plunged off into the thick of the crowd.

Across the roof of the estate car Taffinder Walker's eyes met

Julia's. In a gesture of despair he hurled Cherry Ducket-Penrose's sugar basin through the air. Unable to believe her eyes Julia saw it sparkle and flash rainbows in the sunlight as it curved up over the estate car and down – down – towards her. She put out her hands in a desperate attempt to catch it. She fumbled at it as it fell, half missing it, securing it at last by clasping it to her chest. Her chin went down to hold it firm and unexpectedly tears came to her eyes and ran down, taking her unawares when she could do nothing to reach a handkerchief, falling and splashing on the backs of her hands and the smooth glass held between them.

Policemen were on either side of Taffinder Walker, holding him by the arms. Julia turned away, and found herself face to face with Tom and the Rolls. She looked up at him, tears dripping from her nose, and wished desperately to be comforted.

'Come on,' Tom said gently, 'I'll take you home.'

'What about my moped?'

'Officer,' Tom said politely to the nearest policeman, 'I would like to take this lady home. DCI Southwell will be able to tell you what all this has been about, he is making arrests in connection with a murder. I know that he will want to interview the man your colleagues are holding, as well as the one who ran away. Would it be possible for you to put the lady's moped somewhere safe until she can come for it?'

Julia was always to think that Tom's car had its own brand of magic. Once their names and addresses were noted, no objection was made to them turning in a stately fashion to the delight of the enthralled crowd, and heading out of the city once more, towards Clifton. She subsided into the front seat beside Tom and went on clasping the sugar basin to her breast.

When they reached the Dutch House again after a silent ride, Tom said, 'I suppose you won't want to come out for a drive now?'

'I don't really, Tom dear. I feel all shaken up.'

'There are things I can do in the garden,' Tom said gloomily. 'Why exactly are you clutching that glass object?'

'There must be something special about it.' Julia held it away from her body and gazed at the bowl. She explained about Duncan's request to buy it and thrusting down a five pound note after snatching the basin up. 'Well, he wouldn't have done that,

I shouldn't have thought,' she went on, 'unless there was something special about it, but I haven't any idea what it is.'

Again they sat in silence.

'I suppose I might as well go,' said Tom.

'Would you like a cup of tea? I need one.'

'I won't come in for tea ... It's hard to leave you,' muttered Tom.

Julia didn't say anything.

'We won't see each other again, then?'

'Don't you think it would be best not to? For a while anyway? We are bound to meet in the normal course of things.'

'We were too intense too soon, do you think?'

'No, oh no! This all hurts so much. It has been so wonderful, Tom. Such a wonderful thing to happen. Perfect. We could have gone on, but ... It is natural for you to want to be married with children. Ten years ago I would have said yes, let's have babies. I just can't now, and that has come between us, somehow.'

Tom had taken one of her hands and was playing with it. 'It has been a wonderful summer,' he agreed. 'Soon it will be autumn and it will all be a memory.'

'A beautiful memory. Won't we still be friends?'

'Oh! Friends! Women always want to be friends!'

'Well, I do want to.'

'Yes, all right.' Tom faced her and the sugar basin lay on her lap as they clasped hands. They kissed. 'Friends and no hard feelings,' said Tom.

'Friends and no hard feelings,' said Julia.

At that moment they were both wanting each other desperately, but overriding that was the strange sweetness of renunciation.

After the Dutch House closed at five o'clock Bob Southwell rang Cherry Ducket-Penrose from the police station and asked if he could call to see her.

'There are one or two things I would like to say,' he told her.

'Can you explain what has been going on?' asked Cherry, 'because if so I think everyone has a right to know. They are all here, because we'd planned to have a bit of a celebration at the end of the first day, so we are having it, despite everything. We'll wait for you in the drawing room.'

When Bob Southwell arrived the residents of the Dutch House had all managed to find a chair in the drawing room to suit their individual tastes, ranging from deep mahogany-framed Victorian chairs in crimson plush to dainty silk-covered painted chairs and a bead-stitched prie-dieu which looked most uncomfortable for anything except saying prayers. The tom-cat Oberon was there too and sat looking impressive on the white sheepskin rug in front of the marble hearth. Bob joined him, leaned on the mantelpiece, and gazed round at them all. The windows were open and the herby air of the garden drifted in.

'As you may know,' he began, 'we arrested three people today – your neighbours Doctor Bright and Miss Wilmet and Mr Taffinder Walker's driver, Duncan Fraser. I would like to assure you that Mr Walker is not under arrest and as far as we know at present is not involved in any way with the matters we have been investigating. Doctor Bright and Duncan Fraser are charged with stealing and illegally exporting antiques. I believe Doctor Bright and Miss Wilmet to have been responsible for the murder of your neighbour, Mrs Honor.'

'*Susannah?*' It was a general cry from everyone, appalled, disbelieving.

'But the doctor is such a nice man,' added Cherry.

'He appears to be a very pleasant man, I agree with you,' said Bob Southwell, 'although he wasn't very pleasant when we arrested him – we saw a different side to him altogether. But the evidence we have been collecting on the illegal export of antiques has pointed irrevocably to him. He retired early, I gather. He is not as old as he appears. His wife, who is younger than he is, genuinely has chronic bronchitis in the winters, and it may have been this which led them gradually into a life of crime. She lives extravagantly when abroad. She also holds a pilot's licence and is very skilled. She is one of the very few women who have been test pilots. We found this in old newspaper references. I don't imagine it has been mentioned by the Brights recently. She is also under arrest, in France.'

There were murmurs of amazement at this. They saw so little of Mrs Bright, but what they knew of her disposed them to believe that she might well fly planes, she was the sort of person who might do anything, anything at all, climb Everest, for example. The main thing they remembered was her penetrating voice.

'It was probably her flying experience which led to a friendship between her and Mr and Mrs Honor before the Honors ever came to live here. When Mr Honor wanted to buy a special present for his wife, Mrs Bright said a friend of hers was selling some early Dresden china at a good price. He bought the pieces and gave them to his wife. We think neither of the Honors knew they were stolen. When we identified the Dresden as stolen goods, we noticed that in the description Mrs Bransby gave us, she said that Mrs Honor always used the same words, "Mrs Bright so kindly found my dear shepherd and shepherdess and the other Dresden for my dear Toto to buy for me."'

'She always said that,' agreed Mrs Robinson.

'So we had several reasons to connect the Brights with the smuggling. To recap, Mrs Bright has kept up her flying and we believe that a small private plane was used to transport the goods. Some stolen goods from several years ago were in Mrs Honor's possession, bought from Mrs Bright. She spends a great deal more money when abroad than can be accounted for, and stolen items have been known to turn up at times and in places she has visited. So much for the continental end of the operation. Now, Doctor Bright. He has been responsible for locating suitable antiques and organizing burglaries. Of all the residents in the Dutch House, none of you had such easy access to all layers of society as did Doctor Bright. Mrs Bransby reminded me that one person who can walk into any house is the doctor.'

'But he said he knew nothing about antiques!' cried Julia.

'On searching his flat we found a concealed bookcase with all the standard reference books on antiques. He said that he was looking after the books for a friend. They are very well used, and his finger marks are all over them. He does locums in various parts of the country, and it is noticeable from his diary that he does them exclusively in the richer areas. At one time he was in partnership with a doctor who collected jade. That collection of jade was stolen and none of the pieces were ever traced.'

202

'It does look black for him,' said Cherry.

'It doesn't make him a murderer, though,' said Adam.

'Now we come to his partner in crime, Duncan Fraser. They do not seem to have been together very long. Duncan has never before been in serious trouble. He is energetic and capable, and he is learning about antiques fast. We don't think he was involved with Mrs Honor's burglary at all. None of his fingerprints were found and there are some differences between that crime and the others in this recent series.'

'Suppose we have a cup of tea,' said Cherry. She and Mrs Robinson went out and came back with a loaded tea-trolley. Cherry was becoming quite proficient at serving refreshments. In no time everyone had a cup of tea and the break was very welcome. There was a buzz of talk.

Bob too drank some tea. His voice had been getting hoarse. 'The thing is,' Bob went on, 'we don't know whether Mrs Honor ever knew her beloved Dresden was stolen.'

'I know she did,' said Mr Markhall, who until then had not said a word. 'She found out during the early evening of the day she was murdered.'

'You told us you had heard a row,' said Bob Southwell.

'I heard it because I had the floorboards up in my living room. Our insulation is good because the wing is well-built. The floorboards are nearly two inches thick. Normally I never hear a sound from Mrs Honor's, but I was wiring up my new hi-fi system and that was how I came to hear the argument. The boards were up and I was lying on the floor threading wires through and connecting things. I couldn't help hearing their voices clearly.'

'Go on,' said Bob, and everyone else was very quiet.

'It was Doctor Bright and Mrs Honor. She had obviously tackled him about a conversation she overheard when his wife was with him. She said he and Mrs Bright must stop stealing things or she would inform the police. He was talking to her in a hectoring tone I didn't like at all, telling her that she was in possession of stolen property herself and needn't get on her high horse. He said unless she agreed to help him he would shop her to the police over the Dresden china.'

'What did he want her to do?'

'I think he was planning to steal some of your antiques, Miss

203

Ducket-Penrose, because he wanted her to discover what was most valuable. She refused. He said he would make it worth her while.' Mr Markhall added diffidently, 'I feel she was hard up, you know.' Then he went on, 'She said that she didn't want to have stolen property and she wouldn't help him in any way. Doctor Bright said she had better, but she refused.'

'Why didn't you tell us about this conversation before?' asked Bob Southwell sharply.

'I did tell you that I had heard a row,' the thin, shy man said, 'but my mind had gone on to thinking about a difficult chess problem and I couldn't remember what they had said, not exactly. I had heard scraps and missed the beginning. After a while, concentrating on trying to remember, it began to come back to me. It is only with hindsight that I realize what the conversation was really about. In fact it is only today, with you telling us about Mrs Bright and so on, that I have made sense of what I heard. I have given it to you as it must have been, now that I understand it, but at the time I heard it in disjointed snatches and if I had told you of it before today you would have been as puzzled by it as I was.'

'So you heard a quarrel but didn't really understand what it was about?'

'That is right.'

'Now that you know what has been happening you realize what it all meant?'

'Yes.'

'Perhaps you will make a statement giving us the original words as closely as you can remember them.'

'I will.'

'Anyone else been hearing things and not telling us?' asked Bob.

'She did say something to me, actually,' said Gawain Lloyd, 'on the very afternoon. She said there was something she wanted to consult the police about. I asked her what. She said it was to do with one of the other residents. Then she shut up like a clam and wouldn't say any more. I must admit, I thought it was about you, Mr Spicer, because she'd been cutting the flowers again.'

Mr Spicer made a grunting noise intended to express disgust.

Cherry cried out at this point, wanting to know how Susannah Wilmet was involved – the very question which was ringing through everybody's mind. 'She is the last person I would have suspected,' she said.

'The last person anyone would have suspected,' Bob said wryly, 'but there you go. One thing we learn about murderers is that they are egoists. Completely and utterly self-absorbed. Would you say that was a good description of Susannah Wilmet?'

Without saying a word they all nodded their heads.

'Exactly. So we should have suspected her at the beginning. Bemused by her charms, we did not suspect her.' His voice was bitter.

Once again there was a silence.

'Before the murder,' Bob said, his tone now much lighter, 'my wife and I were talking about the Dutch House and all of you, perhaps because we had bought one of Oberon's and Titania's kittens, and because Julia here is a friend of my wife's. Linda happened to say that none of the tenants of the different flats were related to the tenants of the others. I had no reason to challenge her statement. But we now know that not only are the tenants of the two attic flats, Ms Haygreen and Ms Hodson,' here he nodded to the two ladies, 'first cousins, but the new tenant of one of the garage flats, Miss Wilmet, is Doctor Bright's niece.'

Everyone looked surprised, but again no one spoke.

'She is the daughter of his wife's sister. They did not declare the relationship to Miss Ducket-Penrose, who has the freehold on the flats, or to any of you, as far as we know.'

There was a general muttered chorus of, 'No, they didn't.'

'Doctor Bright hoped to work with Susannah Wilmet in the antique burglary business, if you can call it that. Since being arrested he has been singing like a bird, otherwise we would have no idea what her motivation was. As you know, Mrs Honor made a pet of the much younger woman.'

As he paused to drink a second cup of tea, Mrs Robinson, who had never liked Susannah, said, 'Mrs Honor flattered her and buttered her up abominably. Susannah came out of that flat looking like the cat that ate the cream.'

'Exactly. But there was one occasion, the day of the murder, when she left the flat and did not haste away. Adam saw her. Once outside Mrs Honor's door, Susannah bent down to fasten a loose shoelace. The hairdresser had just arrived, and the door had been left open. Full of the delicious flattery, Susannah now heard Mrs Honor say in very sarcastic tones to her hairdresser, "*She* thinks she's going to be a concert pianist. Blue Moon has more talent for playing the piano in his front paws than she has in the whole of her body. She is absolutely useless." That was the gist of it. Those words sealed Mrs Honor's fate. They burned themselves into Susannah's brain and she repeated them to her uncle, not once but several times with more and more anger. Now of course he has repeated them to us.'

'No wonder Susannah snapped at me when I spoke to her,' said Adam.

'The uncle had planned the burglary in order to get back the Dresden china. It was evidence against the Brights which Mrs Honor could have produced to the police. Luckily, we found records of each piece, the date and place of the theft, and the name of the person who lost them in that break-in. Doctor Bright thought Mrs Honor was in bed and assumed she was asleep. He knew that she was taking sleeping pills, prescribed by her own doctor. Unfortunately, Blue Moon raised the alarm, and she must have forgotten to take her pills. She was knocked down to prevent her recognizing them in the darkened room, but it was Susannah who picked up the bronze bust of de Gaulle in a fit of fury at the old woman's two-faced words and sarcasm. They must have been corroding her ever since she overheard them. She probably also attacked the dog. Is there any more tea in the pot?'

The talk became more and more noisy as the residents reacted to what they had heard. DCI Robert Southwell found a spare chair and enjoyed the last of the rather stewed tea, then stood up and raised his hand for silence.

'Before I go,' he said, 'I will tell you about the sugar basin, which I see you have on your lap, Julia. Walker, who is not a bad sort of chap, has told us what it is. It is a rare piece of English seventeenth-century glass.'

Here Bob took a notebook out of his pocket and consulted it. 'It was made by one George Ravenscroft in either 1677 or 1678, and has his raven's head seal. There are believed to be only seventeen pieces of glass with his seal still in existence, according to Mr Walker, seven of them drinking glasses. This bowl must be the eighteenth, and it is in perfect condition. He said museums will be falling over themselves to buy it, and that it is probably the most valuable thing in the house, Miss Ducket-Penrose. He had told his assistant of its probable value in the course of educating him in his trade, and was intending to tell you today and ask for the loan of it so that he could have it examined by an expert. Duncan obeyed a sudden mad impulse.'

'But it's not cut glass,' said Cherry in surprise. 'It is only my old sugar basin.'

'If I were you,' said Bob, 'I would put it in the bank's safe deposit. It is worth a fortune.'

There was silence in the drawing room of the Dutch House. For once all the inhabitants were united. How could this humble sugar basin be a rare treasure? The contrast between appearance and reality took tangible shape before them in this small object of glass, full, it seemed to them, of imperfections.